Social Actions: A Vietnam Story

by
Donnie Henriques

Social Actions:
A Vietnam Story

by
Donnie Henriques

Copyright 2018 by Donnie Henriques
Social Actions: A Vietnam Story

Published by Yawn's Publishing
2555 Marietta Hwy, Ste 103
Canton, GA 30114
www.yawnsbooks.com

This book is a work of fiction. References to real people, events, establishments, organizations, products, or locales are intended only to provide a sense of authenticity, and are used fictitiously. All characters and incidents, including dialogue, are drawn from the author's imagination and/or experiences and are not to be construed as real.

All rights reserved. No part of this book may be reproduced or transmitted in any form, electronic or mechanical, including photocopying, recording, or data storage systems without the express written permission of the publisher, except for brief quotations in reviews and articles.

Library of Congress Control Number: 2018960455

ISBN: 978-1-947773-36-3

Printed in the United States

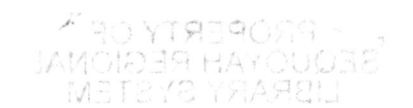

Thanks to my wife, Jan, for continually pushing me to write and publish this book. As well as my children, Derek, Jeremy and Maddie, for the constant encouragement. A special thanks to Chase King, a local artist who painted the cover. I am grateful for his vision.

Table of Contents

Chapter 1: Things Came Easy	1
Chapter 2: James "Juicer" Forest	25
Chapter 3: In Country	38
Chapter 4: Hope for Christmas	58
Chapter 5: Getting into the Conspiracy	72
Chapter 6: Pulling Out: Nixon's Withdrawal Plan	84
Chapter 7: Electric City: One Week in Saigon	95
Chapter 8: A New Setting: Thailand	108
Chapter 9: Testing and Crashes	119
Chapter 10: A Little Slice of Home	133
Chapter 11: Ninety and a Wake Up	142
Chapter 12: Implications and Eradications	151
Chapter 13: "The World"	158
Chapter 14: Trying to Get Things Right	174
Epilogue	182

Chapter 1
Things Came Easy

May 14, 1973

Sitting in the stockade, staring up at the bare cement ceiling with the smell of stale human waste in the air was not his idea of preparing for an early release homecoming. His time was up. He had spent his year in hell, and it continued here in Montgomery. It was only fair that he should be going home soon.

"How the fuck did I get myself into this mess," he said to the empty room. His mind drifted…

November 22, 1971

He stepped off the plane in Cam Rahn Bay, Vietnam, and was hit with a blast of hot air that felt like a furnace. Jesus, I sure was a dumb-looking newbie, decked out in winter dress blues in a 90-degree steam bath… and at two in the morning, he thought.

"Hey asshole, ya' never get used to it," the grizzled returning vet yelled in his ear. "My third tour, glad to be back! Get the fuck outta the way pussy! Let the real grunts through!" he said as he pushed past Haney.

Patrick looked at the staff sergeant as he rolled past. Decked out in his jungle fatigues with a red beret cocked to one side, Haney knew the guy had been there even before he had said anything. He had that crazed look in his eyes. Patrick's friend, Bobby, had warned him about the type.

"You have to keep a look out for the VC, but don't trust anybody that's been there longer than they have to be, even if they're supposed to be on your side," Bobby said.

Haney knew Bobby was familiar with the breed, having done a tour in Da Nang.

May 14, 1973

"HANEY, FRONT AND CENTER!" the stockade sergeant bellowed, shaking Haney out of his thoughts. "OSI wants to see you, NOW!"

Patrick jumped up, snapped to attention, and followed the sergeant down the hall to the commander's office. Seated behind the desk was a short, stocky, balding man in civilian clothes. "Sergeant Patrick Haney?" he asked in a barely audible voice. "Yes, sir," Haney responded, thinking he was looking at a human bowling ball. "I'm Colonel Pierce, Office of Special Investigations. Sit down and let's talk." Haney took a seat at the desk opposite the officer. His mind wandered as the colonel started talking in a drone nasal speech…

* * *

All during high school, Patrick Haney had trouble keeping himself busy. It was as though things came too easily for him. While his grades didn't set the world on fire, they were good enough to get by without burning up too much energy. He excelled in many different sports, but found that playing on organized teams meant practice every day, and that was out of the question.

New Orleans was a great place to grow up during the '50s and '60s. This was mostly due to the small neighborhoods that dotted the city and separated it into smaller towns. The Irish Channel, Garden District, Carollton, the Ninth Ward, and the "Projects", among other various public housing scattered throughout the city.

The Irish Channel, bounded by the Mississippi River, Louisiana Avenue, Magazine Street and Annunciation Square on the downtown side, was considered the ugly stepsister to its neighbor across Magazine Street – The Garden District. With its palatial mansions being protected from the 24-hour shipping activity of the Riverfront by the five-block width of the Channel, it was a completely different world. Across Magazine Street the mansions gave way to "shotgun" doubles dominating the streetscape. Occasionally, a single-family home would creep into view, with its occupants considered well-off by the neighbors.

The residents of the Channel had a fierce reputation throughout the city, going back to the early settlers straight off the boat from Ireland. This reputation made it the kind of area where neighbors sat out on the porch, visiting with each other, and not having to lock the doors at night. Its teenagers were known to travel in large groups, projecting a "militia" feel to the area which intimidated outsiders. Patrick grew up in this environment. Running the streets at night with friends, never in serious trouble, but always on the fringe of meeting a different future by way of the court system. His father passed away when he was fourteen. His mother, trying to make ends meet, went back to teaching, moved in with her father, along with Patrick, in the only two-story double on Laurel Street. He started going steady with the first girl that showed any interest in him. While they dated steadily for three years, he never even considered it a possibility to be with someone other than his girlfriend.

His senior year was one of absence. By the time March had rolled around, the school counselor summoned him to the office.

"Patrick, you've been absent 22 times so far this year. If you keep this up, there will be no graduation in May," the counselor said.

"Mr. Vitrano, you know I'm helping my mom out by working more these days, besides, I'm still passing all my classes," Haney hurried to say.

"That doesn't matter, son," Vitrano responded. "The school board has a rule about attendance. You can't graduate unless you attend class. It's either class or the job, take your pick."

Haney thought for a moment, thinking some counseling job this guy does, not even considering the circumstances at home. Standing up, Patrick started walking out the door, "Mr. Vitrano thanks for nothing, but I'm making more selling clothes at Sears than my mom is teaching, and she has a degree. I think I'll take the job." He walked out and never returned.

* * *

"What are you going to do," his mother asked. "You can't survive in this world without *at least* a high school diploma," she said in her teacher's voice. "Mom, I know you wanted me to go to college, but I can't seem to concentrate on school right now," he said. "I'll figure out something, and maybe... no definitely, I'll get my diploma, I promise." His mother sighed and shook her head, "I wish your father were here; I never could handle you."

* * *

"Why don't we join the Air Force on the Buddy Plan," Timmy said. "Bobby told me he's having a great time. They're teaching him electronics, and we'd be guaranteed to stay together at least the first year." Patrick looked at him from a different view. Is this the same guy who barely scrapped though high school and has refused to look for a job in over two years? Timothy O'Riley would never be confused with someone voted most likely to succeed. He was more often thought of as a modern day Maynard G. Krebs, the beatnik from the old "Dobie Gillis Show".

Timothy O'Riley, while running in the same circles as Patrick, always seemed to be in trouble. Although they became best friends in high school, Timmy was the one to always get caught at whatever trouble they were causing. He had many minor brushes with the police, but only twice was he actually arrested. Naturally, when something bad happened in the neighborhood, he was always the first one everyone would blame. But he was just like the rest of the group; a fierce pride in their heritage, and a quick temper to trigger it. There was usually a fight of some sort brewing, and Timmy was always in the middle of it. Being less than five foot ten, and a mere 160 pounds, he usually found himself the underdog in any scuffle he was involved with. This made him even more defiant, verbally challenging his opponents until they couldn't back out gracefully.

"Timmy, think about what you're saying," Patrick said. "We'd be stuck for four years without any control over our lives." As he sipped the last of his Dixie beer, Timmy looked at him and asked, "How much control do you think you have now?"

The next day the recruiting officer on Canal Street in downtown New Orleans was rambling on about all the good times they would have seeing new countries and experiencing strange cultures when Haney interrupted him and said, "Can you guarantee, in writing, we'd be together for the first year and that we'd be sent to the technical school of our choice?"

"Without a doubt young man, the Air Force believes in the judgement of its own people," the captain stated without blinking an eye. "Mr. Haney, since you won't be 18 until just before you leave, I'll need your parents' signature just below the line where you sign," the career officer said as he pointed to the document in front of him. He stood up and reached across the desk, hand outstretched and said, "Congratulations men, you won't regret it."

*   *   *

Three months later they were on a plane bound for Lackland Air Force Base, San Antonio, Texas, and basic training. Haney leaned over and whispered to Timmy, "How come they never found out about your irregular heartbeat?"

"Beats the hell out of me. I was counting on having an out just in case I got cold feet," Timmy replied.

Basic training was everything they had been told it would be. Anybody wearing a Smokey the Bear hat will try to intimidate you, so just play along with the game. Unfortunately, Timmy had just read an article on responding to that kind of treatment through defiance.

"WHAT ARE YOU, SOME KIND OF HIPPIE PROTESTOR MAGGOT?" the burly technical instructor yelled into Timmy's face.

"No sir, Sergeant," Timmy responded, "I just don't like meat. I'm committed to being a vegetarian."

Sergeant Walk's neck veins popped out and he turned a shade of purple Haney had never seen before.

"YOU WILL EAT EVERYTHING THE COOK PUTS ON YOUR PLATE, AND YOU WILL LIKE IT. IS THAT UNDERSTOOD SCUMBAG?" the sergeant screamed.

"Yes sir, but I do it under protest," Timmy said. Wrong answer, Patrick thought.

"YOU FUCKING COMMIE, PINKO FAG. YOU WILL NOT TALK BACK IN THIS MAN'S AIR FORCE. FALL OUT TO THE PC FIELD, ON THE DOUBLE," bellowed the technical instructor.

That would only mean one thing, Patrick thought. Timmy wouldn't be relaxing in the rec room after a day that started at 4 a.m. As Haney walked back to the barracks, he glanced over to the physical conditioning field. As the sun set behind it, Haney could see Timmy jogging around the track, the technical instructor sitting in the stands watching him. "Jesus, Timmy," he said to no one in particular. "If he'd just learn to keep his mouth shut for once."

The next morning came all too quickly for Patrick. He felt like he had just hit the rack when that irritating, nasal voice came over the loud speaker,

"0400, GET-UP, GET-UP, GET-UP!!!"

Two weeks down, four to go, he thought. Patrick looked across the room and saw that Timmy's bunk had not been slept in.

After breakfast, Haney returned to the barracks before the rest of the flight. He could never stomach much food that early in the morning, so he promised Plimpton, a rather large guy from Rye, New York, that he would help him shine his shoes if he would eat the rest of Haney's chow. It didn't take much arm twisting. As Patrick walked into the large dormitory style room with eighty beds crammed together, he stopped. There, in front of Timmy's locker were two security policemen stuffing the contents into a duffle bag. "Hey, you fucking thieves," he yelled, "get away from there." As he started running toward them he heard a familiar bellow,

"AS YOU WERE AIRMAN," Sergeant Walk screamed.

"These men are working on my orders. If you've got a gripe, go see the captain."

"But, Sergeant…" Haney tried to say.

"You got a hearing problem, Airman? I said take it up with the captain," Walk insisted.

Patrick went straight to the captain's office. He found the captain in conversation with First Sergeant Mack. "Sir, excuse me for interrupting, but Sergeant Walk said to come see you about what's going on upstairs in the barracks," Haney said rather aggressively.

"Airman, can't you see…" the captain started to say when Sergeant Mack leaned over and whispered in his ear. After a brief exchange between the two that Patrick could not hear, the captain said, "Haney, step into my office."

Not knowing what to expect, Haney stood at attention in front of the captain's desk.

"Take a seat, son," the captain said. "Haney, we here at Lackland are tasked with taking untamed, raw and restless individuals, and turning them into disciplined, productive airmen who can proudly serve their country as she sees fit. Sometimes, in doing this duty, a recruit slips by the weeding process, and makes it here, when, by all rights, he shouldn't have." Patrick's patience was growing short, but the captain continued. "I'm afraid that's what happened to your friend, Airman O'Riley." He paused to gauge Haney's reaction, then continued, "We'll need you to identify the body before we ship it back to his parents." Patrick leaned forward in disbelief.

"What are you saying… what happened to Timmy?" His voice cracked as he spoke.

Sergeant Mack stepped forward, "We think he must have had a heart attack while doing extra PC training for Sergeant Walk. His body is undergoing an autopsy right now. I'm sorry, son. I know you two were close. These things happen."

* * *

It was Haney's first time at the base hospital. Hopefully, he thought, it would be his last. Sergeant Mack and the security police escorted him down into the basement. Mack and Haney waited while the SP went through double glass doors at the end of the long grey hallway. After what seemed like an eternity to Haney, the SP reappeared with a major in a sterile white lab coat. The major and Sergeant Mack conferred out of Haney's earshot for a moment. Then the major motioned over for Haney to follow him. As the doors swung open from the force of the SP's shove, Haney's nostrils were engulfed with an odor he had never in his life experienced.

"Formaldehyde. Gets all newcomers," the major said.

The SP stood at attention by the door as the three walked toward a stainless-steel table in the middle of the room. As Haney approached he could tell it was Timmy. But something was different. He stood staring down at his friend he had known since kindergarten, noticing dark purple circles on his face, shoulders and down his chest. He also couldn't help but see the incision that had been made from his Adam's apple down to his naval.

"What'd you do to him?" Haney asked.

"Standard procedure. Suspected heart attack victim, inspect the heart, found severe damage to two chambers, probably caused by an irregular heartbeat," the doctor replied matter-of-factly. "This man should have never been allowed to enlist."

"Excuse me, sir," Patrick interrupted, "I knew O'Riley for a long time.

He played football and ran track in high school. Hell, he ran at least ten miles a day for training. How come this doctor in New Orleans let him do all that, much less at his level of ability? I'm also trying to understand what all those dark spots on his face and chest are from."

"To answer your first question Airman, these conditions are subject to change without warning," the doctor said. "Secondly, those bruises must have been caused when he fell after having suffered the fatal attack."

Haney looked at the doctor, not believing what he was hearing. The doctor was nervously exchanging glances with Mack. Then Mack said, "About face Airman, back to your barracks."

On the walk back to the barracks, Haney started to ask Mack a question when Mack blurted out, "Drop it Haney, I know what you're trying to do. There is nothing more to this than a simple heart attack."

"But Sarge…" Patrick started to say before Mack had him by the throat and up against a brick wall, screaming within inches of his face,

"I SAID DROP IT, you read me?"

"Yes, sir," Haney responded.

As Patrick walked up the stairs to his barracks, he knew he had to talk to that doctor, this time alone.

* * *

It was the hardest thing Patrick had to do since telling his mom that Dad had died suddenly. Back then, he had the support of his grandfather to get him through it. This time he was all alone. The captain had allowed him to call Timmy's parents with the news. Haney felt hearing it from someone besides an impersonal telegram might soften the blow. The captain stood next to him, so Haney thought it better to not mention anything else other than a heart attack. Mrs. O'Riley dropped the phone when she heard the news. Mr. O'Riley, after calming her down, told Patrick to bring Timmy home; his Uncle Clarence's funeral home would handle the arrangements. After hanging up, the captain got on the phone to arrange transportation for the body. When he was finished, he informed Patrick that he could escort the body back and stay for the funeral. The flight left the next morning at 0900.

* * *

Faking sick was easy. The TIs are trained not to doubt a recruit's illness.

Maybe if Walk hadn't, Timmy would still be alive. Haney decided it didn't make sense to speculate. He just had to see that doctor. Sergeant Mack figured Patrick was just upset by what had transpired.

"Here's your sick call pass, Haney," Mack said as he handed him the pink slip. "On the double, it's 1800 hours now, lights out at 2100. Be back in your bunk by then."

"Yes, sir," Haney replied.

It took longer than Patrick thought to see a doctor at sick call. He had to report or the pass couldn't be stamped and signed. After getting a dose of bicarbonate, Haney realized he only had twenty minutes to get back. As he ran down the stairs to the basement, it suddenly occurred to him the doctor who did the autopsy probably went home by now. As he walked through the double glass doors, he almost knocked the major over as he was leaving. Startled, the doctor said, "My God son, you almost ran over me. What's the big hurry?"

"I'm sorry sir, but I don't have much time," Haney wheezed as he tried to catch his breath. "I don't think you were telling me everything earlier. What really caused those bruises, Major?"

"See here, Airman..." the doctor said before Haney stopped him.

"Sir, he was my best friend, I've known him all my life. Either you tell me, or I go to the base commander's office."

Patrick knew it was a long shot, but he had to take the risk. The major looked at Haney pensively.

"Son, you haven't been here long enough to understand, but let me try to explain... What I am about to say was never said. I'll swear in a court martial that I never said it, understood?" the doctor said.

Haney nodded yes. "Now I'm not saying your friend died of unnatural causes," the doctor started, "but if I had the equipment and experience, I'd run more tests to find out exactly what happened. This isn't a civilian coroner's office, and I work for the same commanding officer you just threatened to go see. He's the one who told me how your friend probably died. I just confirmed heart disease. Hell, your friend probably would have died in a couple of years anyway. There was just too much damage done."

After letting the words sink in, the major continued, "I was ordered not to go any further with the investigation. Do you understand?"

Without saying another word, the doctor walked through the doors and out of Haney's sight. Patrick didn't have much time to think about what the doctor had said, he only had ten minutes to get back to his barracks, or he might not be permitted to make the trip back to New Orleans with Timmy's remains.

* * *

It was a typical Irish Channel wake. The women held down the crying duties while the men congregated in the bar across the street to do their own method of grieving. At the first opportune moment, Patrick pulled Mr. O'Riley to the side, saying, "You've known me a long time Mr. O'Riley. You know me to be honest, right?" O'Riley nodded in approval. Patrick continued, "Don't ask me why, I can't tell you, but I think there was more to Timmy's death than a heart attack. He had bruises on his face and chest when I saw him in the morgue. I was told it happened when he fell, but I don't buy it." He signaled for two more Falstaff beers.

"Paddy, why you think such a thing?" O'Riley asked. "The Air Force wouldn't lie to me. That's our government, why would they do that?"

"I don't know," Patrick answered.

He grabbed the elderly man by the shoulders and said, "You have to promise me, don't mention me if you decide to have his death investigated, at least not until I'm finished with basic training. Promise!" he insisted.

"Yeah, Paddy, I promise," O'Riley said seeing the fear on the young man's face. "But you gotta understand laddie, people like us, we don't have things investigated. We are too poor, nobody listens to us. Besides, I'm a good American, been that way ever since me Da walked me off the boat in '24. If Uncle Sam say accident… then I believe him."

Mr. O'Riley grabbed Haney's GI haircut and rubbed it saying, "Get drunk with me tonight, we bury Timmy tomorrow, then you go be a good soldier, OK? … OK?" Haney nodded gently. He then grabbed his beer, climbed up on a chair and yelled to the crowded bar,

"TO TIMMY, THE BEST FRIEND I COULD HAVE HOPED FOR."

He raised his bottle as the rest of the bar said, "Here, here." Patrick could see the pride wash over his friend's father. They proceeded to drink to Timmy's memory. The wake lasted until daylight, only giving the last of mourners a few hours to clean up. Patrick knew he could sleep on the plane.

* * *

The trip back to San Antonio was a headache in more ways than one. Haney had spent the last 36 hours mourning and burying his best friend and consuming more alcohol in two days than he had in two years. Some of the younger mourners had passed around a joint outside the bar, but Patrick decided it wasn't a good time to try something new.

Sitting in the seat next to him was a young mother with a crying infant. The shrill sounds coming out of the child lasted the entire flight, contributing to an already pounding head. He also wondered if there was something else he could do about Timmy's death. Who could he go to? Should he carry it any further? He knew without the family's help, there wasn't much he could do. He remembered Mr. O'Riley's words about people "like us" not making waves. The older man was probably right. The Air Force would protect its own.

But it wasn't his makeup. He knew he'd have to talk to someone about it. Not knowing who to trust, he went to the only place he knew his inquiry would be safe… the chaplain. Father Conlin had been a priest for over twenty years, fifteen of them in the Air Force. He had reached the rank of lieutenant colonel and was looking for more before retiring to a parish church back in his home diocese of Kansas City.

"Do you want to make this a confession, son?" the priest asked.

"No, Father, I just need some advice," replied Patrick.

After relaying the whole story, Patrick asked, "What do I do? Who can I go to?" The priest sat back in his chair, looked pensive for a few seconds, and then said, "Do you really want to pursue this? It could bring more trouble than it's worth and you could still wind up with the same result."

"I have to Father, I have to know what happened," answered Patrick.

"Well, then your next stop is the base Inspector General's office. I can set up an appointment for you if you would like, son," the priest said, hoping to sound helpful.

"That'd be great Father, when can I expect to see him?" Patrick asked.

"It will take a few days, you go back to your squadron and wait for me to contact your captain to release you for the meeting," replied Conlin.

Haney felt better about what he was doing after leaving the priest and walking back to his barracks. He knew he could trust the priest. Something he didn't feel about anyone else on the base.

* * *

Reporting back to squadron headquarters, he found they had placed him in another flight.

"Can't miss any time in basic," the captain said. "You've got three days to make up, and I can't keep the rest of your old flight behind until you catch up."

At first, Haney was angry. He had met several nice guys in his original flight, and he wanted to continue on with them. His new instructor, Sergeant Knuckles, made the delay bearable. The name described his look. A balled-up fist, skinny as a rail. The Korean and Vietnam veteran looked like he would bite your head off for no reason, but Haney found out the first day that Knuckles had been heaven sent.

Patrick walked up the stairs alone after lunch that first day with his new flight. As soon as he turned the corner, a large hand grabbed his throat and slammed him against the wall.

"You scared, BOY?" growled Sergeant Walk. "You better be. I know you been to see the doctor before you left. Leave it alone, BOY. I got 23 years invested in this career; I don't need no fucking rookie fucking things up for me. GOT IT, BOY?"

From the next level a different voice shouted, "GET YOUR HAND OFF MY TOY, SERGEANT." It was Knuckles.

He pounced down the short flight of steps and got right in Walk's face as he released Haney. "NEVER, ever let me catch you putting your hands on ANY recruit, much less mine. Remember Walk, my five stripes to your four means something. Now get the fuck out of here before I report this little incident to the captain."

Walk glared intently at Knuckles, but knew better than to argue with a superior. Haney started to thank the TI when Knuckles said, "get up to your bunk and make it right, we got an inspection in one hour." Then he was gone, leaving Patrick grateful for his timing… and courage.

* * *

He had waited a full week before hearing from the chaplain concerning an appointment with the IG. Although he knew not to trust anyone, even the priest, he decided to follow up with the meeting anyway. After waiting in the reception area for almost an hour, the short stint spent in the IG's presence seemed a ridiculous waste of time. The colonel, acting on behalf of the Inspector General of the Air Force, had already determined that no further investigation was warranted in the matter of Timmy's death. He was satisfied with the coroner's report and that the matter was put to rest. At that point, Patrick knew that it was now up to Mr. O'Riley… if he even wanted to do anything. There was nothing further he could do. The lesson learned was to never trust anyone.

He already knew that Walk was notified about his request for an inquiry. Whether it was the chaplain or the IG, it didn't matter. Patrick knew that the IG had already made its mind up before Haney had arrived. Add in the fact that Walk had added him to his list, he knew that basic training had the potential to get much harder. Even deadly.

* * *

The next few weeks were spent learning the way to survive in the modern Air Force. Physical training, testing, marching, testing, physical training, and on and on it went. In week five, the results of the testing came in. Haney was determined to be qualified for Interpretation School. That meant the next 26 months in upstate New York learning Russian. He reported for his last hurdle before assignment: security clearance. Everything seemed to go well during the interview. The lieutenant conducting the session seemed pleased with his background. Just before the interview was over, the lieutenant said, "I see you came in on the buddy plan, who is your friend?"

"He died of a heart attack the first week," Haney replied.

"I'm sorry," the lieutenant offered as he scribbled in the file. "That'll be all Airman."

Two days before graduation; orders day. Finding out where everyone would be going. Haney was excited. He knew his assignment to Russian language school would mean no leave until Christmas, four months away, but he was thinking of all the possibilities. Being assigned to the U.N. or some foreign embassy. Then discharge and a high paying job as an interpreter. As he opened his envelope, the anticipation rose. The words on the orders were like a sharp tack in a worn tire: Administrative Specialist, 70100, Charleston AFB, South Carolina. He couldn't believe his eyes. What happened to New York? Language school? The U.N.? He walked over to Sergeant Knuckles saying, "Sarge I believe I got someone else's order. I was supposed to be going to language school."

"The key word there is WAS, Airman," Knuckles replied. "You fucked up your security interview. You have to be able to get a top secret clearance for that job. You didn't qualify."

Dumbfounded, Patrick said, "So what does this administrative specialist mean?"

"It means you go home for 10 days, report to Charleston, and then learn how to become a 70250," Knuckles said.

"What is that?" Haney asked.

"Titless WAF," replied Knuckles. "You gonna be a male secretary, Ace."

* * *

Graduation day was something every recruit looked forward to from the first day. Six weeks. Thirty "business" days. The Air Force didn't count the Saturdays used for training purposes. Up until the late '60s, even Sunday was used until the Chaplain General's complaints to the Pentagon found a sympathetic ear. Patrick's flight was a little unlucky by drawing a 1700 hours (five o'clock) ceremony, meaning most of them wouldn't leave until the next day. The only saving grace being the ability to enter the Airman's Club and get a few drinks to celebrate… as long as they could sew on their first stripe in time.

It was as wild a time as a place with a jukebox containing the complete collection of Perry Como and no females whatsoever would allow. Patrick had several seven and sevens with a group from his flight but decided to head back early due to a 0700 departure. The walk back wouldn't take long due to the brisk night air for a mid-November Texas evening. He was motoring along quickly and reached the grounds of his barracks compound in less than five minutes. He imagined later if he had ordered another drink or walked a little slower he wouldn't have run into Walk. Or was Walk waiting for him? It really didn't matter. It took Patrick about five seconds to realize the sergeant was stone drunk. He couldn't understand what the man said as the veteran lunged at him. Instinctively, Patrick side-stepped him and used his weight to pull him down over Patrick's leg. A basic move learned in hand-to-hand combat class.

Before he could feel too good about himself, the sergeant's experience took over and he whipped his right arm around and caught Haney in the back of the head, sending him falling forward to the sidewalk. Then before Patrick could turn over and get up, Walk was on top of him, grabbing his neck in a hammerlock from behind. Patrick felt consciousness leaving rapidly. He tried to grab Walk's hair, eyes, anything he could, to no avail. Just before his body went limp, he felt the wind rush by his right ear and Walk's grip on him suddenly loosened. Patrick looked up and saw the slender frame of Sergeant Knuckles diving over his head and hitting Walk with a flying tackle that the New Orleans Saints would be proud of. Normally, Walk's sheer size advantage might have allowed him to overcome Knuckle's surprise attack, but the alcohol slowed him down enough for his adversary to knock him down and deliver a blow to his chin… putting him out.

The Security Police Jeep had already stopped by the time Knuckles had delivered the final blow. The sergeant gave them a brief rundown on what had happened and Walk was placed in handcuffs as an ambulance was called. Patrick regained his composure and said, "Thanks for coming by when you did, Sarge." Knuckles shook his head, saying, "I knew he was coming to look for you. Overheard him bragging at the NCO Club how he was going to kick your ass for blemishing his record. Shit, his record was crap already. Just glad I followed him."

After statements were given, Knuckles gave Haney an escort back to the barracks. It was 0100. As Patrick opened the door to the stairs leading up to the dorm, Knuckles said,

"Try to make your flight without any more trouble, OK?"

"No problem, Sarge," Patrick answered, "and thanks for everything."

* * *

As Haney stepped off the plane back in New Orleans, his thoughts of the last 12 hours were lost as he was engulfed by friends and family. Everyone was excited to see him and had gotten a head start on the festivities. Little Bobby, Timmy's younger brother, was the first to greet him.

"Hey man, pretty surprised by all this, huh?" he said as he grabbed Patrick around the neck with his arm. "We got a present for ya over there," he pointed his finger as the crowd parted to reveal Big Bobby, his friend who was supposed to be in Vietnam. Haney ran over to him and shouted over the noise, "I thought you were still over there for two more months, what happened?"

"Got early rotation. Need an operation on my knee," Big Bobby said. "We been partying since I got in this morning. Figured we'd just wait here for you." They hugged each other as childhood friends do and proceeded to continue the party back in the old neighborhood.

Sitting at Mura's, the corner bar, it seemed like 1968 instead of 1970 to Patrick. All the good ole' boys were there. Louie behind the bar. Seems like he started back there when he was in diapers. Glen, always playing the pinball machine, hoping for the big payoff. The two Bobby's. Timmy wanted to distinguish between the two so he took the easy way out and gave them each a prefix. Yeah. Timmy. The thought of him jolted Haney back into the conversation.

"Man, you wouldn't believe how much of it they have available over there. Dirt cheap, too," Big Bobby said. "You can't help but get involved in it, it's everwhere."

"Wh—What are you talking about, I must have missed something," Patrick asked as he shook the cobwebs from his head.

"Grass, man. Dope," Little Bobby replied. "Where you been?"

Big Bobby continued, "I mean everybody does it. Gotta get high on something. My second looie on the flight line was the best connection I had. He always had some righteous stuff." When did he start talking like that, Patrick wondered. Sounds like he spent some time with the hippies in California.

"Bobby," Haney said, "you mean to tell me you bought grass from an officer?"

"Yeah, man," Bobby replied, "and smoked some with a major one time. I'm tellin' ya man, EVERYBODY does something. If it's not dope, then it's the lifers and their booze. Guys stay stoned all the time; only way to cope, know what I mean?"

No, Haney didn't, but he knew to let the subject drop. Little Bobby couldn't, saying, "Hey, big Bob, you got any stuff on you?" Bobby looked around to see if anyone else had come in, "Yeah, I got some. Who's game?" As he looked around the room everyone said yes except Patrick and Louie the bartender.

"I can't leave the bar alone," Louie said. "Go ahead Louie," Patrick said, "I'll watch it for you." "Man, this is your chance to get a sneak preview of what you'll be getting," Big Bobby said. "You may get the chance one day."

"No, thanks," Haney answered, "I'll pass." He walked behind the bar and grabbed an apron. "You guys go on." As they walked out the door, Haney thought that he didn't realize all his friends fooled with that stuff, especially Little Bobby. The guy just turned 18, for Christ sakes!

* * *

The ten-day leave went all too quickly. As he was saying his goodbyes at the airline gate he said to no one in particular, "Seems like we were just doing this." Everyone nodded in agreement and laughed. As Haney got to the end of the line of saying goodbye, Big Bobby stood there with a sullen look on his face. "Don't let 'em send you over there, man," he said. "Nothing good happens to people in 'Nam."

"I won't," Haney said. "They at least owe me a safe four years." As Haney was about to step on the walkway leading to the plane, Big Bobby grabbed him by the neck and while hugging him said in his ear, "I mean it, DON'T LET THEM SEND YOU." As Patrick gently pulled away he nodded to Bobby, and saw that the guy he always believed to be tough as nails was actually crying. He didn't remember getting to his seat, he was too stunned.

* * *

Arriving in Charleston at night, he had no feel for the layout of the base. The clerk checking him into the temporary barracks was helpful in giving him specific directions to the chow hall and Fleet Services, where he was assigned.

After breakfast, the five-minute walk to his duty station gave him a chance to understand where everything was located. The base was a dream for those without a car. All the streets were flat and the essentials were centrally located around the Base Exchange in the middle of the base.

Fleet Services was a small, raised one-story cinder block building located on the edge of the flight line, next door to the Military Terminal. Master Sergeant Frank Wills was happy to see Patrick, saying, "We've been asking for a 702 for six months. It's been tough doing the paperwork and running services at the same time." His elation was quickly extinguished when he learned Patrick wasn't even trained yet. "I suppose you can at least type?" Wills asked. "Yes sir," Patrick replied, "Fifty words a minute." The smile returned to Will's face. "At least that's a start," he said. The master sergeant was a career man, what the troops called "a lifer". Twenty-eight years in and he was looking forward to retirement in fourteen months. He was a tall man, slender with a Henry Fonda look and persona. Almost looked identical except for the horn-rimmed glasses.

Charleston wasn't a bad place to be. It reminded Haney of New Orleans. Cobblestone streets, rich European flavor, and great seafood. Charleston was also flat, just like New Orleans. The locals didn't call it "low country" for nothing. Besides the obvious tourist attractions, Charleston was also known as one of the largest military areas in the States. The Navy base was located, naturally, on the water, close to Atlantic Ocean access. Outside of Newport News, it was the largest naval base on the east coast. The Air Force Base was centralized inland, sharing the airstrip with the commercial flights in and out of Charleston International Airport. The air base was the main point of embarkation on the east coast for military personnel stationed in Europe. Needless to say, the personnel based there inundated the nightlife on weekends throughout the area. Most of the GIs congregated in the outlying bars featuring dancers and strippers. Patrick was different.

Every other Friday he met up with a few other office guys and rode out to the wharf area and enjoyed a seafood dinner. Every week would have been nice, but sixty bucks once a month for pay doesn't go far. They enjoyed their time away from the base and the constant harassment from the rest of the troops. It was tough on administrative people in a predominately blue collar squadron. The rest of the barracks was full of flight line workers who preferred bologna and beer to trout and Chablis. Haney found he was more comfortable with the dining crowd. It was something of an education for him. Back home, the closest he came to this was crawfish and a Dixie beer. He found he enjoyed their company even though he was ribbed for being the youngest in the group by some seven years. Weekends were spent on the golf course, learning more about the game he had started to play as a kid with his brothers. It didn't take him but a few months, and he was winning the enlisted man's tournament.

Everything was running smoothly for Haney. He was learning how to do his job the Air Force way; through a correspondence course. It was a piece of cake. Like being in junior high, he thought. Breezing through the first half, he got upgraded from 70100 to 70230. With it came a promotion to airman first class (two stripes).

"Great!" he said to himself. "Means a raise I hope."

Another let down when he got his next paycheck; a whole eight dollars more. Master Sergeant Wills said, "It's the next step to 70250 that means buck sergeant and more money. I think we're getting a non-com administrator in here. He'll be able to help you with your second half course studies."

Staff Sergeant Morris was a real pain in the ass. From the first day they met, he and Patrick developed what seemed like a severe case of the hates for each other. Haney couldn't figure it out. He did everything Wills or Morris asked, but Morris still gave him bad performance appraisals. His nice, easy job turned into one of being a personal man-servant to Morris. Pick up his laundry. Get his lunch. It never seemed to end. Plus the fact, Morris deemed it his personal mission in life to have Haney get his 70250 rating with more than just a passing score. He rode Haney about studying every day. He even made him show up early for study lessons and stay late every night. Haney couldn't figure it out.

"If this guy hates me so much," he asked Wills, "why is he pushing me to get such a good grade?"

"You have to understand where he comes from, son," Wills answered. "He's colored, from a ghetto in Philadelphia, and has had to fight for everything he's achieved. Hell, when I joined the Air Force, Negroes usually didn't get past three stripes, much less make staff sergeant in four years like he has. He just wants to see you get as much out of yourself as you can."

"Well, why didn't he explain things to me, instead of riding me all the time?" Patrick asked.

"Remember, he's colored," Wills replied, "I don't think he's had much experience giving orders to white people. Tell you what, with the holidays coming up, we'll need help on the flight line with all the leaves scheduled. I'll tell Morris I need you out there. It'll give you a two-week break from each other. Whadda' say?"

Haney jumped at the chance to break the monotony.

* * *

Sergeant Wills was right. After the first two days of his temporary duty,

Haney started to get to know some of the guys assigned to Fleet Service and the jobs they had to do. He never realized before that someone was responsible for the delivering of box meals, playing cards and crossword puzzles, and the flight manifest to each plane upon its arrival in Charleston. He also didn't realize that they were responsible for cleanup and restocking of the latrines on board the mostly C-141s and gigantic C-5As. He received a rude welcome on his third day while helping Chastain, a young buck sergeant from Wyoming, empty the bowels of a C-141.

"See that screw top cover," Chastain said as he pointed to a six-inch pipe sticking out of the bottom of the plane. "Twist it off and stick this hose in there when I tell you to," he said as he handed Patrick a large, six-inch in diameter, flexible hose that was connected to the waste truck they were riding in.

"What's this for?" Haney asked as he grabbed the end of the hose and started investigating a plunger type contraption on the connecting end.

"Don't worry about that now," Chastain replied, "just unscrew the valve when I give you the signal."

Chastain ran around the truck and jumped in the driver's side, giving Haney the thumbs up. Haney leaned down and unscrewed the cover as he had been instructed to do. Before he could turn to grab the hose for proper placement in the pipe, he was engulfed in a flow of greenish-blue liquid which gushed out of the pipe he had just uncovered. Kneeling there, soaked from head to toe in the vilest smelling liquid he had ever come across, Haney heard a roar of laughter and applause from behind him. He turned to see the other guys from his shift enjoying a ridiculous sight at his expense. The rage started to build up and was about to explode as he spotted Chastain joining in the laughter. He lunged at Chastain but was intercepted by Staff Sergeant Whitman, the shift supervisor.

"Whoa, partner. Before you go off half-cocked you should know that you've been accepted into the fraternity."

Calming, Patrick asked, "What are you talking about?"

"Delta Alpha Delta, or what we call Derelicts After Defecation," Whitman replied. "Everyone goes through it, even Sergeant Wills. We just forget to tell you about the doughnut that is pushed up the pipe to stop the flow until you're ready for it. Works every time."

Wiping his uniform off with a towel someone provided Patrick asked, "What is this stuff?"

"When it goes in, its blue anti-freeze and deodorizers," Whitman said, "its greenish now because of the mixture… piss and shit."

Suddenly, Haney's anger turned to nausea as he leaned over and launched his breakfast on Whitman's shoes. When he finished, Patrick looked up at Whitman and said, "Guess that happens a lot, too." They stood toe-to-toe staring at each other as the rest of the shift prepared to break up the fight when they suddenly started laughing and shook hands.

"Come on, Haney, I'll give you a ride so you can clean up," Whitman said, "I guess I can use a change of socks."

At the end of the shift, Whitman said, "Haney, we're all going over to my room for a little R&B. Why don't you join us?" Not knowing what R&B was, Patrick accepted anyway. He was glad to be accepted by his new peers, as temporary as they were.

* * *

The sun was setting as Haney entered the barracks where Whitman lived. As soon as he got to the head of the stairs, he could smell a pungent odor that he had come to recognize. It got stronger as he approached Whitman's door. He could hear muffled voices being drowned out by the music coming from a stereo. He'd heard the music before, but couldn't quite remember who it was. As he knocked, he heard the music lowered and voices being shushed. The door opened, and Whitman peered out through the crack.

"Who is it?" he said as he squinted to recognize the visitor.

"It's me, Haney," Patrick replied. The door swung open and Whitman charged out, hugging Haney, "Our rookie has arrived boys. Glad you could make it, man. Come on and settle in."

As Haney entered, he had to step over guys lying on the floor. As Haney sat, a can of beer was shoved in front of him. He gladly took it. The music, smell, darkness. It was all new to him. Beer was something familiar.

"What's R&B stand for Whit?" he asked. "The music?"

Whitman snorted as he choked back the beer he was swallowing. "No man, reefer and booze. Where you been all your life," he replied as he passed Haney a half-smoked joint. Haney thought for a moment then took the dope and puffed amateurishly.

"No, no, man. You gotta caress it in and down your lungs, like this," Whit said as he grabbed the joint and demonstrated for Haney. "Caress it, man."

Haney took it back and slowly dragged on it.

"Hold it in your lungs as long as you can," Whit said. Never having smoked anything before, Haney found this extremely hard to do and coughed up the smoke and a little beer at the same time.

"Don't worry about it man. It happens to everybody the first time," Whit said as he patted Haney on the back.

The others had started a new round of joints, so Haney was left to experiment with his own. It wasn't long before the combination of the drugs and beer took its desired effect on him. Feeling more relaxed he asked, "Whit, aren't you guys afraid of getting caught? I mean you can smell and hear this group all the way down the hall."

"Nah," the Sergeant answered, "nobody bothers us as long as we do our jobs. I mean, everybody does it in one form or another anyway. So they leave us alone. Com'n man, relax. You like The Doors?"

The rest of the evening seemed to float away for Haney. He didn't know how he got back to his room. Next thing he knew, it was morning and he was riding out to meet another C-141. This time, he knew better.

* * *

Haney's remaining time working on the flight line was a blur. Twelve hours of cleaning and restocking the planes, and twelve hours mixed with dope, beer and sleep. He felt a part of the group. Each shift stuck together, sharing everything. Haney was disappointed his time was up when he reported back to the office the first Monday of 1971. Sergeant Morris was actually glad to see him for a change.

"Although it was hard on me, Haney," Morris said, "I can appreciate your volunteering for flight line duty. It was something most airmen wouldn't have done. I'll certainly remember this come evaluation time."

Haney thought maybe Wills was right. This guy might be human after all. Perhaps it was Morris's new attitude about Patrick, or maybe it was the fact they were getting used to each other, but Haney really enjoyed the next few months of preparation for his administrative exam. Morris pushed hard, but with a different set of priorities. He was placing more emphasis on Haney's overall development instead of the strict ABCs of Air Force administration. When the test results came in May, Morris walked in Haney's office and stuck out his hand saying, "Congratulations Airman, you scored a 98 percent. I'm damn proud of you."

"Thanks Sarge," Haney replied. "I guess my third stripe will be coming soon."

Morris, with mixed feeling, replied, "Yeah, with the last evaluation I gave you it's a cinch. But, you gotta understand with sergeant's stripes you automatically go on the transfer list. You'll probably get orders in the next three months. Just pray for somewhere besides 'Nam."

"You been there Sarge?" Haney asked.

"Yeah. Spent one tour in Saigon. Wasn't too bad there. But I had plenty of buddies on smaller bases. If it wasn't the VC rockets that had 'em worried, it was the drugs or the black market. If God intended for the world to have an asshole, 'Nam is it."

Morris just shook his head saying, "I just hope you go somewhere else."

* * *

The next week Haney was asked to help out on the flight line again. The stint would only be for a day while every Military Air Command base participated in a series of events that comprised the annual competition measuring each base's effectiveness and readiness. Fleet Services did their thing on each entry while the planes were refueling.

Patrick approached a C-141 from Wright-Patterson Air Force Base and noticed three officers wearing "judge" arm bands. Patrick knew there was a chance of the "doughnut" not being in place, so he asked the officers to step back to a safe distance just in case. Two of them immediately complied. The third, a major, took a more active approach telling Patrick, "I'm a judge, I have to observe everything."

"But, sir…" Patrick started to say but was cut short by the major.

"Get on with it son."

"Yes, sir," Patrick replied and proceeded to shove the hose and connector onto its counterpart underneath the plane. When he shoved the plunger up, he felt no resistance, telling him there was no doughnut in place. As soon as he turned the flow knob, Patrick jumped back as quickly as he could. The force of the surge blew the hose off the connection and the greenish liquid flew out and splashed on the concrete flight line, sending it upwards right into the officer's face, drenching him from head to toe. He stood there as still as a statue while Patrick jumped in the truck and drove off, trailing the hose behind him. Looking back in his rearview mirror he could see the other two officers laughing so hard they were falling backwards to the ground. The dry portion.

* * *

Patrick didn't have long to wait for his next assignment. Three weeks later a set of orders came through. Promotion: E-4, effective September 1, 1971. Relieved of current duty October 15, 1971. Thirty days leave granted. Report to port of embarkation, Seattle, Washington, November 16, 1971. New assignment: Office of Social Actions, Cam Rahn Bay, Vietnam. The words seared into his mind, like the brand on new cattle.

When he called his mother with the news, she asked why. Patrick couldn't answer the question. He gave the timeline and between sobs she asked, "So you'll get your GED before you leave?" He tried to make excuses, but she reminded him of his promise to get his diploma. How can you argue with your mother? he thought.

The next six weeks were spent in classes preparing for the test. Taking the exam, he felt it to be elementary. His grade proved him right. A 92 was more than enough for him to send his freshly minted diploma to his Mom.

Chapter 2
James "Juicer" Forest

Spring 1962, New York City

James was a junior at Brooklyn's Stuyvesant High School. Attending in name only. He had missed over half the school year already. When a letter was sent home for his parents to attend a meeting with the school principal, it was thrown in the trash… by his father. A 44-year-old mechanic, James Forest, Sr., did more drinking during the day than working. At night his favorite pastime was beating on his wife. When he got tired of that he started in on his three sons. James Jr. was 16, Steven 14, and John 12. But now, James Jr. was getting too big for him to get away with it without retaliation. The night the letter from the school came, his mother arrived at home about 7 p.m. and was met with a verbal and physical barrage from James Sr. for not having dinner on the table. After the second closed-fisted punch delivered to his mother, Jr. gave the old man a roundhouse right that sent him crashing through the bathroom door. Jr. was now equal in size to his father. Given the age difference and the elder's sobriety state, laying him out wasn't hard.

The next day James Sr. left… for good this time. Mrs. Forest held a job at a local laundry and figured without the drain of paying for booze, she could make it without the no good sonofabitch. Jr. had other plans. Against his mother's wishes, he left with $90 in his pocket and the address of a cousin in Los Angeles. James had grown up in the last year. He stood 6 foot, two inches, with blond hair and blue eyes and a thin, but athletic frame. In his neighborhood, you either were part of a gang or a homosexual. The Dragons were his choice, but he didn't tell any of his brethren about his hopes of one day going to Hollywood and making it in the movies. He promised his brother he would make a life out there and then send for them. It was the last they heard from him until 1968.

His cousin Jeff was an extra on the Universal lot. He didn't make much but was able to pay his rent, buy food, and enough reefer to keep him happy. Once James was able to get on with the studio, they moved out of their small, studio apartment in Television City and got a run-down, two bedroom a block off the ocean in Venice Beach. Jeff was happy to lie around smoking dope all the time, but James immediately got into the body-building clique that was just starting to form on the concrete boardwalk. James didn't shy away from joining his cousin, but taking care of his body was becoming a priority.

* * *

After four years of feeling stagnant, James started trying out for more important roles instead of just being background fodder. Without an agent, it was hard just to get a reading, but when he did the answer was always the same… rejection. By this time, his relentless workouts were paying off. He looked like he belonged in the movies. Six foot four, two hundred thirty pounds of sheer muscle. One thing was keeping him from his big break…he couldn't act. The two would collide in 1969 when one director too many rejected him. James tried to wipe up the floor with him, before his assistant called the security guards to throw him out. The police arrested him during a workout on the beach. He spent 90 days in jail and lost any hope of even being an extra. Now he had to figure a way to make a living. His cellmate, serving a possession charge of six months, gave him the idea. George was already making a living as the largest distributor of weed on Venice Beach. Now he was branching out to the source and eliminating the middle man. His connection in Mexico could supply him whatever he needed. George's friend would fly it in on a small plane. Flying low and under the radar was all it took. James asked him if he needed a partner, but George already had three. If James was willing to take the risk, George told him his supplier was looking to unload some heroin he had come across. George was too scared to fool with it. The big question was could James come up with the five grand to buy the stuff. If he could, he would probably make fifty or sixty grand.

* * *

Women were easy to come by for James. His sleek body and rugged good looks were all it took for the best looking girls on the beach to be more than willing to spend the night with him. There never were any repeat customers… James found a way to get angry at his companion and usually threw them out using more force than was necessary. Word got around, and it didn't take long that the only girls interested were the ones without background knowledge of the physical abuse.

* * *

Jeff had experienced the blackball effect being James' cousin, so he was up for anything. The rent was already two months behind, and he was getting tired of bologna and PB&J. James proposed a quick and easy score... an armored car when it picked up at the convenient store near the Universal lot. He knew it came every day at three o'clock, and the guards were over sixty years old. The proprietor was a little Asian man who was always there by himself. It was just before school let out and the shift change at the studio lot. A couple of ski masks and they were there. James pulled out a .38 caliber he had bought while he was still employed, and they decided tomorrow was the day.

It was a Thursday and pouring down rain. James hadn't seen it come down like that since he had moved to Southern California. When three o'clock rolled around, the thunder and lightning made their job that much easier. After the guard entered the store, the two made sure that the driver wasn't following. They entered the door, masks on, and James immediately pointed the gun at the guard and said, "Don't fucking move." Jeff started to move around the counter when the owner went for a shotgun hidden under a shelf. He never got close to getting the gun leveled off. James immediately and without hesitation shot him in the left eye. The guard stood there with his hands in the air, not moving. Suddenly, a crash on the floor over to James' left made him look towards the upright cooler. Standing there, frozen in his tracks was the director that had James blackballed. A sneaky smile came over his face, and without warning he shot the guard through the forehead from only three feet away. He told Jeff to get the money bag and check the register, and he pointed his revolver at his nemesis and walked towards him. Knowing the director couldn't tell it was him, he pulled off the mask and smiled at his prey. Having been in the store that many times, he knew there was no camera system. When the director saw who it was, his face lost all blood and his bladder forced him to piss in his pants. Looking down, James said, "I knew you were a wimp." The director started to beg, "Please, don't." Before he could say any more, Forest shot him in the crotch and watched him collapse on the floor. As he rolled back and forth, holding his mutilated privates, he begged for his life. It made it all the more pleasurable for James... a slug in the left temple from three inches away.

Jeff's voice jolted James back to reality. He realized their luck with the strongest thunderstorm in years would make their escape almost undetectable. Without the guard, it would be impossible to get the driver to open the door of the armored car. They decided to take what they had, exited the store and saw the driver still sitting behind the wheel, probably hoping his partner took even longer.

As James blended the car into the afternoon traffic, Jeff opened the bag and immediately started to hit the dashboard. "What's the matter?" James asked. "Nothing, man," Jeff said, "We hit the jackpot." He pulled out stacks of twenties and hundreds bound with bank wrappers. Making a quick calculation, he said, "There's gotta be over twenty grand in here." They had no idea that their luck that afternoon extended beyond the storm. The store was a drop-off point for an illegal gambling operation run by the Chinese mafia. All they needed to do now was steer clear of Chinatown.

* * *

George introduced James to his connection in Nuevo, Mexico, Jimenez Gonzales. Together they started to import as much heroin as "Gonzo" could get out of South America. Gonzo was happy to be making fifteen to twenty grand a month, and James, after stepping on the product by adding other ingredients to expand the amount, was clearing over two hundred thousand a month. Gonzo felt he had to give his new friend a nickname, since he had saddled him with one, so he settled on "Juicer" because of James' ability to squeeze the juice out of an orange with his bare hands. Their partnership was profitable for two or three years, until Juicer got greedy.

James had persuaded his cousin to not spend the money foolishly, drawing unwanted attention. They did upgrade their living quarters by buying an apartment building on the beach but used their paid accounting connection at Universal to verify their employment and paid the monthly note out of their proceeds. James was smart. He knew to try and look legitimate in all facets of their life.

* * *

Juicer did the math. He knew if he made his own connection in South America and started importing more he could quadruple his monthly take, easily. Getting Gonzo to agree to do the introduction was easy. Their relationship had grown into one of trust… at least on Gonzo's part.

Diego Dorr was living the highlife in Bogota, Colombia. He lived in a virtual castle on a hill in the jungle. He had every law enforcement and politician paid off so his operation was running without any interruption at all. He and James hit it off immediately. He sensed the same greed in James that he knew was inside him. Diego also had no loyalty to Gonzo. He let Juicer know this when they happened to be alone after dinner that evening. Juicer promised Diego he would be back in a week to talk turkey.

* * *

James sent Jeff to take care of Gonzo upon his return to Venice Beach. Jeff was happy to do it. He saw the upside for himself. Jeff figured a few months with the new deal and he could go out on his own. Unfortunately for Jeff, Juicer knew his plans. Jeff had gotten high and drunk one night with a few of the many goons that Juicer had been able to hire. More than one of them had let Juicer know, hoping to move up in the organization. Besides, Juicer had suspected him of skimming off the top when he did the daily pickups he was assigned.

Jeff's trip to Nuevo was uneventful. He and Juicer had become licensed pilots and had the planes rigged up with enough false compartments so that if they were stopped on either side of the border, the patrols would find nothing. Little did he know that another plane took off from the desert airstrip Juicer had bought a year ago, just fifteen minutes behind him.

Gonzo, being the trusting soul, had no personal guards with him. He relied on his mutual trust with his clients, and the fact that his children were always around the hacienda, all twelve of them. This day was no different. Jeff landed on the outer field from the house so he wouldn't be heard. He took Gonzo completely by surprise. With all twelve children watching, he walked up to his friend with his hand out like he wanted to shake. Gonzo, looking down at his friend's right hand, never saw the left come up to the side of his head. The shot dropped the man to the floor and his children stood there frozen in fear that the intruder would come after them next. Jeff didn't have orders to kill anyone else, so he stole away back to his plane and was surprised to find one of the goons there.

"What are you doing here," Jeff asked him suspiciously.

"Juicer wanted insurance," the goon said, "In case you lost your nerve."

Being more at ease he let the goon know the job was done and he started to enter his plane for the trip back. Jeff didn't see the other goon coming from behind the plane. He never knew what hit him, but it was a .45 to the back of the head. Without saying a word, the two got the body inside one of the planes and took the passenger door off. It was easy pushing Jeff out the aircraft over the Mexican desert.

* * *

With Jeff out of the picture, Juicer knew he needed reliable help. The only place to go was a blood relative. His brother Steven was out of high school and working a meaningless job at a hardware store. He had followed James into the Dragons, but knew he had to help his mother bring in money. When his older brother called, there was no hesitation. Ms. Forest knew where James was getting his money and refused to accept any of it. The middle son was another story. He was on the next plane out to Los Angeles the next day.

* * *

Venice Beach 1970

Steven proved to be a great asset to the organization. He had Juicer's intelligence along with his ruthlessness. He also had developed his older brother's affection for body building. The two of them spent almost every day sculpting their shapes, to the delight of the bikini-clad beauties who hung around, hoping to catch their eye. They were known all over the beach as the party animals. At the close of each day, thirty or forty people would adjourn to their ground floor apartment for fun and games. The brothers were smart. They never allowed any drugs in their house, not wanting to give any undercover cops a reason to suspect they had become the largest heroin dealers in Southern California.

The beginning of the New Year brought a new idea from Diego. One he had already implemented in Australia. Shipping smack back from a new source in Asia. The supply was capable of producing a much greater yield than their South American contacts, and it was delivered in a foolproof manner: body bags of the Killed In Action from Vietnam. Diego assured Juicer that obtaining contacts on both ends of the route was as easy as tipping a waiter after a gourmet meal.

Juicer, as always, only trusted blood. He did find corruptible contacts on each end of the route, but wanted to assure himself that nothing would go wrong. Naturally, his youngest brother was enlisted to help the operation. Juicer knew he didn't have the intelligence of Steven, but was as strong as a bull as well as fearless. It was a longer-term plan than he wanted, but Juicer knew if he could bribe John's way to Asia after basic training, he could better control the source. He was stunned at how easy it was to find the right people in the right locations. It would cost him about fifty grand a month, but it was worth it. He and Diego figured the final would exceed two million dollars per month… each.

By the time the end of 1970 rolled around, the system was running like a Swiss timepiece. John was stationed in the Philippines and, with another goon's help, was able to set up the operation, having that much money to throw around. John let his brother know that if he could get them transferred to Thailand, the Philippine middleman could be cut out. Juicer liked the way his brother was coming around. After the transfer was arranged, John was sent to deliver a message to the Filipino middleman… but he exceeded his instructions and cut the young man's throat. When the police found his body, the head was nearly detached.

* * *

The year of 1970 had been a profitable one for Juicer and Diego. Juicer was earning so much money he was having trouble hiding it all. He was setting up dummy corporations with the help of the many sleaze ball law firms in L.A., who were more than willing to take a chance with the law given the payoff available from Forest. Some of the money was run through legitimate banks scattered around the country, but most of it was deposited in offshore accounts in the Caymans and the cliché Swiss banks. After his first trip to Geneva, Juicer said, "I thought these secret accounts were only fiction made up by Hollywood." After his third trip, his account totaled over 30 million. Needless to say, the FBI was interested in Juicer, but couldn't pin anything on him. He had groomed loyalty within his non-blood organization by being very generous. Occasional reminders to his associates how ruthless he could be by putting a bullet in someone's head as an example didn't hurt loyalty either.

Christmas of 1970 brought an invitation to Rio De Janeiro by an associate of Diego's from Colombia. Being leery, Juicer persuaded Carlos Mantenga to come to L.A., promising to show him around Hollywood. Carlos was convinced, hoping to meet his movie heroes.

The meeting took place at the Hollywood Hilton in the Presidential Suite. Carlos was impressed by the surroundings and pleasantly surprised to know he would be staying there for as long as he wished. Carlos was a man of few words, something Juicer could appreciate. In a nutshell, he told Juicer he was expanding his cocaine operation out of Bogota and wanted to offer him the opportunity to be the initial distributor in the States. "What about Diego?" Juicer asked. "This does not concern Diego," Carlos answered.

Juicer had just finished reading "The Godfather" by Mario Puzo, and his mind immediately went to the part where the drug dealer made a similar offer to the Don. He knew this was bad news for Diego and didn't want to be caught in the middle.

"I'm sorry," Juicer started, "but my organization is geared for smack… different customers."

The Colombian looked at him and smiled, "I've heard you were smart, that's exactly what I wanted to hear. It will be no problem setting up my own people here in the States. Our businesses will complement each other, not conflict."

When he said that, Juicer knew that Diego's days were numbered.

"Now," Carlos said, "can we go see Hollywood?" Everyone in the room laughed.

* * *

The word came the first week of January. It was a personal courier from Carlos, telling Juicer that Diego was dead and that he was now the sole proprietor of the operation. Carlos also promised to keep in touch, that maybe they could do favors for one another from time to time. Juicer knew this would be a request he could not refuse.

With Diego out of the picture, Juicer's take doubled, making it that much harder to hide the money. The lawyers were being very creative in doing that for him. He owned so many businesses around the country, he kept a log in his safe hidden in the floor of his building. He had completely renovated the building, moving out all tenants and making it the first opulent house directly on the beach. Local codes did not allow for single occupancy housing, but the city fathers were easily persuaded to change the zoning laws after large contributions to their campaign coffers.

Venice Beach in the early 1970s was a mixture of the bodybuilding crowd along with the fun-loving dopers that included his old friend George and what seemed like every stewardess based in L.A. George mentioned to Juicer his desire to branch out into the new "hot" drug: cocaine. Juicer liked George, so he agreed to set up a meeting with Carlos, knowing this would circumvent any hostilities between the two. George was grateful and showed it by introducing Juicer to some stewardesses who, like all the others, never came back for an encore.

* * *

April 1972

Although he had suppliers all over Southeast Asia, he knew he couldn't let the disruption in flow from Cam Rahn Bay go unpunished. This Doctor on the payroll was managing to get an assortment of drugs from the hospital and traded them to the black market for the heroin he needed. Juicer had one of the goons speak directly to the doctor and ordered him to take the cause of disruption out. The Doctor explained that his position was compromised, but Juicer ordered him to find a way to get it going again, and that Juicer would send someone to make an example of the person responsible. The Doctor begged the goon to have Juicer allow him to do the job himself, thinking that since his medical career was over, he may have an opportunity to show he might have a place in the organization in another capacity. Although Juicer gave the OK, he also ordered to take the doctor out once he had done his job.

Within twelve hours of it happening, Juicer knew that the Doctor was dead. He also knew his hitman wasn't the one who did it. Who was this person who dared to fuck with his livelihood? He ordered his Saigon representative to pay 10 thousand dollars to the VC mafia to take care of the problem. Juicer didn't know the name of the party responsible for his problems in Cam Rahn, he just wanted it wiped out.

Three weeks later his contact in Saigon said the job was done and the local police had already termed it black-market revenge. Their system was safe. The contact didn't know the assassins had gotten the wrong person.

* * *

Summer 1972

Korat, Thailand was becoming Juicer's most productive outlet. With the war slowing down, he started to worry about not enough body bags to fill his needs. He started investigating other ways to keep the supply going. In the meantime, he was still having trouble hiding the money. The FBI knew he was into something, but just didn't know what. By the time August of 1972 rolled around, two years had been spent on the case. After so many man hours spent by the agency, it was a tip from one of Juicer's former one-night stands that gave them their first break.

The one - night stand was Sue Marino, a beautiful, 26-year-old stewardess who supplemented her income by occasionally working for a high-priced escort service, all to service her coke habit. Her date that muggy August night was staying at the Beverly Hills Hotel. She knew the protocol. Let the john instigate the conversation to avoid any undercover cops. But, tonight she was in a hurry. After two minutes of small talk she started stating the menu and its prices. Under interrogation at the station house, she offered information in exchange for release. The lieutenant in charge listened to her story about a muscle-bound guy who lived on the beach. He seemed to have an unlimited supply of money but no real job. Always on the phone, she figured he owned his own business. After roughing her up that night, she was gathering her things to leave. When she was about to walk down the stairs, she heard Juicer talking with his brother Steven. The conversation only lasted a few minutes, but she heard him mention the name "Jeff" and a convenience store robbery that included some deaths. The lieutenant put her back in a cell and started the research by notifying the other law enforcement authorities in the area. Only 30 minutes went by before the local FBI office called and confirmed that the big muscle guy went by the name of "Juicer". This could be the break they needed. Now they just needed to find out which robbery.

* * *

It was fairly easy paring down the number of unsolved convenience store robberies. Most of them did not involve shootings. Over the last five years, there were only three that fit the bill. That's where they concentrated their efforts. All three robberies had slugs dug out of the victims, and ballistics had identified the caliber of each weapon. One .38, a .22 and a .45. But was this enough to get a search warrant and would Juicer be dumb enough to still have the gun? They had to try.

Juicer had just kicked his latest bimbo out the door, literally, when the FBI showed up. It was 4 a.m. After they had finished the search, six hours later, the house looked like it had just gone through another renovation. Not a mattress or piece of furniture was left untouched. The lead agent was about to call it quits when he noticed something in a shadowbox frame lying on the floor. Turning it over and finding a painting pushed up against the glass made him curious.

"Who inspected this?" he asked, holding up the frame. No one took responsibility, but that didn't matter. He popped off the back of the picture and there, taped onto the back of the oil painting, was a chrome plated .38. Juicer, it seems, was a packrat and couldn't get rid of anything. Especially when he considered it a trophy symbolizing his first kill.

The FBI informed his lawyer, who had arrived by this time, that they would like his client to come down for questioning. Not seeing any reason to avoid it, the lawyer agreed. One police officer was assigned to rush the pistol down to ballistics and determine if it was a match. They knew with such a high-priced attorney, the time they would be able to question Juicer was limited.

After two hours of getting nowhere, the attorney issued an ultimatum: charge him or release him. Luckily, the lab called just before the door was opened to let him free. It matched the robbery and murder of three outside Universal Studios back in 1966. It was enough to book him, but now they had to make the case against him. Knowing he could probably afford any bail set, they implored the State's Attorney to ask for bail denial. But, this being California, the most liberal state in the fifty, bail was set at $500,000. He was out before dusk fell.

* * *

Pre-trial motions were exchanged over the next few weeks. The only one granted was the state's request to fast track the case due to the nature of the crime and the information from the FBI suspecting Mr. Forrest to be involved in a large drug dealing operation. The trial was set for November 15, 1972. Juicer, however, already had other plans for that period of time.

At 9 a.m., Los Angeles Superior Court A, the trial of James "Juicer" Forrest was to begin. The courtroom was full, mostly with reporters. Both legal teams were there. One thing was missing. It seems Juicer had gone underground.

* * *

Getting out of the country was easy. With enough money, there were ample border guards eager to help him cross over into Mexico with his truck full of all the necessities of his stay, including the ready cash he would need. His brother, who stayed behind, could access any account if necessary.

The trial was not his first concern. His complete operation in Asia had now been halted and he wanted the head of the individual responsible. Ten days before Christmas 1972 was the first time he heard the name Patrick Haney. If he hurried, his source told him, he could cap the guy while he was on leave in New Orleans. If not, Juicer would have to chance hitting him on a federal base, giving the FBI the power to exert more effort in their efforts to nail him.

Juicer knew a guy in New Orleans, Ray Boudreaux, who would hit anybody for a price. It was reported he freelanced for Carlos Marcello, the crime boss there, from time to time. Juicer gave him a down payment of $25,000 with another $75,000 upon completion.

Boudreaux started tailing Haney as he came out of his Mom's house. Traveling down St. Charles Avenue, Haney always admired the large mansions lining the street all the way to Jackson Ave. At first he didn't notice the car trying to pass him on the right on a one lane road. Haney caught a glimpse in the side view mirror of the crazy driver trying to get by. As the sun glimmered off the chrome plated pistol, Haney knew he had to do something. As Haney slammed on his brakes, the hitman's car sideswiped his, causing him to veer onto the tree-lined neutral ground where the streetcars rode. He missed the first one but couldn't avoid the second. The force of the collision made a large dent in his front left bumper.

The police were on the scene quickly, causing the hitman to take off without finishing the job.

* * *

Christmas and New Year's came and went. Juicer was losing his patience. After confirming that Haney had left for Maxwell AFB, he demanded his $25,000 to be refunded. Boudreaux refused. The next day the New Orleans Times-Picayune ran a story about a mafia hitman being found in a grain barge on the riverfront with the back of his head blown out by a .357. The FBI immediately interviewed Marcello. He was furious. Boudreaux was one of his best contractors, so he gave the FBI what they wanted: Juicer Forrest ordered the hit as revenge. That was all Agent Rison needed to hear. He ordered the twenty-four-hour surveillance be doubled in manpower so as to not lose their bait.

* * *

Montgomery, Alabama - April 1973

Rison knew they were getting close. The surveillance on Steven Forrest had paid off. The FBI had tracked him driving to Alabama with three goons. Rison knew they weren't going for the boiled peanuts. The assistant director had already assigned him to take over from the Birmingham office, but he chose to be where the action was, in Montgomery. The office was too small, so they took over a wing of the Holiday Inn on the South Bypass. Things were going to come to a head, and soon.

The tail on Steven told Rison that they had met another car with four more goons at the Travelodge just down the street from the FBI's command center. At least they made it convenient for them, Rison thought. But there was no sign of Juicer.

* * *

Juicer was smarter than Rison gave him credit for. He knew the FBI would be tailing his brother, so when he arrived in Montgomery and he and his bodyguard checked into the Rodeway Inn, he was in disguise. The two of them never left the room. Communication from his brother was done through whatever fast food delivery service came to Juicer's room that night. It helped that he already owned a couple of them through dummy corporations.

Acquiring a few spies on the base was as easy as ever. A couple of hundred dollars a month wasn't much, so an additional thousand was too attractive to pass up. Upon learning of the cookout planned by Haney and his barrack mates, the plan was set. Steven and his car would take the FBI on a wild goose chase while Juicer's hired hands and their car would take its place on the dirt road. Juicer and his bodyguard would stay behind, waiting to hear the job was done. Steven led the tail downtown making unnecessary turns around the Capitol Building until he felt the time was right. The car entered a covered, multi-decked parking garage where Steven and two of his friends jumped out and dove into a waiting vehicle. It worked. The FBI continued following the original car as Steven and his boys made their way out to the dirt road to take their place and await Haney and his girlfriend.

* * *

May 15, 1973

When Juicer didn't hear from his brother after a couple of days, he knew there was a problem. The newspaper didn't uncover the story until a reporter overheard a conversation about a shootout on a dirt road out in the sticks. By the time it ran, Steven had been in custody for some time.

Juicer's bodyguard had found out about Haney's departure day from one of the paid snitches. He knew they would have to take care of it themselves. The bodyguard tried to talk him out of it. He had millions to live off in some country without an extradition agreement; they should just go.

"Fuck you," Juicer said, "this guy cost me two brothers and my livelihood, he's going down. Besides, the FBI thinks I'm out of the country, they won't be following him anymore."

By 8 a.m., they were parked in the outer lot of Maggie May's, waiting for a brown Mercury Capri to come through the gates. The plan was to hit him on the interstate so their escape could be easy.

Chapter 3
In Country

New Orleans, November 15, 1971

He never was a good traveler, especially by plane. So Haney was relieved when the going-away party lasted until sunrise. Probably wouldn't have slept a wink anyway, he thought. The party was great. What started out as an intimate gathering of close friends at the Silver Slipper lounge turned into an orgy of booze and reefer with what seemed like the entire Irish Channel. At 6 a.m., Joey the bartender threw them out so the cleaning crew could start getting ready for the day shift of neighborhood drunks. Good thing. Haney's plane left at 7:30 a.m.

Airport security was alerted before Haney even made it to the gate. Seems a couple of the good ole boys took offense to the cocktail lounge refusing to serve drinks to them just because they couldn't stand up without assistance. The entourage was escorted to gate 5, concourse B only after Haney's mother and uncle pleaded the case of a "soon to be defender of the democratic way of life in a far land." The security officer in charge knew he was being fed some BS, but he had a son in Pleiku, so he allowed the group safe passage, as long as they behaved themselves.

Haney was scared. Looking back, he couldn't remember all the goodbyes. There were too many people. He did remember the look on his mother's face like she would never see him again. Normally he never was able to sleep on planes. This wasn't normal. The effects of the grass, booze and beer took its toll. Sleep came easily.

* * *

Seattle, Washington, November 16, 1971

It was everything he had learned in geography class. The rain not only came down the entire time he was there, but did so sideways. It wasn't cold, so he decided to put on his summer uniform with the light windbreaker. He was told to check into the temporary duty enlisted barracks, catch some sleep, and report to the terminal at 2100 hours for flight boarding.

When he arrived at the barracks, he took one look at the situation and started to scout for a phone to call a cab. The room he would have been assigned to was about 30 x 30 with portable cots jammed in next to each other so that almost every inch of floor space was taken up. Each cot was covered with a two-inch foam mattress that you could tell let you feel every spring and wire support. On top of that was neatly folded, dingy gray linen with holes the size of apples. The attending airman informed him that no one was allowed in a bunk until after 2100 hours. Haney told him he was scheduled to catch a plane at the time and needed some sleep before that.

"Tough shit, man. You can catch some shuteye in a day room. They got some chairs in front of the TV," the airman said matter-of-factly.

"No, thanks," said Haney as he walked to the payphone.

The taxi smelled as bad as the TDY barracks, and was just as dirty and littered with trash. The driver told him his friend managed a motel right outside the gate. After exiting the base and driving about a mile past several suitable motels, the cab eased into a shell driveway that revealed a broken neon sign flashing Oasis Motel, except the "a" and "m" were not blinking.

"Are you sure this place is OK?" Haney asked apprehensively.

"Yeah, no problem. Don't let the outside fool ya. Say, you want some company?" slurred the cabby.

"Depends on what you mean," Haney answered as he got out of the cab and left two bucks to cover a 75-cent meter. Without waiting for an answer, Haney entered the lobby which looked more like a mop closet. The cabbie's friend told him it would be six dollars until 7 p.m., and the TV was free since he was only a two-striper. Good thing he didn't get his stripe sewed on yet, Haney thought. Apprehensively, he took the key and decided to check out the room. After struggling with the key for a few seconds, he entered and was pleasantly surprised to find a fairly clean place, though sparsely furnished. It did have a color TV and a waterbed. First time on one of those, he thought. He proceeded to settle in and try and get some rest before reporting for his flight that night. Glancing at the 1:35 which showed on the clock, he figured five hours of sleep might just be enough.

Not even having had time to settle the constantly flowing water, he was shaken out of a shallow slumber by a constant chatter and continued knocking on the door. Looking over at the clock, he quickly figured he'd only been sleeping for about 45 minutes. Grudgingly, he stumbled to the door and opened it. Standing there in matching hot pink pants and halter tops were two of the most well-endowed women he'd seen in some time, if ever.

* * *

DeDe and Candy invited themselves in and plopped down on the bed. Haney stood there in his Air Force issue skivvies and asked nervously, "Did I die and go to heaven?"

"Honey, Charlie the cabbie said you needed some company but didn't get a chance to ask what flavor," DeDe said.

"Flavor?" queried Patrick.

"You know… vanilla or chocolate," DeDe answered, pointing to Candy. It was then that Haney noticed Candy was black, albeit very light skinned. He hadn't noticed because he had been concentrating on her ample breasts straining to jump out of a top two sizes too small.

"Well, what'll it be, honey?" insisted DeDe. Having just turned 19 a few months ago, Haney had never encountered a prostitute before. Hell, sex was a relatively new phenomenon to him. Throw in the fact he came from one of the most racially biased areas of the South, he wasn't sure what to do. DeDe spoke first, "Look, Honey, its 20 bucks for either one of us till 7, 10 more if you want anything other than a roll, as they say, time is money."

"How much for both of you?" Haney blurted out, not really thinking about what he was saying. Both of the girls looked at each other slyly and smiled. Candy said, "Baby, if you can handle it, we'll do it for $60."

Haney did a quick calculation and decided to go for it. Hell, he'd only read about such things, never knowing anyone who actually got two at the same time.

What seemed like a few moments to Haney was in reality all the time he had allotted for rest before his flight. The clock read 6:30. He jumped up off the bed and in doing so made the water rotate so violently that DeDe was thrown to the floor and Candy jostled awake. He grabbed his wallet and counted out three $20 bills and handed them to Candy. Quickly counting the rest, he saw that $220 was left from his travel pay.

"Gotta take a shower and catch a plane. You girls can have the room until the manager throws you out," he said as he grabbed his wallet and towel and headed for the shower. While he was trying to scrub his back he heard the door open and DeDe say, "Sorry, gotta pee." A few seconds later the toilet flushed and the door closed. Haney quickly pulled back the shower curtain and grabbed his wallet and started counting.

"Bitch took a hundred," he said to himself as he grabbed the towel and stormed out the door. Before he could take two steps out of the bathroom, Candy was standing there with his money in her hands.

"I'm sorry honey, my friend has a problem she can't seem to shake. I hope you can forgive her," she said.

"No problem, thanks," he answered, smiling. When he came back out of the bathroom after finishing his shower, the girls had left. All of his belongings seemed to be there so he proceeded to shave and get dressed. Then he noticed that they had left him something that brought another smile to his face. Smeared on the mirror in candy apple red lipstick was his goodbye; "Take care in Vietnam, look us up on the way back."

* * *

The flight left two hours late. Although the military chartered civilian airlines to make these trips, they didn't act like a civilian airline. It did have a few attendants, but that was as far as the creature comforts went. The head stewardess told the 170 passengers that their flight would take them first to Anchorage for a refueling stop, then on to Tokyo. After stretching their legs, the final trip to Cam Rahn Bay. Actual flying time was about 18 hours. Haney nodded off as soon as everyone settled down. He was jolted awake two hours later by the airplanes' gear touching down at Anchorage International. After coming to a stop some 200 yards from the gate, the stewardess informed them they would have to disembark for refueling purposes and that the jetway was unavailable for use due to severe weather conditions. As he stepped through the frozen door and started to walk down the stairs, Haney experienced what it meant to be in the frozen tundra. As warm as it was on that plane, as soon as he hit the night air the hair on his arms was immediately frozen due to the mild perspiration collecting there.

"Jesus, Mary and Joseph!" he yelled to no one in particular. He started to run but noticed those ahead of him who thought the same thing and promptly ended up hitting the deck in a very ungraceful manner. The ice covered everything. He looked up and saw a time and temperature sign reading 4:22/-1 F. As quickly as his feet would allow, he made it into the terminal. He decided to take his winter blues from the bag he carried and change in the restroom. No sense in freezing again he figured. When he emerged, blood again flowing, he noticed he had about an hour before having to board the flight again for takeoff. His stomach suddenly reminded him it had been at least 24 hours since he last ate. Problem was there were no restaurants open at that hour. He had one of the passengers who was a mess hall jockey and knew how to operate the coffee machine round him up something. Haney gingerly passed his way through the crowd looking for a seat. His eyes were burning from all the smoke in the air. He thought he smelled reefer but decided that no one was dumb enough to light up in public like that.

The only spot he could find was a booth in the corner occupied by three black guys in Army fatigues. "Mind if I sit down?" Haney asked. "Knock your lights out, man," answered the one with an unlit cigarette dangling from his mouth. Haney took his place next to him and looked at the uniforms of his bench mate and two friends across from them.

"What's that insignia for?" Patrick queried pointing to a patch on the guy's shoulder.

"Cavalry," said the smoker. "We headin' back to our outfit for our second tour. Gonna' meet up with 'dem in Da Nang."

Patrick remembered Big Bobby's words; "don't trust anybody that goes back for more". The words seemed to linger in his mind as the one sitting next to him continued. "Yeah, 7th Cav. We 'da baddest motha's in country. We take care of all the dirty work you fly boys don't wanna do. Name's Cyril, man. This here is Leo," he said, pointing to the guy across from Haney, "and this here is brother Charles." Haney shook each hand as it was thrust out to him, letting each know his first name. When he came to brother Charles, Haney experienced a handshake like never before. The man wearing a sort of beret made of woolen material alternating red, black and green, grabbed his hand with force and did a strange movement on Haney's hand. Grabbing, holding and tapping to some sort of rhythm was not only foreign to Haney, but extremely uncomfortable. As brother Charles let go of his vice grip, he slapped the back of Haney's hand and pointed his index finger at each of his friends. They all stared at Haney for a few seconds and then snickered between themselves at what was obviously Haney's expense. Cyril spoke up, "Don't worry 'bout it man, we knows you a rookie. You'll get the hang of it 'ventually."

With that Cyril broke out what looked to Patrick like a finely rolled joint. As he lit the stick, Cyril sensed Haney's fear and said, "Look man, everybody does it. That's why we going back. Can't beat the reefer and other goodies available to the brothas. Price is right, too."

As he passed the joint to Haney, he noticed Patrick looking around suspiciously and eased his fears, "Look at that lifer over there," he said pointing to another 7th Cav nom-com. "He going back for his third tour. Ya' know why?" Haney looked at the career man and noticed him sweating profusely and nervously dragging on a Marlboro. Cyril didn't wait for an answer. "He got a monkey on his back, man. Couldn't kick it so he gave up and he's going back, man. Probably die before he gets back to the world." Haney was completely puzzled.

"What in the world are you talking about," he asked. In the meantime, Cyril had bypassed Patrick and passed the joint to his friends who eagerly took their turns. Cyril answered, "The guy is hooked on smack, man. You know…heroin, man!" Haney said with the shock evident on his face, "That guy's at least 40 years old. And look at all those ribbons on his chest. The Army wouldn't let that happen to someone," he insisted. The others smiled at each other and Charles chimed in, "The Man don't give a fuck as long as he can use you. You best remember that rookie. Might save yo' life one day." The other two nodded, and Leo handed Patrick the half-smoked joint saying, "It ain't as good as you get in country, but it'll pass the time." Haney grabbed the reefer and thought, what the hell, maybe it'll stifle my hunger pains.

* * *

The next thing Haney realized, the plane was touching down in Cam Rahn Bay. The flight had been an eye-opener for him. He had changed seats to be by his new-found Army friends. The reefer never stopped coming. Haney was still nervous about it until he saw others, white and black, puffing on whatever was pushed in front of them. He also noticed many a bottle of Southern Comfort making the rounds between the lifers sitting a few rows in front of him. It didn't take long for him to feel more comfortable. Hell, it was better than playing pinochle, he thought.

As he stepped off the plane, the blast furnace hit him in the face. He suddenly felt that the interior of the plane was more pleasant, even though thick clouds of smoke had made the temperature feel more tropical than it was. The cobwebs were shaken from his head as the grizzled veteran shoved his way past Haney, spouting obscenities to anyone within earshot.

By the time he made it to his assigned barracks, it was 3 a.m. Orders stated to report to his duty office at 0800. He wasn't sleepy, so he just sat outside his barracks door on top of the cement bunker four-foot-high wall that surrounded the two-story structure, watching the sun rise over the South China Sea.

* * *

Haney had left his barracks in plenty of time to eat breakfast at the chow hall and still have enough time to find his duty office. It was his first experience with powdered eggs. He hoped it would be his last. The mess sergeant told him they usually had real eggs, but supplies were lagging behind orders. "How'd you know it was my first time here, Sarge?" Haney asked as he signed his name to receive his meal. "Easy, rookie" the staff sergeant answered, "you signed your full name, everybody else just scribbles something. Besides, your fatigues are new. Get used to it, newbie," he laughed. Haney had forgotten about the jungle fatigues he was issued last night when he arrived. The olive garments looked two sizes too big with the oversized pockets that were tilted inward, and the shirt came down below his crotch.

After breakfast he tried to get directions to the Social Actions Office. Everyone he approached looked at him strangely and said they didn't know, never heard of the place. A second lieutenant directed him to base administration, they should know, he said. After what seemed like an eternity, a major came out of an office and gave Haney directions to his new duty office. "Major Daly has already called looking for you, Airman," he said. Haney glanced at his watch and saw he was already twenty minutes late, causing him to hurry out the door and down the road to the hut at the end. The sign hanging on the door was hastily scrawled with a black marker: Social Actions Office.

* * *

As Patrick stood at attention, he quickly noticed his boss was probably the skinniest officer he had ever come across. Major Stan Daly was an 18-year veteran doing his first tour outside of the U.S., or the world, as those in Asia had come to call it. A picture of a handsome woman and four daughters was the only thing on top of his desk besides the phone. As he rose, Haney noticed how tall he was. At least six foot three he guessed, making him appear even more slender.

"At ease, son," the major said in a kindly voice. "I was beginning to get worried about you."

"I'm sorry, sir, no one could give me directions to get here," Patrick said, "I had to stop at admin to find out where to go."

"Don't worry about it, Patrick… May I call you Patrick?" the major asked.

"Of course, sir," he replied.

"It's no wonder no one knows we're here, son," the major continued. "You see, the Office of Social Actions is a brand new arm of base administration tasked with two goals: implement a new drug and alcohol abuse program that President Nixon has ordered the Pentagon to begin, and establish a race relations course that all personnel will attend to better the interaction between us all. I myself have only been in the country for one week. Today is the first day we even have an office."

"Patrick," the major continued as he took his seat, "you might ask yourself why you would be chosen for this assignment."

"Yes sir, the thought crossed my mind," he answered.

"Well, we were looking for someone with administrative skills and a high degree of intelligence who could possibly develop into a counselor for our program. We feel you could fill that role very nicely."

A little puzzled, Patrick answered, "Yes sir." The major went on, "Although I'm a career officer, you'll find that I like to dispense with routine military titles within the confines of our office, that is of course, when no one else is around."

"If it's all the same to you Major," Haney replied, "I'd just as soon stick with normal protocol, sir, cuts down on the confusion."

"As you wish, son," he said. "You'll be in the outer office here," he said as he walked into the reception area.

"What are those other two offices for, Major?" asked Haney.

"Those are for our two full-time counselors who are arriving next week," answered Daly. "A Staff Sergeant Norton and Master Sergeant May, if memory serves."

The rest of the day was routine with Haney and the major setting up files and drawing essentials from Central Supply to stock the office. The major pitched in and got his hands dirty. Patrick decided he was going to like this guy.

* * *

That night after chow, Haney sauntered back to his barracks, taking the time to get his bearings about the base. He finally made his way to the primitive dirt road marked by a crude makeshift sign saying Miami Ave. and walked the few hundred feet to his barracks.

His barracks on Miami Ave. was just like all the others. The living quarters had been laid out in a grid and sat closest to the beach. Every building was identical to all the others; two-story wood frame with screens for walls with roll down canvas. Each building was surrounded by a four-foot concrete wall that protected the residents from rocket attacks. The only roads that were paved were the main ones leading to the business areas, including the BX. The closer you got to the flight line, the more paved streets you came across. The dust from the dirt roads tended to fly into the barracks, making it impossible to keep anything not covered clean, including the beds.

Outside the two-story wooden structure with no windows, a handful of guys sat on top of the cement bunker wall whistling and catcalling as the day maids left their assigned jobs. Most of the local women were nothing to be foaming over, but these guys had obviously been there much too long. He could tell by the faded nature of their fatigues.

"Hey newbie," one of them yelled to Haney, "you the guy that moved in downstairs?" Haney looked around to see if he could be talking to anyone else. Not seeing anyone he answered, "Yeah, just got in last night."

"Well newbie, protocol says the rookie pays for the hookers the first night," the largest of the group continued as he jumped down from his perch. "And that means YOU!" he said poking a finger into Haney's chest. Since he was doing this at a distinct downward angle, Haney thought it best not to get off on the wrong foot. He figured it might take the guy 10 seconds to pound him to a pulp.

"Sorry guys, I'm a little tired from my flight," Patrick said as he tried to step around Godzilla, "I'll give you a raincheck, OK."

No luck.

Godzilla stepped in front of him again and poked even harder, "That ain't a request newbie."

By this time Haney was getting very anxious, and was contemplating what his next move might be, short of getting killed, when a somewhat short, red-haired buck sergeant stepped in between them and pushed Godzilla away.

"That's enough fun, Alvin," the red-haired stranger said, "This rookie probably has to change his shorts now."

With that, the stranger turned and stuck out his hand to Patrick and said, "Chuck Danton, don't mind Tiny, he just forgot his manners back in Texas. Or maybe he was an abused child… take your pick."

"Uh, yeah, uh, hi Chuck, Patrick…Haney," he responded, thanking his stars for the intervention.

"C'mon," Chuck said, "I'll walk you to your room."

Room, Haney thought to himself. That was a joke. As they entered the barracks, the first room was the latrine. It seems the Air Force didn't build them for aesthetics as much for function. Passing through the latrine you entered what was, in reality, a large room separated by sheets of plywood. Each cubicle was considered a room. This would be about as much privacy as Haney would see in his time there. Even the toilets had no doors, only half walls. Some of the cubicles had padlocks on them.

"You might want to get a lock from the BX tomorrow," Chuck said as they walked into Haney's room, which was the closest to the latrine.

"Not that it makes your valuables any safer, but it may give you a sense of security."

As they sat down, Haney took a mental inventory for the first time. Steel frame bed with a standard six-inch mattress. Upright metal locker with a lock frame to secure everything he owned. One metal folding chair. Chuck took the chair and Haney flopped on the bed.

"Thanks, you probably saved my life out there," he said to Chuck.

"Nah, Tiny's all talk, Chuck answered, "He was just having fun with the new guy. Besides, if he wanted to hurt you, nobody could have stopped him."

"Well," Haney said, "he seems to respect you a lot."

"He'd better," Chuck replied, "I let him call home every week for free.

I figure it's better than buying insurance."

Puzzled, Haney inquired, "What do you mean?"

"Oh yeah, you wouldn't know what I do," Chuck answered. "I'm the operator at the base switchboard. I can call anywhere in the world... for free. Nobody else is around, so I let a few select friends call home every once in a while."

"Aren't you afraid of getting caught?" Patrick asked.

"Nah, they can't trace the calls," Chuck said. "Besides, they don't want to. Chalk them up to the war effort."

Chuck noticed Haney's eyes getting heavy and said, "I'll let you get some sleep, you've got jet lag. It'll take a couple of days to adjust. I'll meet you after work tomorrow out on the wall for the shift change." With that, Chuck was out the door before Patrick could ask him about this shift change. He was too tired to get up and find out. He was in a deep sleep in a few seconds.

*　　*　　*

The next day was much like the one before; except Haney knew how to get to work. That evening after chow, he made his way down Miami Ave. and just as the day before, the same group were lounging on top of the wall.

"Hey, Patrick," Chuck shouted, "how's it going?"

Without waiting for an answer he continued, "Guys, this is Patrick Haney. You remember him from last night." He started introducing everyone on the wall for Haney's benefit, even though Patrick couldn't remember anyone's name five seconds later. Last on the wall was Tiny who said, "Hey man, no hard feelings about last night... I was just yankin' your chain, OK?"

With a quick wave of approval, Haney shrugged it off and climbed up to the top of the four-foot barrier with the help of a chair. Sitting next to Chuck, he asked, "What's this about a shift change?" Chuck smiled and answered,

"You see, every day at 0700 the local women who clean the barracks come in to their day's work. Most of these women are older and uglier than they need to be. That's why they do this work. At night, their daughters and nieces come on base to do their job."

Still puzzled, Patrick asked, "You mean, they clean rooms for guys that work at night?"

The whole row of GIs snickered at the rookie's question.

"No man," Chuck said, "their daughters service the needs of the flesh… you know… whores. They're here all night. Leave in the morning when the gate opens up. Spend a few minutes with Mamasan on her way in, go get some shuteye, and come back that evening. Six days a week. Most of them are Catholic, so they take Sundays off."

"What does the brass have to say about it?" Patrick asked.

"Nothing, man," Chuck replied, "they just turn their heads the other way as long as there's no trouble. That reminds me, your Mamasan wants to know if five bucks a week is OK."

Another puzzled look came over Haney's face. Chuck didn't even wait for the question, "She's assigned to your floor. Cleans your room every day and does your laundry twice a week. Hell of a deal."

"Does her cleaning meet inspection standards?" Patrick asked.

"What inspections," Chuck laughed. "This is 'Nam, Patrick. There are no inspections. Save that stuff for when you get back in the 'world'."

"Is that enough money for them to live on, Chuck?" Haney asked.

"You do the math," Chuck answered, "Seven or eight GIs… that's 35-40 bucks a week. Man, these people are living high on the hog for that amount. Hell, your Mamasan supports a husband and nine kids plus other relatives on her salary."

Patrick was about to ask more when Tiny shouted, "Hey Chuck, let's bring the newbie up to the Veranda."

"Great idea," Chuck said. "C'mon Patrick," he said as they jumped from the wall and headed inside.

The "Veranda" was the roof of the barracks. Getting up there was easy with a ten-foot, built-in ladder rising from the latrine on the second floor. Once up, you had to negotiate the slanted tin roof over to some benches the guys had installed. If you went up too early, the soles of your shoes would start to melt. As it was, the roof temperature was over one hundred degrees, and this after 1900 hours, or 7 o'clock. Patrick knew that getting back down after imbibing would be a bit more difficult.

As they sat down Haney noticed for the first time what was beyond the few square blocks that had become his new world. Because there were no buildings higher than two stories, it was easy to survey the area from there. To the east, over some dirt mounds topped by barbed wire fences known as the 'perimeter' was the South China Sea. Haney thought it was the most beautiful scene he had ever experienced. The water was crystal blue, even from the few hundred yards where he was sitting. He compared it with the murky waters of the Gulf Coast of Mississippi and Florida, or the polluted Lake Pontchartrain and Mississippi River which surrounded New Orleans. He speculated that one day after the war, the beach would be jammed with resort hotels. The clean, white sand would be covered with surfers waiting for the next perfect wave. To the west was the flight line, where he could see C-141 transports coming and going on their 24-hour-a-day missions. Beyond that, Cam Rahn Bay. It separated the Air Base from the Army post situated at the bottom of one lone mountain. Coming from South Louisiana, he had never seen something that big. It looked to him to be part of the Rockies. Covered with trees, it seemed majestic to Haney as the sun was starting to set directly behind the peak.

As he started to take his seat, a burning sensation jolted him back to his feet. The others laughed and Chuck said, "Come sit over here on the bench. The tin roof stays hot for several hours." Haney took a seat next to Chuck and was about to ask what they were doing up there when a joint was shoved in front of him and a light appeared.

"Go ahead, man," Chuck said holding the lighter. "It's the best you'll ever have."

With that, Haney started to drag on the weed with a new-found intensity. He had never smoked cigarettes, so smoking weed was something he tolerated to get to the plateau he was looking for. Immediately, he sensed this time was different. It tasted like nothing else he had experienced. Mild, a bit of a fruity flavor he thought. And the rush! Never before had weed affected him this quickly. He wasn't finished with half the joint before the familiar feeling of giddiness and slurred speech came over him.

"Wow!" he said to no one in particular. "Look at that sunset, man!"

"Now you know why we come up here every night," Chuck said.

After an hour of nonstop smoking, Haney knew if he didn't go now, he could never negotiate the ladder to get back down. He managed to make it back to his room and flopped down on the bed. Darkness was just about complete. His mind drifted off on a drug-induced joy ride. It seemed like hours but in reality just a few minutes had gone by. He was startled back to consciousness by a faint knock on the door as it slowly opened. With just the power of a 40 watt bulb it was difficult to make out who it was walking into the room. His sense of smell was the first to recognize that at least it wasn't a GI. It took him several seconds to finally focus on his unexpected guest. She was small, under five feet tall, with beautiful shiny, dark hair. Her body was compact, but he knew she was well endowed, by Vietnamese standards.

"Hey Joe," she said softly, "you friend say you wanna good time tonight. Fuckie, fuckie, ten dolla."

The lightbulb in his head went off. Chuck had told him to never give the price they ask. Always negotiate.

"No, I'll give you five," he answered holding up his fingers.

"No five, I do for eight," she countered.

"Seven and you got a deal, sweetie," he answered.

"Ok, Joe," she said looking a little dejected. "Hope you no take too long, I gotta make money tonight," she said as she started to disrobe. Just as quickly as she said it, she was naked laying in his bunk... arms and legs spread.

"C'mon Joey, I don' got all night."

Hell, he thought, I'm not in the mood for foreplay anyway.

* * *

The first blast came about five minutes into his session. It reminded him of the explosions that went off around him on the obstacle course in basic training, and felt that close, too. It was followed by a loud siren lasting about ten seconds. Then a voice over a loud speaker announcing, "red alert, red alert. Take cover immediately." Haney didn't have to be told twice. He jumped up, pulled his pants on, grabbed the girl and ran outside to duck behind the wall. Seemed to be a big night for visits in the barracks. There were just as many girls as GIs crouched for cover. Suddenly, a whooshing sound got closer and someone hollered, "INCOMING!" Haney grabbed his head and tried to get closer to the ground and wall. The sound was deafening. It was so close mud and rocks flew over the wall and covered Haney and a few others. Everyone stayed in place for an hour. More blasts were heard intermittently at varying distances. The "all clear" came about fifteen minutes after the last blast was heard. The voice over the loud speaker announced, "Yellow alert will remain in effect until further notice."

It wasn't until then that Haney saw Chuck. He was standing by the opening of the bunker wall, staring at the crater left by the closest blast. It was thirty feet away and left a hole three feet deep and ten feet around. It hadn't hit anything but he could tell Chuck was upset by its closeness.

"Fun like this every night?" Haney asked.

Chuck, without even turning around said, "Just lately. Seems like Charlie is getting more daring from his mountaintop retreat. Sending down 140s now. A lot stronger than the 122s he's been using."

As Chuck turned to Haney, he said, "You better check out some protection from supply tomorrow. You're gonna need it."

"What do you mean?" Patrick asked.

"These, man," Chuck said as he grabbed his flak jacket and helmet, "just might save your life one night."

Haney went to supply on the way to work the next morning. Work seemed less routine than usual. A greater sense of being had settled in after the long night before.

* * *

The rest of the week bored Patrick, except for the nightly intrusions from the VC based on the mountain across the bay. He learned that daily missions by the Army failed to root out the enemy or the site where they were launching their nightly assaults. By Friday, the Air Force had convinced allies with the Korean Army to aim their 55mm artillery at the mountain and spend five hours a day pounding the mountainside, hoping to ferret out the VC that were holed up in the series of tunnels running throughout. It only took a few days and the once pristine, tree-covered mountain started looking more like the Rock of Gibraltar.

While Patrick never totally got used to the nightly attacks, by the end of the week they didn't seem to bother him as much. The same was true for the rest of his barrack mates. Tiny even got so smoked up one night, he completely slept through one particularly vicious attack.

The following week started out the same. Things were starting to shape up for the Office of Social Actions. Haney was glad for Major Daly. He had come to genuinely like his boss. A good family man with an overall decency towards everyone he came in contact with. Haney especially liked the fact that the major allowed Haney to do his job with little oversight. The only time Patrick had to consult with his boss was when the Air Force red tape got in the way of getting supplies. Haney then let the Major's rank run interference for him.

About mid-week, two black non-commissioned officers walked in the office. This, in itself was unusual, since no one had come in since Haney had arrived. They both said hello to Haney and started checking out the other offices that sat vacant. Somewhat timidly, Haney walked into the first office where one of the sergeants was crudely measuring the size of the office by walking along each wall. Haney spoke,

"Can I help you, Sirs?" The taller of the two turned to him and stuck out his hand saying,

"I'm sorry, Airman, I'm John Norton, and this is Quinton May. We're assigned to this office. Just got off the plane about an hour ago. Is Major Daly in?"

"Oh, yes, sir. I'm sorry sir," Patrick fumbled, "We weren't expecting you until tomorrow. Right this way." As Haney led them back to Daly's office, Master Sergeant May said,

"What's your name, son?"

"Patrick Haney, sir," he replied.

"Haney," May exclaimed, "what did you do, get busted as soon as you got promoted? Where's your third stripe?"

"No, sir," Patrick replied, "didn't get busted, just haven't had time to get them sewed on."

"Well, Sergeant Haney," May continued, "see that you are in proper uniform by tomorrow. Is that clear?"

"Yes sir," Haney replied, knocking on the door frame and sticking his head in the Major's office saying, "New personnel you've been waiting for Major."

As the two men stepped into the office they both came to attention and saluted the Major, introducing themselves.

"At ease, men," the Major said as he stuck out his hand to greet each of them.

"Have a seat and tell me about yourselves. Patrick, would you like to sit in with us?"

"No sir," Haney replied, "If you don't mind, I need to run over to Admin to pick up some forms."

"As you wish, Patrick," Daly said.

One jerk, one nice guy, Patrick thought on the way to base administration. It could have been worse. Could have been stuck with two "lifers" instead of one.

* * *

The next few days were spent helping Norris and May set up their offices and getting them acclimated to their new surroundings. They both had started counseling patients at the hospital almost immediately. That freed the major up so he could work on implementing a testing procedure for drugs and a Race Relations Course. It became more apparent every day that Norris was a genuinely nice guy. He would actually take the time to talk to Haney about his personal life and how his days were going. May was another subject.

There were obvious physical differences between the two sergeants. One was a 30-something black man proud of his heritage, but not to an overbearing fault. The other was extremely light-skinned, with an overload of Dap smeared through his hair to straighten out the natural curls. His mustache was trimmed and clipped until it appeared as a thin pencil line above his mouth. The uniform, whether fatigue or khaki, starched until it appeared to stand on its own.

May ran Haney through his paces. Constantly giving him errands to run to base supply, the finance office, the hospital. It seemed as though he would think up places for Patrick to go, just to keep him out of the office. On one of his down occasions, while sitting in Norris' office talking about the sergeant's role as the base recreation director, May walked in and verbally berated him for not doing his job at his desk.

"Sergeant Norris, please do not encourage the young sergeant to be a slacker. I'm trying to instill good work habits in him," barked May.

"Will do, Sergeant May," replied Norris as May left his office. As Haney stood to leave, Norris said, "Don't worry, Patrick, he'll calm down in a few days."

"That's nice to know, Sarge, I just thought it was my sparkling personality that brought it out in him," said Haney.

*   *   *

One of the things Chuck had warned him about were the insects that would invariably infest his room. Each morning brought a boot inspection to make sure a black widow hadn't taken up residence overnight. The real problem was the cockroaches. Patrick had seen some big ones in New Orleans, but these looked like those little breakfast sausages that the corner grocery liked to sell. One evening, Haney was awakened by the feel of the sheet he used for cover being moved. He opened his eyes and saw a three-inch roach walking across the top of the tea colored sheet toward his face. After successfully ridding his bunk of the monster, sleep was impossible for the rest of the night.

Another evening found him going to sick call to have a doctor remove a baby roach that had decided to start a nest in his ear. Yes, 'Nam was an unusual place, Patrick thought. Unusual being used diplomatically.

*   *   *

That evening after work was a carbon copy of every other since he had arrived in country. Chow hall, back to the barracks, lots of reefer, a little beer, and an occasional dalliance with one of the working girls, then fast asleep, usually by 11 p.m.

This night was different. Haney was startled awake by the thin plywood door as it creaked open. Still rubbing the sleep from his eyes and the fog from his brain, he glanced up and caught the silhouette of a familiar figure in his room… Master Sergeant May. Patrick glanced at the wind up alarm clock and said, "Sarge, it's 1 a.m., what's going on?"

May stumbled in and got close enough that Haney could smell the reason he was here.

"Sarge, you're plastered, you should go to your hut," implored Patrick.

"Naw, not till I say what I came to say Haney. I wanted to apologize for the way I been treating you," May slurred. "Norris had a talk with me and convinced me that I was treating you poorly, I'm sorry," he finished as he reached his hand out to complete his apology. Patrick, still lying in bed, reached up to shake his hand and hopefully get him out the door. As the two men shook, the alcohol took over and May collapsed on top of Haney.

"Get off me you drunk," Patrick snarled. Before he could say or do another thing, he got the shock of his life as the veteran started kissing his arm mumbling further apologies.

"What the fuck are you doing, you old bastard!" Haney shouted. But he didn't wait for an answer as he sprang out of the bed and walked out into the hall just outside his cubicle. Still groggy from being awakened in the middle of the night, he tried to figure out if this was a dream or if it was really happening. He didn't have long to ponder, as the drunken sergeant followed him out the room into the hallway. Luckily, he turned right and started walking into the latrine area. Haney didn't even hesitate. He pushed the man from behind, forcing him to fall face first into a commode. Patrick then retreated back into the cubicle and thanked his stars that Chuck had installed a slide bolt on his door that afternoon. He sat back in his bed and wondered what to do next. The knocking on the door told him that a bad drunk never gives up.

"Get the fuck away from the door you fag," Haney screamed. With that the lights started clicking on throughout the rest of the floor. Haney thanked his barrack mates silently as he heard the stumbling sergeant leave the building.

He sat there not knowing what to do, when he was suddenly bounced out of bed by the unmistakable concussion of a 140mm rocket hitting right next to the wall outside his room. He quickly donned his helmet and flight jacket and spent the rest of the night huddled against the outside wall of his room, feeling somewhat protected by the four-foot concrete wall surrounding the barracks.

* * *

The next morning, he was again startled awake by a knocking on his door. Realizing he was still on the floor with his combat gear in place, he felt his knees pop as he pulled himself to his feet. At the last minute, he hesitated opening the door, remembering his late night visitor. Another knock prompted him to unlatch the door. It was Norris. Thank God, Haney mumbled.

"Patrick, the major sent me looking for you, do you realize its 0900?" barked Norris. "Get dressed, I've got a Jeep outside, I'll give you five minutes."

On the ride to the Social Actions hut, Patrick tried to explain why he overslept to Norris.

"Before you start Patrick, the whole base was under attack last night, so I wouldn't use that excuse with the major," Norris interjected.

"That's not all that happened Sarge," Haney protested. Although he was reluctant to share the rest of the story with May's friend, he knew he had to in order to protect himself. At the end of the story, Norris pulled the Jeep over a few hundred yards shy of the office.

"Then that would explain why May was found a few barracks down from yours this morning." Norris said.

"What do you mean, found?" Patrick asked.

"He's dead," Norris replied. "At first we thought he was hit by some shrapnel, but we only found a few scratches on his face. The hospital is doing an autopsy right now. Did anything else happen that you know of, Patrick?" he asked.

Patrick was stunned. And his face showed it. "No, he walked out of there on his own, I'm sure of it," he answered.

The rest of the day was a blur. Haney didn't get any work done. He silently thanked Norris for informing the major, so even he didn't bother Haney for the rest of the day.

* * *

The next day word came from the Security Police. May died of a heart attack brought on by severe alcohol poisoning. Norris told Patrick that May was a recovering alcoholic. He was supposed to be on the wagon for the past six months. He was even going so far as contemplating a new medicine being used to combat the disease that, when taken, would make the patient violently sick if alcohol was ingested. Norris told the SP investigator this, hoping that it might shed some light on what happened. A few days later, toxicology reports confirmed it… May was self-medicating. Being the lead counselor for the office, he and Major Daly were the only two who had access to the drug. You would think the Air Force had more sense than that, Patrick thought.

Chapter 4
Hope for Christmas

December 1971 – January 1972

The holiday season takes on a whole new meaning in this part of the world. While every work space on the base, including the mess hall, had some sort of Christmas decorations afoot, it was hard to imagine the 25th was a few days away. Especially hard when Patrick was lying on the pearl-white sand beach working on a tan that any California surfer would be proud of.

On the walk back to the barracks, Chuck and the rest of the crew were talking about "the show". After several references to it, Patrick had to know. Tugging on Chuck's shirt he asked, "What are ya'll talking about?" Chuck looked puzzled at first, but then recognition came over his face and he said, "That's right, working over there among those civilian business huts you wouldn't be in the know. Consider this an invitation… Bob Hope and his road show are going to be at Bien Hoa on Christmas day… interested?"

Patrick, not one to pass up on an adventure said, "Sure, but how do we get there? It's a few hundred miles away."

"Not to worry my friend," Tiny cut in. "Working in the flight ops traffic has its perks. The show is at noon, but the only time I could get a C-130 was 3 a.m., so be ready to go."

Christmas Eve dinner wasn't too bad, given the fact these were the same cooks in the mess hall the rest of the time. The base commander had arranged for ten frozen turkeys to be shipped in. The cooks, knowing this would not be enough meat for all the troops, made a deal with some local merchants for some additional meat products to be available. By the time Chuck and Patrick got through the line, very little turkey was left to be had. There were several trays on the steam tables full of what looked like steak, but they weren't sure how that had gotten there. The boys looked at each other, simultaneously shrugging their shoulders, and dug in with ample supplies on each of their trays.

Joining the rest of the crew at a long table, the two hesitated as they noticed the rest of the boys staring at them.

"Nobody had the balls to try it," Tiny said. "The cook said it was water buffalo."

Chuck looked at Patrick and said, "What the fuck, you only live once."

With that, they both stuck large pieces in their mouths and started to chew. Without saying a word, both started smiling and shaking their heads in unison, giving the rest of the table the thumbs up. Not missing a beat, Tiny led the crew on an assault at the steam table. Before Chuck and Patrick had finished their portions, the rest of the mess hall had cleaned out all the buffalo left on the buffet. At least they had their share first, Patrick thought.

* * *

Back at the barracks, the crew had already decided that going to sleep would be harder than trying to wake up by 2 a.m. So, they did what they usually did when the hookers weren't around… play poker. Being the end of the month, everybody's beer stash was perilously low, considering a two case per month allotment. It was decided that sharing was the order of the day, Christmas and all. Naturally the reefer was plentiful and the time passed quickly. Before long, the clock told them to trudge over to the flight line and catch a ride to Bien Hoa.

Walking into the hangar, the boys were taken aback by the crowd waiting for them. Chuck looked at Patrick and said, "Guess Tiny couldn't keep his mouth shut." Nodding in affirmative, Patrick did a quick count… "There must be over 100 guys in here," he said. Just then, Tiny walked up and reported, "135 to be exact, we'll have to all take a seat on the deck of the plane just to get everybody on board." He wasn't kidding… jammed in on every inch of cargo plane deck, the crowd had to fold up their knees and sit on as little space as possible. As the plane taxied out the runway, Patrick wondered if the stewardess would allow everybody to take the flight without fastening their seatbelts. He chuckled, knowing that a flight crew on this bird was not in the cards.

Although the flight was relatively short, it was hard on everybody. A C-130 was a slow moving, low altitude cargo plane designed for carrying equipment, not 135 guys sitting on the flight deck. It would take more than two hours to get to Bien Hoa.

After thirty minutes of flying, the plane was suddenly rocked by an explosion that sounded like it was just outside the right side of the craft. Everything appeared to return to normal as the load master assured everyone that it was random anti-aircraft fire shot at the engine noise from the ground. They were flying too low to be picked up on radar. But the next sound put the fear in the heart of everyone on board.

At first it sounded like a woodpecker going to town on a hard oak tree. But when the passengers saw the load master run to the cockpit, and the plane suddenly bank to the right, Patrick knew this was not something they were expecting. The rat-a-tat of shells hitting the fuselage was met with a fear that could be felt throughout the cabin. Everyone collectively held their breath as the plane straightened out after the sharp banking and continued its flight toward Bien Hoa. The load master stepped through the huddled troops, checking to see if anyone was hit. Patrick could see the fear on his face as he realized that a few of the troops were hit.

Running back to the cockpit, he retrieved the first aid kit and started immediate care of the injured. A couple of medics joined in to lend a hand. Their jobs were made harder by the constant banking from side to side of the plane, attempting to avoid the ground to air fire that continued to trail the aircraft.

After an hour of zig-zagging, the plane leveled off and the pilot came over the loudspeaker to say the airstrip was in sight. The crowded cargo floor gave a collective sigh of relief. Patrick looked over at the staff sergeant next to him. Being one of the unlucky who had gotten hit, he was lying down on his stomach in order not to cause further damage to his injury; a small caliber slug imbedded in the right cheek of his ass. While not severe, the blood had poured out of him causing a small flood covering the deck around him. Thankfully, the medics were able to stop the flow, and administer some morphine. This caused the non-com to chuckle at where he got hit instead of writhing in pain. As soon as Haney said the word "gluteus maximus" the injured man started laughing and said "Please don't make me laugh, it hurts."

Patrick, smiling down at his plane mate said, "What are you going to tell your family where you got shot."

The sergeant shrugged his shoulders, "I dunno."

Patrick helped him by saying, "You tell them Vietnam. If they still want to know, you tell them in the ass, the perfect metaphor for this war."

The sergeant couldn't take it, laughing so hard the dressing on his wound fell off. Patrick promised him he'd stop.

Upon deplaning, everyone groaned as they got up and stretched their legs for the first time. Some, like Chuck, actually toppled over before regaining their balance and getting the strength back in their legs. It was also the first time the bright white lights were turned on and Patrick could see the line of holes in the left side of the plane. Nudging Chuck, he pointed to the damage and they both sighed relief as they realized how close they had come.

Waiting less than 100 yards from the plane were six-deuce-and-a-half trucks, diesels running. At least the soldiers could sit on benches for the rest of the trip. Driving to the show site, Patrick was struck by the sheer destruction of the villages along the road. Not one hut had a full roof on it. Some had cardboard cut into makeshift roof panels. The stench was unworldly, Patrick thought. Nothing could possibly smell this bad. Everyone on his truck lifted the neck of their fatigue tops over their noses, hoping against hope that it would help deflect the odor. It was probably for the best that the young men didn't know the source of the stench: dead bodies and human waste.

* * *

By the time the trucks arrived at the site for the show, the sun was in full view. Before jumping off the deck of the two-and-a-half-ton transport truck, Patrick paused to view the arena. It was a natural amphitheater built into the side of a hill. A large broadway-style stage sat at the opening of the horseshoe-shaped hill with crude wooden benches lined up in rows. Being just after 6 a.m. in the morning, the only other people already there were crew members of the show setting up the massive amount of equipment and scaffolding that would be needed. The boys decided to go ahead and grab some seats as close as they could get, plopping ten rows in front the stage. Chuck said if they got any closer they would all get neck strain from having to look up to the fifteen-foot-high stage.

The morning went by slowly. By 8 a.m., all the guys had shed their fatigue tops. The mercury was already approaching 90. The only thing to occupy their time was watching the setup of all the equipment. Patrick started a conversation with one of the stage hands and found out that all the equipment was due to the filming of the show for a Bob Hope Christmas Special to air before New Year's back in the States. Every hour or so, the guys would take turns heading to a makeshift snack area run by some young enterprising Vietnamese. Although disappointed that nothing stronger than soft drinks were available, they still welcomed anything cold... By 11 a.m. the temperature was over 100 degrees.

The noon hour was approaching, the stands had steadily filled throughout the morning. Precisely at 11:30, just as the guys were getting lathered up with excitement, the Security Police Squadron moved in and surrounded the first 25 rows in front of the stage. An SP major got on a bull horn and started ordering everyone who was sitting in these rows to move to seating further back. Needless to say, no one was moving too quickly, stunned that after braving the searing heat all morning, they were being asked to give up their seats. On the verge of a near riot, the SPs started moving in with fixed bayonets, pushing the crowds out of their seats. Chuck looked at Patrick and said, "I think they mean business pal, let's go before we get stuck without any seats."

Patrick nodded in agreement, and they both rounded up their buddies and started the trek to the nearest seats they could find.

When they finally found some empty benches, they turned and found out not only were they a good 150 yards back from the stage, but the TV cameras were perched on platforms directly in back of the first 25 rows. In addition to that, rising on each side of the bank of the cameras were the tallest speakers they had ever seen, looming at least 40 feet into the air. Taking their seats they found their view of the far off stage to also be almost completely obstructed.

"Crap, they're probably going to put the brass into our seats," Chuck said.

"Hope we get to see a little of Miss America."

It was Patrick's turn to run for snacks, so he took off, mumbling under his breath about how they got screwed by the brass. He was still muttering to himself as he stood in line for drinks, when he started to feel the wind and vibration before he could hear the unmistakable sound of Huey helicopters coming over the hill. They landed in twos just outside the arena next to the snack area.

"I guess it's just the brass coming in to claim our seats," Patrick said to no one in particular.

"Wrong newbie," said the guy behind him. "Those are the grunts from the front. They swoop in to pick them up, see the show, and back to the bush they go."

As they started to deplane, Patrick could see the guy was right... every guy humping off the Huey looked like they had just rolled out of a mud pile. Some were completely covered with dirt to the point he couldn't make out if they were black or white. The same SPs who routed Patrick and his friends out ushered the grunts to their front row seats. As he gathered up the drinks to bring back to his group, Patrick felt as inconsequential as he had ever imagined he would. Relaying the information to Chuck, they both looked at each other with the same resignation on their faces.

As the show started, the smell did too. There was over 10,000 screaming GIs in the amphitheater, so it made sense that the reefer would start to flow. The brass had wisely decided that alcohol would only inflame the already randy crowd, and seeing Miss America, Miss Universe and the Golddiggers from Dean Martin's show would be incentive enough to live up to the reputation that all GIs had. When Jim Nabors was introduced, most of the crowd booed, wanting to see Joey Heatherton and Jill St. John. But the boos turned to cheers at the booming voice singing "God Bless America" telling the crowd that this wasn't Gomer Pyle on stage. Hope was funny, and played off Martha Raye perfectly. By the time the finale started, the group, having smoked the entire time, were caught up in the cheering and chanting that wailed throughout the arena. As the show ended, Chuck and Patrick started walking back to the pickup area. They looked at each other before donning their fatigue tops and started laughing uncontrollably. Having their shirts off and no suntan lotion produced beet-red skin tones, even with the solid tans they both had acquired on the beach at Cam Rahn Bay. But the laughter turned to pain as they pulled their shirts on and realized this was not going to be pleasant.

Having been up for more than 24 hours, the plane ride home found just about all of the now less than 135 leaning on each other, knowing their crutch or not, fast asleep for the two-hour trip. A quick bite in the mess hall and everyone hit their bunks before 8 p.m. By 3 a.m., just about all of them were in the latrine sharing the only jar of Noxzema that Chip from California had. The rest of the night was spent trying not to move in their beds or suffer the sharp and sudden pain that a sunburn would bring. Patrick thought what a mess, sunburn on Christmas Day.

* * *

Luckily the next day was Sunday, so Patrick could lay low and soothe his aches with his own jar of Noxzema from the BX. The only time he left his bed was to go to the chow hall. That night, the boys were back to the veranda, killing their mutual pain with as much smoke as possible. Tiny, knowing everybody felt as bad as he did, decided they needed a little extra help. Without telling the rest of the group, he had added a little something extra to the perfect joints he had rolled earlier… heroin, in powder form.

Patrick didn't even remember going to his bunk that night. All he knew was he wasn't in any pain. It was the best night of sleep since he had arrived in country.

* * *

That week was easy on Patrick. While he had to man the office every day, activity was limited. Both Major Daly and Sergeant Norris were on R & R. Daly had met his wife in Hawaii and Norris was off to Tokyo. Patrick, outside of answering the phone, found the hardest thing would be attaining a comfortable position to take a nap.

Extra time around the office found him sitting inside the hut, watching his neighbors go about their daily routine for the first time since arriving. Just before lunch he saw a vision sitting outside the hut next door. She was typically slender, like most of the Vietnamese women, with the same straight black hair down below her shoulders. She wore the traditional Ao Dao, colorful silk dressing gown over the silk black pajama-looking pants. He thought she was different. He had seen many a beautiful girl in Vietnam, but this one had a look that set her apart. Her eyes, he decided. That was the difference. They were perfectly set apart, framed by thin black eyebrows and just a hint of natural-looking make-up. But it was the color that truly made him stare… azure blue. An eye color he had not seen in country.

Just as he was trying to figure out a way to strike up a conversation, two men walked out of the hut, chatting in Korean. They both looked over at Patrick at the same time. After a few awkward seconds, the older of the two waved to Patrick. He waved back. Then the man waved him to come over to their hut. Patrick jumped up as quickly as he could and strode over extending his hand to the friendlier of the two. Shaking hands, they introduced themselves to each other.

"My name is James Hang, my friend. And this is my partner John Na," the friendlier one said.

Patrick told them both his name and then asked what they were partners in.

Social Actions: A Vietnam Story

"We are the distributors of Stars & Stripes for the whole Na Trang sector," James said. "We here six day a week, rest on Sunday."

Patrick glanced inside the hut and saw rows of desks and piles of newspapers. "How many people work in this office?" Patrick asked.

"We have eight women and the two of us," John finally spoke for the first time.

"Where's your Korean accent John?" asked Patrick.

"I spent high school and college in the States, graduated from Oregon State. I guess I lost it," he replied.

Just as he was preparing to ask about the girls sit-kneeling in front of the hut eating their lunch, Patrick was startled back to reality by the phone ringing from his office.

"Excuse me guys, duty calls, I'll talk to you later," he yelled back as he ran to his office.

* * *

On the other end of the phone was a harsh sounding Colonel Bolden from OSI.

"Where's Major Daly?" he bellowed. Holding the receiver a foot from his ear, Haney thought he didn't need the phone.

"R&R sir," he replied.

"I'm ordering you to report to my office on the double, sergeant," barked the officer.

"Sir, my orders are to man the office ever day while the major is out," Haney countered.

"I'm a colonel son, you will appear immediately or face some brig time, you got me?" ordered Bolden.

"Yes sir, right away," Patrick replied.

What in the world is going on, Patrick thought to himself as he placed a sign on the door after locking up. He didn't have long to wonder as the walk over to OSI was only a hundred yards or so. After checking in at the reception desk, he was told to sit and wait on the rough bench available in the outer office. Before being called back by a second lieutenant,

Patrick had noticed he had spent 45 minutes on the pine bench, and felt like he had the splinters to prove it.

As he entered the colonel's office, he was immediately struck with a feeling of intimidation: The colonel was seated behind a long mahogany table with three other officers and a staff sergeant who apparently was there to take notes on the pad in front of him.

"At ease Sergeant Haney," Colonel Bolden said.

"Do you know why you're here sergeant?" inquired one of the junior officers seated with the colonel.

"No sir, no idea," replied Patrick.

"We are investigating the death of Master Sergeant Quinton May, who worked in the Office of Social Actions for approximately one month," the officer said.

"Do you have any knowledge of Master Sergeant May's personal life… his habits, what he did during his off time, that sort of thing," he added.

Patrick paused momentarily, wondering if he should divulge the only off hours contact he had with May, the night before he was found dead. "No sir, I didn't have any contact with him outside the office," Patrick replied.

He had quickly decided that this wasn't anything he wanted to have a part in. The panel of officers never said a word… just sat there and stared for what seemed like eternity to Haney. Finally, Bolden spoke up,

"Son, are you sure of your answer, think carefully?"

"I'm sure, Colonel," Patrick said, "I never had any contact outside of the office, I really didn't care for the sergeant all that much."

"That's strange sergeant," interjected a Captain on the end of the table. "His body was found near your barracks, across the base from his own, and we can't find anyone else in that area he knew, only being here such a short time."

"I can't help you captain," replied Haney.

"What do you know about May's work…? Who was he working with in his counseling at Social Actions?" asked the Colonel.

"I don't have access to personnel files at the office sir," answered Patrick, "Major Daly and Sergeant Norris would be the only ones authorized besides May."

"I see," said Bolden, "And who had access to the prescription medications used to treat alcoholism?"

"As far as I know, Major Daly and the flight surgeon were the only ones having that access," Haney said.

"Are you sure May didn't have access, sergeant," asked the Captain.

"I'm not sure," replied Patrick.

After sharing inquisitive glances with each other, the Colonel said, "That will be all sergeant, get back to your post."

"Yes sir," Haney said as he snapped to attention and saluted before leaving. As he walked back to his office, he wondered what they were digging for. Were they after Major Daly? His mind was allowed to backtrack over the past few weeks, exploring whether he had missed noticing something he had been privy to.

* * *

The counseling at the office had started within days of May's arrival. Norris was mostly involved in setting up the Race Relations course. That left May and Major Daly as the two primary counselors. They made their own appointments in order to keep the patient's privacy intact. The files were kept in a locked cabinet in Daly's office. They each typed their own reports and sent Patrick to the Base Hospital with a copy in a sealed envelope. Doctor Heath was the supervising physician who received the reports and would send medication over to be dispensed by the counselor's according to his directions. Most of the meds were kept under lock as to not give the patient a chance to abuse the drug. Patrick didn't know how many patients or how much medication was stored in the office.

The rest of the week, he tried to put the questioning out of his mind. He had decided to see if he could get to know the dark-haired beauty working just a few yards away at Stars & Stripes. And he had decided to do it through his newfound friends, John and James.

The first two days, he had invited both of them to accompany him to the mess hall for lunch. Being civilian contractors, they were allowed to eat there as long as they were accompanied by military personnel. The third day, he had purposely gone over to their hut after the traditional noon hour to see about lunch… his timing paid off. She was there, sitting at her desk, eating a bowl of noodles. He startled her at first, not expecting anyone back in the office so soon.

"Hello," he said. "My name is Patrick…"

Before he could get any further, she interrupted, "I know who you are," in perfect English.

She continued with her noodles, with lowered eyes, the same way most of the Vietnamese reacted to GIs, except for the hookers. They had learned to be bold and aggressive, mostly from the movies that played occasionally in the open air theater outside the base. Movies that were at least three to four years old by the time they made it there. But speaking to the rest of the population was generally like pulling teeth, and she was no different.

"What's your name," he asked.

"Lee Mai," she reluctantly said, only being polite.

He wondered if this was going to be worth it, but he answered himself by looking at her again. She was the most beautiful Vietnamese woman he had seen. Beautiful, shiny, straight black hair. That dark blue eye color. Alabaster skin that was flawless. Although small by American standards, her body was perfectly proportioned, outlined by the traditional smock. His admiration of her appearance was interrupted by the other seven ladies who worked there coming back from a walk around the compound after lunch. Their giggles told him that his presence was embarrassing Lee Mai, the last thing he had wanted to do. He quickly waved goodbye and retreated back to his hut. Settling back at his desk, he had resigned himself to not being able to continue his pursuit of the lovely next-door neighbor, when suddenly she appeared in the doorway and said, "I come eat with you tomorrow." And just as quickly, she was gone before he could utter a word.

* * *

The next morning seemed to go by at a snail's pace. With no one else in the office, and the phone not ringing, Patrick couldn't help but watch the clock. When noon finally rolled around, he was glad to see that she was right on time. He hadn't known what to expect, but was pleasantly surprised to see she was carrying two covered bowls, one on top of the other. She smiled sweetly, with a half bow, and put the bowls down while she cleared papers from his desk and spread a beautiful colored silk scarf across the desktop. She motioned for him to sit, placed a bowl in front of him and handed him a crude metal spoon which reminded him of a baby's utensil. Lifting the top released the pent up steam from the noodles. Forgetting the possibility of burning his mouth, he scooped up some noodles and was surprised by the first taste he recognized… garlic. He had missed its aroma and distinctive flavor. But the next instant caught him off guard… flaming hot spices. It reminded him of his first taste of boiled crawfish back home when he was young. Great taste followed by extreme pain from the cayenne pepper imbedded in the crawfish. Somehow, she had been able to duplicate the pepper taste without having access to a spice not known in this part of the world. His face told the story… eyes as wide as they could go and sweat pouring out of his skin. She started laughing out loud while handing him a cup of water. After dousing the flames in his mouth, he joined her in laughing at his own expense.

The half hour went by much too quickly. They immediately felt a connection with each other, being so close in age. Lee Mai was 19, the oldest of seven children, still living with her family in Na Trang, 30 miles away. She took the job at the Stars & Stripes because it paid her 25 dollars a week, enough to feed the entire family. She spent every night during the work week with her aunt in the make-shift village that cropped up outside the gates of the base. Their 'apartment' was a cubicle in a former barracks belonging to the South Vietnamese Army before they moved onto the U.S. Army base across the bay. It wasn't much she said, but it was better than taking the two hours to travel home each night to Na Trang. She collected her bowls and they made a promise to do it again the next day, Saturday. Patrick felt sympathy for his new friend. Nineteen years old and supporting six siblings and two parents, while not being able to see them except on Sundays.

* * *

Saturday was his last day before Major Daly and Sergeant Norris got back. He meant to make the most of it. But his intentions were short circuited when John and James joined Lee Mai in his office for more garlic noodles she had prepared. James mentioned to Patrick that he should join them that evening at the NCO club. The band playing there was from Korea, and he and John both attested to how much they sounded like Led Zeppelin. Besides, they could drink for free by sitting at the band's table near the stage. Patrick looked at Lee Mai and said, "Could you join us, too?"

Demurely she shook her head and replied, "I am sorry, I must got home in Na Trang to see my family."

The rest of the meal was filled with James talking about their friendship with all the bands who came through the circuit of bases throughout Southeast Asia. He promised that Patrick could party with them every Saturday night and then spend Sunday with them as they hosted the bands on a beach party. Patrick stole a glance at Lee Mai and knew instantly that she felt as he did… wishing she could stay and spend the time with each other.

As the lunch came to a close both James and John reminded Patrick to meet them at 7 p.m. and thanked him for a pleasant lunch. Lee Mai took her time washing out the bowls and when she was sure her two bosses had left, she gathered up everything, looked Patrick soulfully in the eyes and leaned up to kiss him. He was more than ready for the exchange. While it didn't last but a few seconds, Patrick felt the urge to take her in his arms and not want to let her go. But, his manners got the best of him, and allowed her to steal away, leaving her scent of perfume to remind him of what might be on the horizon.

* * *

That evening Patrick enjoyed himself more than he had since being in country. The band was full of fun-loving, perfect English-speaking twenty somethings that traveled with their own entourage, groupies and go-go dancers. By the time midnight rolled around, everyone had decided to meet on the beach at noon on Sunday where James and John would be waiting with ice chests full of beer and a large hibachi loaded with thinly sliced water buffalo meat and a distinct Korean delicacy: Kimchee. Patrick had never even heard of it but was goaded into trying it. No sooner had he had in his mouth before he was reaching for a bucket of water used to soothe the flames on the cooking pit. Knowing what to expect, the band had gathered around to wait for his reaction. They weren't disappointed. Watching him pour the water down his throat made them all roll in the sand, egged on by the effects of the Korean beer they had consumed.

After recovering enough to be able to see through the tears, Patrick grabbed James and hoisted him over his shoulder, running to the water's edge and dumping his fully-clothed friend in the South China Sea. The rest of the group must have seen this as the thing to do so they each grabbed one of the girls and followed suit. By the time Patrick got back to the picnic area, there was one particularly buxom dancer sitting on a towel laughing at the events unfolding. Patrick stood over her, shook his finger as if to scold her, then picked her up and ran to join the others. Once reaching ankle depth, he stood her up in the water, grabbed her by the arms and tried to pull her into the water with him. But the alcohol had taken its toll, and she started to wiggle out of his grip. Falling towards the water he desperately reached for whatever his hands could grab and continued the plunge. He knew he had something in his hands but didn't know what until his head came back out of the water... the bikini top of the well-endowed Korean beauty. His first reaction was embarrassment beyond belief, for himself and his victim. But before either one of them could turn red, the rest of the band grabbed the tops of the remaining dancers and groupies and ripped them of. The women and Patrick were momentarily shocked before joining the guys in uncontrollable laughter. Even though there were several other groups on the beach that day, the tops remained off as the rest of the beer was downed just before the sun set over the mountain across the bay. Patrick had thoroughly enjoyed his day.

* * *

Monday morning started out just as expected. Major Daly and Sergeant Norris were already in the office when Patrick got there. Before Patrick got a chance to tell them of his visit to the OSI office the week before, James came through the door and looked like a ghost even though his skin had been tinted pink the day before.

"Patrick, something terrible has happened," he said. "Lee Mai was killed in a mortar attack on the road home Saturday night. We just found out from the local police. I thought you should know."

Patrick was motionless. The feeling in his stomach was one of nausea followed by a sheer bolt of pain. Daly and Norris were stunned as well. They had met Lee Mai before they left. But they were not aware of Haney's budding relationship with her. Major Daly knew instantly that Patrick was shaken beyond the news of an acquaintance perishing. He put his arm around the sergeant and steadied him. It was just in time, Patrick's knees started to weaken under his weight. Norris grabbed his other arm before he could hit the floor.

Chapter 5
Getting into the Conspiracy

February - March, 1972

The funeral for Lee Mai was held in Na Trang, her birthplace. Patrick asked for and received a special pass to travel there and pay his respects. James and John had gone to bat for him with Major Daly and the base commander. They assured both that Patrick would not leave their side the entire time.

The countryside on the drive to the funeral reminded him of the road to the Hope show. Bombed out buildings being used by squatters who lost their homes and farms due to the conflict. "Conflict". That was the official word for what the U.S. was doing there. Although he had never been in a war, this sure felt like one. The road had been bombed many times by both sides so it was a bumpy a ride as the Wild Mouse back in New Orleans at Ponchartrain Beach amusement park. It was mostly nothing but dirt and mud with the occasional asphalt patch thrown in for more of a wild ride.

As they got closer to Na Trang the scenery changed dramatically. The road was suddenly all smooth asphalt and the buildings were modern brick and stucco structures. But the one thing that stood out was the flowers. Both sides of the road were covered by a multitude of colors and varieties that Bellingrath or Callaway Gardens would be envious of. As they entered the centuries old gateway to the city, James explained to Patrick it was considered "holy ground" by both North and South Vietnam, and not to be touched. Consequently, both sides used the city as an R&R location. One week was north, the next was south. It was just an unspoken agreement between the sides. The city held some of the oldest churches in Southeast Asia. Some dating back to the eighth century. Most were Buddhist temples, but there were some of the newer ones built by the French serving the Catholic population that were introduced in the late 19th century.

The funeral mass was held at Lee Mai's church, St. Francis. It was a simple ceremony that Patrick didn't understand, not knowing the language. He did know when things were said in remembrance because the family would break down anew. It was a very solemn service that had the entire congregation in tears, including Patrick and his two friends.

On the road back, the air rushing in the open windows of the ten-year-old Mercedes James was driving told Patrick that a typical afternoon rain shower was well on its way. As he leaned back on the headrest in the rear, he thought back to his introduction to Lee Mai's family. Their devastation was readily apparent and it had effected Patrick in the same profound way as losing his best friend the previous year. Haney had stared at Lee Mai's siblings, ranging in age from two to sixteen years old. He thought about their future plight of trying to survive on a day-to-day basis. Their father, nearly crippled by his previous time fighting the North Vietnamese, was unable to perform any work. Not even capable of working in the family's vegetable garden next to their three-room hut. A building so small it could fit inside the Social Actions Office. Her mother was able to take in laundry from the local government workers and the occasional Army personnel on R&R in Na Trang. But even working for fifteen hours a day doing laundry only brought in about five dollars per week. Thankfully, the children attended St. Francis School run by the Benedictine nuns and were given two meals a day. Sometimes this was all the food available to them. Hence the importance of Lee Mai's job at the Stars & Stripes office.

At the end of the traditional Catholic Vietnamese funeral, James and John had given the mother an envelope with fifty dollars in it. They took it out of their own pockets. Patrick felt a pride in his new friends and promised himself that he would find a way to help these people.

Just before arriving back at the base gates, Patrick told them of his desire to do something for Lee Mai's family.

"I've got a few hundred saved up I'm going to give them. Can you get it to them for me, guys?" Inquired Patrick.

James pulled the car over off the road just outside the gates. They both turned around and in unison said, "No, you can't do that," James continued, "There are too many families in the same situation, you cannot make a dent in sorrow that affects them all. It's just like what we went through growing up during the war in our country. They will survive until the oldest daughter leaves the school next year and finds work somewhere."

Haney countered, "That's fine, I can help them until she is ready to work. Can you make sure they get the money?"

They both looked at one another and sighed, knowing that their young friend was stubborn and wouldn't accept no as the answer.

"Yes, we'll help you," John said.

At that, James pulled the Mercedes up to the gate and showed the guard their IDs. Patrick asked them to just drop him off at the barracks, since he didn't feel like eating dinner or socializing with his friends. He retreated to his bunk and spent the evening contemplating what he could do for the family until sleep took over.

By the next morning, he had decided to send $200 that he had in the base bank savings account and to stop his $75 per month deduction being sent into the account that he was using to purchase a 1973 Mercury Capri when he got back to the world. He figured the $75 could make a difference in Lee Mai's family's well-being. Besides, it would be temporary and he could still save enough for the car by scrimping in other areas.

Before entering his office, he stopped in to tell James and John of his plan. They both shook their heads and James said, "If you're sure you want this, we'll help you."

"I can't give them everything, but I can give them this," he said. Patrick thanked them both and retreated to his work station next door.

* * *

Just as he noticed on his yellow-faced Seiko that it was 10 a.m., Colonel Bolden and two other officers strode into the office.

"Is Major Daly in, sergeant?" the Colonel asked.

Rising, Patrick replied, "Yes sir, I'll see if he's busy."

"No need, Haney, I'll see myself," Bolden replied.

With that, the three officers barged through the major's door without knocking. Closing the door before speaking to Major Daly made it impossible for Patrick to hear anything that was said.

After a couple of minutes of muffled sounds, Patrick's curiosity got the better of him. Pretending to dig in the file cabinet next to the door, he leaned in as close as he could. Just as he was focusing in on the conversation, he heard from behind, "Curiosity killed the cat, Patrick."

He turned so quickly that he nearly knocked over the cabinet and saw

Norris standing in the doorway.

"Sorry Sarge, I should have known I'd get caught," a still startled Haney offered. He suddenly remembered that Norris wasn't in the office that morning when he told Major Daly of his questioning the previous week. He motioned for Norris to go into his office and Patrick followed him in and closed the door. Norris sat impassionedly while Patrick relayed the story to him.

"Thanks for telling me Patrick," Norris responded. "You better get back to your desk before they come out."

Twenty minutes went by before Patrick heard the phone in Major Daly's office being slammed down. The door immediately opened, and Colonel Bolden rushed out to a waiting Jeep. The other two officers waited in Daly's office for a moment until two security policemen entered the building. They immediately went into the major's office and a moment later exited leading Major Daly out of the hut… in handcuffs. Both Patrick and Norris stood there, mouths agape, not knowing what to do. Norris started to speak to his boss when one of the other officers interrupted.

"No one is to talk to the prisoner Sergeant, back to work."

With that they boarded a waiting Jeep and were gone. Norris immediately got on the phone. Patrick didn't know what to do. He submitted to the shock that took over his body.

Not knowing how long he had sat there, Patrick was startled back to reality by Norris donning his cap, and rushing out the door as he yelled back, "Man the fort, Patrick, I'll be back asap!" With that, Haney was left to ponder just what the hell was going on.

* * *

With all the security police Jeeps outside the office, it was natural that the other offices noticed the commotion. Shortly after Norris had rushed out, James peeked his head into the door and asked, "Is everything OK, Patrick?" Shaking his head Patrick responded, "Don't know what's going on James, they just took the major off, in handcuffs." James was not content with so little information and continued to prod Haney on what had just happened. Angrily, Patrick snapped at his friend, "Don't you understand English, I have no idea why they took him away."

Not wishing to push him too hard, James backed off and started out the door. Right before he stepped all the way out, he turned and nonchalantly asked, "Did it have anything to do with Sergeant May and the drugs?" Taking Patrick by surprise, he couldn't respond verbally and just shook his head negatively. James shrugged and walked back to his hut. Patrick didn't know what to think of his question, but he suddenly felt he was beginning to understand some of what had happened.

* * *

The work was nearly done. Patrick was getting ready to close up shop when Norris finally returned from places unknown.

"You can go ahead and go Patrick," Norris said.

"Wait a minute Sarge, what in the world is going on," Patrick insisted. Norris stood tall, pointing his finger at Haney, "You'll find out soon enough, but I'm warning you… don't go nosing around into something that may not concern you,"

Patrick was surprised. This was the first time Norris had acted like a superior to him. For the last couple of months, Norris was the only one he felt would actually talk to him. Sure, Major Daly was cordial enough, but you never forgot that he was the boss. Norris was different. They had spent many a lunch hour talking about family and friends back home and what Patrick had planned for his future. So, he wasn't quite sure how to handle this.

"OK Sarge, I guess I'll see you tomorrow," Patrick said as he turned the lamp off on his desk.

"Good night," he said to Norris already in his office on the phone as he was leaving. He passed by later that evening after chow and saw the light still on in Norris' office and his pickup truck still parked outside.

* * *

Patrick was lying on his bunk staring at the exposed wood beam ceiling as he heard a light knock on his door, and Chuck walked in.

"What have you been up to bud?" Chuck asked. "The boys and I haven't seen you since before the funeral. We're getting a little worried about you."

Even though he knew Chuck was on his way to the switchboard trailer for his graveyard shift, Patrick had to tell somebody. He laid out the entire story going back to his questioning the week before. Chuck sat passively by until he had finished. When he had sufficiently given him enough information, Chuck shook his head and said, "You may be involved in something and don't even know it. Let me think for a minute." Patrick wanted to say something else, but he just didn't know where to go with his thoughts.

Chuck broke the momentary silence, "Are the personnel files from the patients in the hospital or your office?"

"I'm pretty sure we have copies in Major Daly's office. After a session, the counselors always put the carbon copy of their session notes in the file and have me deliver the originals to the hospital," Patrick said.

"Did you ever take a look at the originals?" Chuck asked.

"Nah, they were always sealed in a routing envelope," Patrick responded.

"Then you have to get into the file in Daly's office, that's where the answer is." Chuck insisted. "Come on, I've got about an hour before I have to relieve Shaunessy, I'll help you."

* * *

As they approached the hut, Patrick was relieved to see the light out and Norris' truck gone. Even if he hadn't had a key, getting in the plywood hut would have been easy. Chuck insisted on not putting the lights on, so he retrieved a Zippo lighter from his top pocket and they made their way back to Daly's office. The only file cabinet against the back wall was typical military gray, but it did have a push-in key lock on the top. Chuck immediately whipped out a pocket knife and before Patrick could protest, had flipped out the lock and opened the top drawer.

"I think you've done this before Chuck," Patrick said. Finding the top drawer filled with regulation manuals, they proceeded down until the third drawer yielded what they were looking for… patient files.

Immediately, Patrick knew something was wrong. The two-foot-deep drawer was nearly at capacity with files.

"Chuck, this is impossible, we haven't been here but a few months, there's no way there have been this many patients so far."

No sooner than he said it, Chuck flipped the lighter shut, and raised his finger to his lips. Patrick then heard it… someone had just pulled up outside. They both scooted into the four-by-four closet being used as an office supply and mop storage room. As soon as Patrick had closed the door behind them the light in the major's office went on and someone walked in and immediately opened the file drawer they had just been rooting through. He tried to look through the crack in the door, but he couldn't see the nametag because the intruder was wearing a jungle poncho over it. Then came the unmistakable sound of file folders being pulled and placed on top of the cabinet. Although it felt like an hour to the two hiding out, in reality only five minutes had passed before the intruder closed the cabinet and turned the lights out. The boys waited until they heard the vehicle drive off before they exited the closet and Chuck flicked the lighter back on. Opening the third drawer again, they both stood there staring at the remains. Only about one quarter of the files remained.

* * *

After a nervous walk back toward the barracks, Chuck parted company with Patrick in order to relieve the evening shift operator at the base switchboard. The last thing he told Haney was that things should be slow that evening, so if he wanted to come to the trailer he'd see if he could place a call home for him. Patrick said he would, but he needed to think about what was going on at Social Actions before he could be able to talk to his mom.

Patrick spent the next few hours going over in his head the events leading up to that evening. Why were there so many files in the cabinet? Why were they removed? Who took them? Did Major Daly know about them? And most of all, why didn't the SPs confiscate the files if they suspected Daly's involvement in some wrongdoing. Coming up with questions was easy, he thought, it's the answers that are tough to determine. Deep in thought, he drifted off.

Feeling like he had been sleeping all night, he woke up, looked at the clock reading 3:15 a.m., and suddenly sat up remembering he told Chuck he'd come over to call home. Stumbling into the latrine, he splashed water on his face and started out the door. The switchboard trailer was only three city clocks from the barracks. The walk only took about five minutes. But before he had turned the corner, he immediately recognized the screeching, unmistakable sound of an incoming rocket fired from the mountain across the bay. Diving into the roadside drainage ditch was his only cover. The blast shook the ground with the force of a small earthquake. Too close, he thought. Immediately the base loudspeaker system sprang to life: "Red alert, red alert… Don flak gear and take cover," repeating the message several times.

It was a full fifteen minutes before the "all clear" sounded. The blast had been the only one. Patrick stood up and shook the dirt off his jungle fatigues. That was when he saw the bright orange glow coming from a few blocks away. Rounding the corner, he immediately knew what was burning. He ran the final two blocks as fast as his combat boots would allow. A fire truck and ambulance were already on the scene. He tried to get close to the burning trailer, but the SP's wouldn't allow it. As he stood helplessly by, the trailer burned, with flames reaching well above the two-story rooftops surrounding it. It wasn't until he heard someone yell "Fuck man, give me some help," that he realized the medics were 20 feet to his left, kneeling over a stretcher containing a badly torn up body of an almost unrecognizable figure. He knew who it was before he got any closer. Tears started rolling down his cheeks. He hadn't cried since Grandpa Jake had died three months before he enlisted. The medic noticed him standing there sobbing.

"Can you identify him?" he asked.

Barely able to get it out he replied, "Yeah, but is he going to be OK?"

He shook his head and said, "He's already gone, there was nothing we could do."

Patrick felt like there was a knife slicing through his stomach.

The rest of the night was spent at the hospital, giving statements to the investigators, and helping the hospital staff identify Chuck's relatives who would need to be notified. Although he had never met Chuck's wife, he felt like he had come to know her well. Chuck had talked about his wife constantly when the other guys weren't around. High school sweethearts, Sandra was the only girl Chuck had ever dated. Although he had only seen his daughter for a few days before shipping out, Patrick could tell she was the entire world to Chuck. Her pictures were pinned and taped all over his cubicle wall. Patrick wondered what it would be like for the young mother and daughter to get through the next few weeks, much less the rest of their lives. He knew that the two Air Force officers tasked with delivering the news to their door would be faced with a monumental duty. He was thankful he didn't have to do it. The final thought Patrick had before returning to his barracks was one of self-preservation: Chuck was the only one he knew that had witnessed those files. Patrick was ashamed of himself for thinking so selfishly. But he knew he had to live in the now. He would be drawn into this mess whether he liked it or not.

* * *

After a long, thoughtful time spent showering and shaving, Patrick finally made it to his office. Norris was already there.

"How come you're late Patrick?" Norris inquired. But he could tell something more was wrong outside of yesterday's events. Norris knew of the disaster in the early morning hours, he had already tried to use the phone when the lack of dial tone reminded him of what the rocket had hit.

Haney relayed the story of his friend and his time spent at the hospital. Norris was stunned.

"Another five minutes earlier and you would've been there too!" Norris said. It hadn't dawned on Patrick until he had said it. As badly as he felt about Chuck and his family, a sure sense of relief had come over him.

He didn't have time to dwell on it. Two SP Jeeps pulled up outside the door. Three huge security policemen with forty-fives drawn ordered them to get on the floor with their hands behind them. Right behind them Patrick saw an officer enter and proceed to the back office… Major Daly's. He immediately went to the file cabinet, spent a few minutes rifling through each drawer. Just as quickly as he came in, he ordered the SPs back out the door after him. One of them told the two sprawled on the floor they could stand up. As they pulled off, Norris and Haney both turned and saw the yellow caution tape with: "Security Police-Do Not Enter" printed across in bold black lettering. It was placed over the major's doorway and each drawer of the file cabinet. Patrick looked at Norris with an inquisitive look that Norris did not have an answer for.

"I think it's time we go see the AG," Norris said. With that, they locked up and jumped in the truck for the short trip to the adjutant general's office.

* * *

While neither one had been charged with anything, the Captain who had agreed to see them listened to the events that had unfolded the past two weeks. Captain Glazer didn't look to be any older than Patrick, but the framed diploma on the wall from Georgetown Law School gave them both a sense of relief. After finishing the briefing, the young Captain finally looked up from his constant note-taking on the yellow legal pad and said, "Let me get with my boss, Colonel Turner, and we'll find out what we can. I'll let you know as soon as I have something."

Three days went by before any word about Major Daly surfaced. The information came courtesy of President Richard Nixon. As a campaign promise, he felt it necessary to announce his plan for "peace with honor". While the speech didn't mean much to Haney when he first saw it re-broadcast on Armed Forces Television, the next day it became apparent what it would mean personally.

Without any forewarning, Major Daly strode through the front door of the Social Actions hut. Norris was out at the time, but Patrick was caught between shock and gratefulness. He jumped up and automatically saluted his boss. The Major smiled and gave him a half-hearted return salute, never being one for open expressionism. He then reached his hand out, shook Patrick's hand vigorously, and invited him back to his office. Daly angrily tore the tape from across the doorway and threw his hat on the desk. "Sit down Patrick, we need to talk," the Major insisted.

Patrick cautiously took a seat across the desk from his superior. He quickly reminded himself that he still didn't know who he could trust at this time. So, he decided to do more listening than talking. The Major began.

"What do you know about May's patients and those files that the SPs took?"

Patrick immediately ignored his own advice and answered, "Not a thing… May did his own paperwork. I never saw the actual notes in the files. He only had me deliver copies over to Doctor Heath at the hospital."

"Are you sure you never saw them?" countered Daly.

"Positive sir," Patrick answered. "I never even saw the inside of the file cabinet until…," he suddenly caught himself. He was about to tell his boss that he and Chuck had broken in the night of Daly's arrest and witnessed someone taking off with an untold number of files.

"Go on Sergeant," Daly insisted.

He felt he had no choice. He had to trust someone. Deciding on his own instinct, he felt he knew the Major well enough to know he wouldn't be involved in any wrongdoing. Laying out the story of events after his arrest, Patrick saw that Daly was surprised by what he was saying.

"So, your friend Chuck can collaborate seeing the files before they were stolen?" Daly asked. The look on Patrick's face told the major that would be a problem. Patrick continued with the story including the rocket attack that took Chuck's life and ended with admitting his relief that he had fallen asleep and wasn't in the trailer when it was hit.

"How come they suddenly let you go, major?" Patrick asked.

"I can thank Nixon for that one," Daly said. "The orders have already come down to start the withdrawal process. All investigations have been put on hold. I'm under house arrest until further notice. We've been ordered to shut down operations and prepare for our next base assignment. Where's Norris? He's got to help me organize shipping everything to Korat, Thailand."

"He had a race relations seminar scheduled for today over at the admin hut," Patrick answered. "He'll finish at 1600 hours."

"Go get him Patrick," Daly countered, " tell him I want him to suspend the class and report back here, immediately!"

"Yes sir, but phone service has been restored as of today, you can call him there," Patrick said.

"No, go get him," Daly answered, "I don't trust the phones anymore."

"Yes sir," Haney said, and immediately rose to retrieve Norris.

"Man, this shit must be getting deep," he said to himself.

At first Norris was pissed for being interrupted by Patrick but changed his attitude when he realized the order came from the Major.

"Help me gather up the materials, Patrick," he insisted as he dismissed the class until further notice.

The rest of the day was spent boxing up all files and office supplies. The transportation commander had already started picking up the office furniture. When all the boxes were sealed and picked up by the work detail, the three of them stood in the empty office looking around as if they were waiting for something else to pop out of a closet at them.

"When do we leave for Thailand major?" Patrick asked.

"Sgt. Norris and I leave in the morning. Patrick you have to report to Security Police headquarters at 0700. You've been temporarily assigned to them until your orders are cut," Daly replied.

"SPs? What am I going to do there, major?" he asked.

"Perimeter duty… they're going to need all hands to protect the base while we withdraw," Daly said.

With that, Norris and Daly shook his hand and wished him luck, vowing to see him in Thailand.

Chapter 6
Pulling Out: Nixon's Withdrawal Plan

April, 1972

"Directive from the General Sydney, base commander, Cam Rahn Bay. All non-assigned personnel shall make themselves available for perimeter duty as needed by the Security Police Commander until such time as said personnel have written orders for their next assignment."

The master sergeant reading the order smiled at the group of 20 airmen seated with Patrick in the SP meeting room. He was openly happy that others could get to experience the nightmare existence that his troops had been going through.

"It's now 0815, you will each go back to your bunks, get some shuteye, then report back here at 1800 this evening in full flak gear," the burly sergeant continued, "You will be issued your weapons and receive assignments to a place on the perimeter where you will remain until relieved at 0600 tomorrow morning, that is all, dismissed."

Walking back to his barracks, Patrick said to himself "I joined the Air Force so I wouldn't have to do this shit."

"What are you talking about man?" Smitty asked, startling Patrick.

Terry Smith, an occasional member of the group bedding down in his barracks, was the Chaplin's assistant. A small, skinny kid from Nebraska, he had convinced the personnel people, and more importantly the Chaplin, that religion was his life. He must have been a great actor. He had decided that it would be the safest job he could be assigned to if they insisted on shipping him to 'Nam. But, he occasionally had met with the group to partake in the smoking and whoring that went on, always reminding his friends that his transgressions were to be kept secret. After all, one word from the Chaplin and he'd be joining Patrick on perimeter duty every night.

After telling Smitty about his "good" fortune, Patrick continued walking toward his cubicle.

"Come on Patrick, let's go on the veranda; it'll help you get some sleep," Smitty insisted.

What the hell, Patrick thought, it's probably the only way I'll get to sleep in this heat.

* * *

After being issued an M-16, and boarding the deuce and a half, Patrick found that he would be assigned to the easiest perimeter duty possible: beachfront. There was a walkthrough gate from the base to the beach most of the beach going personnel had used on several occasions that was open only during the day. It was the access Patrick and his friends had used many times, not realizing that before dusk the SPs on duty had secured the barbed wire blockade that stretched across the sandy beach road leading to the base. At night, the opening was a different story. The sandbag-rimmed foxhole was no more than five-by-five-feet square with a green metal tripod sticking up on the wall facing the beach. He exited the truck and found himself alone with a grizzled looking staff sergeant carrying the 20 mm rifle to be mounted on the tripod.

Patrick tried sticking out his hand and introducing himself but was abruptly rebuked with a "don't want to know your name" from his companion. Continuing, he said, "If you make it through the night, I'll be impressed." Patrick, embarrassed by the rejection, withdrew his hand and silently decided to tell his bunker mate to fuck off.

Settling in, the veteran told Patrick to keep his K-rations to himself and under no circumstances was he to catch him sleeping, or he'd put a charge up his ass. Haney decided this guy had been there before, so he might want to pay attention to what he had to say. As the sun quickly set over the mountain, the shadows got longer and the anxiety in the bunker got higher.

"You're not going to be able to see shit, newbie, so keep your ears open," the vet said. "There's not going to be any moon tonight."

The last thing the veteran said before several hours of silent listening was, "If we get lucky, they'll keep coming from across the bay on the other side of the base." Around midnight, Patrick was wishing that his protector knew what he was talking about. Unfortunately, the enemy had decided to take a different tactic that night.

The gentle breeze was forcing the waves to lap lazily against the sand. It was as quiet as a beachfront could possibly be. Patrick was almost in a trance, lulled by the false sense of security offered by the knowledge that the sappers were coming from the bayside. Luckily, his bunkmate was more attentive. It was the sudden splash of water that spurred him into action. Striking the end of the flare onto the flat rock at the top of the sandbag wall, placed there just for that reason, the flare roared from the foot-long tube he was holding. The bright pink ball of light went immediately up to about 100 feet and slowly started falling towards the sand. Patrick still couldn't make anything out on the surf, but the veteran did. Grabbing the 20 mm rifle with authority, he started firing directly in front of them toward the water. Following the tracers of light from the automatic weapon, Patrick finally saw the target: two sappers crawling up the beach from the water returning fire from their Russian-made AK-47 rifles. Patrick's first instinct was to duck behind cover, but saw the veteran continue to fire the rifle with only his helmeted head sticking above the horizon of the bunker. Patrick decided he wasn't going to die without putting up a fight, so he raised his M-16 and joined in firing toward the beach, shooting a weapon for the first time since basic training. Although he had scored "expert" on the range back in San Antonio, firing at live targets was unnerving and he couldn't tell if he was hitting anything or not.

After what seemed like an eternity, he stopped shooting only when his clip was dry. He hadn't realized that the sergeant had also stopped firing. Peering out from behind the bags, Patrick could see that the two figures were motionless lying on the sand, thanks to the quickly dimming flare nearly grounded on the beach. Patrick reached over to slap his partner on the back, and when he did, was startled by the lack of movement from him. He grabbed the sergeant's shoulder and shook him as if he was fast asleep. When he didn't move, Patrick grabbed the back of his flak jacket and turned him over. Haney was confronted by something he had only seen in the movies: a hole the size of a golf ball in the man's face just above his mouth on the right side. Haney first thought it must be a joke because the hole wasn't bleeding. He confirmed the reality of it all by feeling his neck for a pulse. He wasn't bleeding because his heart had already stopped. Patrick felt like his had stopped also, but suddenly felt it about to jump out of his chest when he realized that he still wasn't sure the danger had passed. He grabbed the flashlight that hung on the dead soldier's belt and started shining it out on the sand that was less than 30 feet away. He spotted the two figures, lying motionless on the beach. After fifteen to twenty seconds of watching them he set the flashlight on top of a bag, still illuminating the two, and sent another clip of ammo into each of them. Satisfied that they were no longer a threat, he let out a long slow breath, for the first time realizing that the base sirens had gone off signaling another red alert.

It was only a few more seconds and two Jeeps had skidded across the sand road and come to a halt a few feet from the bunker. Before he realized what was going on, the master sergeant who had assigned him to his location had jumped in the bunker and was accompanied by three other heavily armed guards. Not even saying anything to Patrick, the platoon leader examined the dead sergeant lying next to him and then got on a walkie-talkie for an ambulance and reinforcements. Finally, the leader asked Patrick, "What ya got, Airman?"

"I think we got two on the beach out there, Sarge," Patrick responded. Shining a much larger light toward the water, the master sergeant quickly confirmed what Haney had told him.

"You two get out there and check 'em out," barking orders to his men.

"You hit, Airman?" the master sergeant asked.

"No sir, just a little shaken up, that's all," Patrick told him.

"OK, sit tight, we'll get you some relief in a few minutes," the sergeant reassured Haney.

Almost instantly, several more vehicles skidded through the sand, and Patrick found himself in the back of an ambulance, heading to the hospital with his dead bunker mate. Arriving at the emergency ward, he was hustled to an exam room and seeing that he was in shock, stripped down to his skivvies and examined for injuries. The ER doctor could see that even though there were no physical injuries, the young sergeant was in a state of shock, and ordered the nursing staff to sedate him and put him in a ward for the rest of the night.

It only took thirty seconds for Patrick to feel the effects of the injection given to him. As he was wheeled down a hallway on a gurney, he could barely make out the chatter from the two orderlies taking care of him. He didn't even remember being hoisted onto a hospital bed with crisp white sheets… the first he had felt since arriving in country.

* * *

Haney slept until the next afternoon. He wouldn't have awoken except for the doctor probing his body for any underlying injuries.

"How you feeling, Sergeant?" Doctor Heath asked.

"I'm OK, I think," replied Patrick. After a few more moments of examination, the doctor asked as he shone a penlight in Haney's eyes, "didn't you work in the Social Actions Office?"

Suddenly, Patrick remembered why he looked familiar. This was the doctor he delivered the envelopes to every week containing copies of patient files.

"Yes sir, but the office is in transit to Thailand," he said.

"I know, I spoke with Major Daly before he left," Heath said. "What do you know about that investigation, Sergeant?"

Even though he was still groggy from the medication, Patrick knew not to trust anyone, so he shrugged his shoulders and answered in the negative.

"Well, you don't seem to be hurt," Heath continued, "but I want to keep you for observation today. I'll let the SPs know. You just relax."

Although he felt fine, Patrick was in no shape to argue, the medicine was still making him loopy. Before drifting off again, he heard the doctor give the orders to the nurse that he was keeping Patrick another day. Haney couldn't see the questioning look the nurse gave the doctor, but she answered with a firm, "Yes, sir."

* * *

Several hours passed before Patrick felt well enough to sit up and eat some food. The nurse who had seen to his needs had made sure a tray from the mess hall was available to him even though it was well after the dinner hour. When she came back to remove the tray, Patrick asked her why he was being kept another day.

"I really don't know, Sergeant, but I'm sure the doctor has his reasons," she answered. As soon as she retrieved the tray and walked away, Doctor Heath entered the six-bed ward and made a beeline to Patrick's bed. With none of the other beds occupied, Patrick wondered why the doctor was pulling the curtains around his bed.

"Just going to give you something to help you rest, Sergeant," Heath said.

Before he could ask what it was, the doctor had already injected his arm with the syringe. Almost immediately, Patrick felt his head swimming and his limbs going limp. The doctor threw back the curtains and was startled by the presence of Nurse Baker coming back to see if Patrick had needed anything else.

"Just gave him a sedative Nurse," Heath said, "he should rest comfortably the rest of the night."

"Yes, Doctor," she replied, "I'll check on him from time to time."

As Heath left the ward, it was obvious to Baker that the doctor was giving this patient more attention than needed... he always had the nursing staff give the injections. But he did this one himself.

* * *

Nurse Baker was more concerned when just seconds after receiving the injection, the sergeant had fallen into a coma-like condition. She shook him to see if he would respond, to no avail. Studying his chart, she saw the Doctor had written down 10cc's of a mild sedative, so why did he go out so quickly, she thought. Noticing that he had thrown the syringe into the waste basket, she glanced around the ward and quickly put the used needle in her uniform pocket. Before leaving, she checked Patrick's pulse and breathing, making sure he wasn't in any immediate danger. Reassured, she quickly walked to the lab where she could have the remnants of the medication analyzed by her roommate, who was on duty. She couldn't have imagined that what she would find was done deliberately by Doctor Heath. But, she had no choice but to go to the hospital commander, Colonel Shafer, with the findings.

Since it just before midnight, she ordered the SP sergeant assigned to the hospital to wake the colonel and get him down there immediately. Reluctantly, the sergeant complied. It was only ten minutes before the commander was in his office demanding to know why he was pulled out this late. Baker handed him the lab report on the vial that was analyzed and told him this was injected into the patient in Ward 2 being treated by Doctor Heath. The colonel wasted no time in ordering the sergeant to find Heath, as he commanded the nurse to follow him. Upon arriving at Patrick's bedside, Colonel Shafer studied the chart hanging on the edge of the bed, and then checked his pulse.

"Get the crash cart now, Nurse," he yelled. Without hesitation, he grabbed the manual respirator and shoved the end into Patrick's mouth and started forcing air into his lungs. Seconds later, Baker arrived with the crash cart team and they proceeded to administer to a slowly slipping away Haney.

The colonel had told Nurse Baker later that her gutsy actions probably saved the young man's life. He wasn't sure how she knew to examine that syringe but thanked her for her quick action. Baker started crying, thankful that she didn't take the time to think about what she was doing. Otherwise, Haney would be dead by now.

Colonel Shafer waited at Haney's bed until he was fully awake. The drugs given to him to counteract the heroin were doing their job.

"Welcome back, son," he said to Patrick. "We almost lost you."

* * *

Not needing anything to help him sleep, Haney spent the next ten hours out to the world. He would have stayed in that state if not for the discussion being held at the foot of his bed. Slowly, he opened his eyes and tried to focus on the disturbance a few feet away. It took a few minutes, but his mind and vision cleared about the same time. Colonel Bolden, chief investigator for the SP office, and a young officer were having an animated discussion on whether Haney should be interrogated or not. The stirring from the bed stopped them both. Bolden said, "Guess that answers the question, Captain." It wasn't until they both started moving to the side of Patrick's bed that he realized the young officer was Captain Glazer, the lawyer he and Norris had seen just after Major Daly was arrested.

"Sgt. Haney, I'll be advising you on the colonel's questions," Glazer said. "I won't let you answer anything that could be detrimental to your situation."

"What situation?" Haney asked weakly.

Bolden didn't wait for the lawyer's answer, "What do you know about the doctor treating you after you were admitted here, sergeant?"

Glancing over at the lawyer who was gently nodding in the affirmative, Patrick answered, "Not much. I didn't even remember who he was until I had been in here for a while."

"What do you mean, remember him?" Bolden asked.

"The only contact I'd had with him before was delivering routing envelopes from our office once a week," Haney responded.

"What was in those envelopes Sergeant?" the Colonel continued.

"Patient file notes," he replied. "A copy of the counselor's notes would have to be included in their general medical file here at the clinic."

"Did you ever see these files or notes?" Bolden continued his questioning.

"No sir, they were strictly confidential," Patrick said. "Sergeant May was the only one who wrote on them. But, the file copies were kept in the cabinet in Major Daly's office."

"Major Daly had access to these files?" the Colonel continued.

"I would think so, Colonel, but I never saw him go into the file cabinet, just Sergeant May," Patrick insisted.

"Did you ever have occasion to go in the file cabinet, Sergeant?" Bolden asked.

Again. glancing at the lawyer, Patrick wanted to tell someone about his discovery with Chuck that evening.

"Just the once Colonel," he replied. He laid out the entire story to both officers. At the end Captain Glazer asked, "Where can we find this Chuck friend of yours?"

"You can't," Haney explained, "Chuck was killed later that night when the com trailer was hit."

Both officers looked at each other. Patrick didn't know what to say next, but was prompted by Bolden,

"So, no one else can verify the extra files were there, and that someone came in and stole them. That about right, Sergeant?"

"Yes sir, 'fraid so," Patrick answered.

"Is that all you have for now, Colonel?" Glazer asked.

Nodding he said, "I might have more later. Thanks for your honesty Sergeant."

As soon as he left, Patrick peppered his attorney with questions, hoping to fill in the blanks.

"I don't have all the answers yet, Patrick," the Captain continued, "but we do know that the doctor treating you was involved in the black market, drugs, prostitution, you name it, he was into it."

"Where is he now?" Patrick asked, suddenly realizing he could still be in danger.

"SPs thought they had him cornered in his hut, but when they went in, he had gone out a trap door that was made just for that reason," Glazer said. "They think he's in hiding with his black market connections, probably out in the jungle."

"Do they think that May or Major Daly had anything to do with it?" Patrick asked.

"They know that May's death was not from natural causes," the lawyer continued. "Toxicology reports are preliminary, but it looks like he was given a drug that's normally given to alcoholics to help them stay sober. But, as far as the major is concerned, he is only being accused of dereliction because he wasn't monitoring Master Sergeant May as he should have."

"You get some rest, Sergeant," the lawyer said, "I'll be back as soon as I know more. You'll be kept here for a few more days of observation."

What a relief, Patrick thought to himself. He was in no hurry to get back to perimeter duty.

* * *

The next two days were spent in the motherly bosom of Nurse Baker, isolated from the rest of the hospital population, under twenty-four hour guard. When he asked her why the guards were there, she replied, "Only thing I know is they hadn't caught that good-for-nuthin' bastard that did this to you." This chilled Haney, feeling like a sitting duck at first, until he glanced over at the two SPs standing at the only doorway to the ward, M-16s at the ready. He forced himself to relax and let Lieutenant Baker do her thing.

Although she had other patients to care for, she spent the majority of her twelve hour shift with Patrick, making sure he had enough material to read and his vital signs were taken every hour. Haney had learned she was married, with two children. Her National Guard unit was called up unexpectedly, and her husband of fifteen years was suddenly thrust into the role of Mommy and Daddy. Thankfully, he was a screenwriter in Los Angeles and could work at home most of the time.

Haney had studied her as she went about her daily routine. He guessed her to be in her late 30s, slightly overweight, dark hair and hazel eyes. Although he knew she wasn't, she appeared to be older than her years, projecting the matronly appearance that reassured him. She reminded him of his Aunt Helen back home, his godmother who had helped raise him for most of his young life. Although his parents had never divorced, there were many periods of separation, forcing his mother to leave him with Aunt Helen for long periods of time. Nurse Baker made him feel more secure than the two burly guards standing in the doorway.

On his fourth day of bed rest, the doctor signed his release. Baker delivered a fatigue green bag, sealed at the top with tape lined with Patrick's signature, a sign that his personal belongings were all there. As she handed him the bag, he grabbed her wrist and looked her in the eyes, saying, "I owe you my life, I don't know how to thank you." She smiled down at him as he sat on the edge of the bed.

She placed the bag next to him and said, "You don't have to… just seeing you leaving is thanks enough… I had my doubts for a while." She started to walk away, suddenly turning and saying, "Here is our address and phone number in West Hollywood; my husband said he might be interested in your story when you get back home. Oh, by the way, you're supposed to report directly to Captain Glazer's office from here. Good luck, Patrick."

With that she was gone.

* * *

Captain Glazer was all smiles when Haney sat down in his office.

"Good news, Patrick," he started. "You don't have to go back to perimeter duty. You're being shipped out immediately."

"Where am I going, home?" he asked expectantly.

"I'm afraid not," he replied. "You leave this afternoon for a week in Saigon, then reassignment to Korat AFB, Thailand."

Thinking for a few seconds, he then asked, "Why can't I go home and where the hell is Korat?"

"You can thank Nixon for not going home… the policy coming down is anyone with more than six months in country rotates back to a stateside assignment; you missed it by two weeks," Glazer replied. "Korat is two hours northeast of Bangkok. You'll be safe there, strictly a support unit."

"Two more bits of good news… they have an idea where Doctor Heath is hiding... The SPs are already on their way to pick him up," Glazer said. "Plus, the SP commander is putting you in for a Distinguished Service Medal, with an oak leaf cluster. Turns out they dug nothing but

M-16s out of the two sappers on that beach. Your bunker mate probably was hit early on in the attack. He didn't have a chance to hit anything. Congratulations!"

Haney was dumbfounded. He only remembered firing on the beach out of sheer desperation. He had no idea what he had been shooting at. It was strictly out of self-preservation that he was now in a position to finally get out of this hellhole.

He asked the captain, "Do I have an assignment yet in Korat?"

"The new Social Actions Office being set up there, of course," he replied.

This news also was surprising to him. "I thought the major and Sergeant Norris would be there," Patrick said.

"No, I'm afraid they are both being sent back to the States for Dereliction of Duty prosecution," answered the young captain. "I'm sure Norris will get off with a verbal reprimand, but Major Daly is another story. As far as the OSI can determine, May was falsifying patient files… actually making them up, and they were being approved by Heath and medications were prescribed, then delivered to their underground associates. Daly would have known this if he had been monitoring May more closely."

Patrick took in what he had just heard and asked, "What will happen to the major? He's a good man."

"Probably get an Article 15, or possibly a fine or reduction in rank," Glazer said, "I can only guess."

"Major Daly had recommended you to the new officer in charge."

Patrick didn't know whether to be grateful to the major or not. Would he be getting into a repeat of the nightmare he had just been subjected to?

The captain had wished him well and promised to keep him informed of any developments in the case. He had the office administrator drive Patrick to the flight line to catch a hop to Saigon. His duffle bag was already in the back of the Jeep when he sat down in the passenger seat. The next six hours were spent going back over the last few months in his mind. He had lost two good friends, and thankfully saw a lifer get what was coming to him. He felt lucky to even be breathing, much less on his way to a new start. But he couldn't get that Doctor Heath out of his mind. He still didn't know for sure whether he was in custody or not.

Chapter 7
Electric City: One Week in Saigon

Haney arrived in Bien Hoa Airfield shortly before nightfall. It looked much different from his short visit for the Bob Hope show back on Christmas Day. There were more permanent structures being built by the Army Corps of Engineers. They obviously hadn't heard the U.S. was pulling out. Being fifteen miles from downtown Saigon, he hopped on the shuttle bus as it was just pulling out. All incoming personnel were required to check in with the TDY office in downtown Saigon. He was relieved to hear from the duty officer that they had been expecting him. Although the TDY barracks were full, he was asked to sign for his travel pay, and given a list of recommended hotels in the area. The lieutenant said he would suggest either the Paradise or New World hotels from the ten on the list. He assured Haney they were clean and would fit his budget. Patrick thanked him and was directed to a waiting taxi outside.

The Paradise Hotel was a former department store that had been gutted by a VC rocket a little more than a year ago. The lobby reminded Patrick of the YMCA on Lee Circle back in New Orleans. A few chairs scattered about and a short counter served as the check-in desk. The clerk behind the counter was smarmy looking with slicked back hair like the kind Patrick had seen walking the French Quarter peddling their stable of girls to the tourists. When he found out the room was only seven dollars per day, he figured it couldn't be much to look at.

The climb up to the fifth floor was dotted by the sight of on-going construction on nearly every floor. No bellhops... what did he expect at that price? Entering the double doors to his room, he was shocked by what he saw... the biggest suite he had ever been in. With an elaborate Roman-style formal living room leading into a separate bedroom holding a round, king-size bed that was as big as his bedroom back home. He felt he had entered the Garden of Eden. The bed was placed in the middle of the room under a fully-mirrored ceiling. The bathroom held a heart-shaped porcelain tub and Patrick immediately knew the marble tiled room was larger than the living room he grew up in back in New Orleans. Not having a phone in the room seemed to be the only convenience not in place. Patrick made a mental note to make sure there was no mistake on the room rate... but that could wait until morning.

Even though he had spent several days lying in a hospital bed, he felt the effects of the drugs still in his system, and plopped face-first on the satin-sheeted bed and immediately fell asleep.

*   *   *

Morning came early in his suite. Overlooking one of the busiest streets in Saigon, it was in the heart of the shopping district, so the street traffic started just after daybreak and grew louder as the sun rose. After a quick bath, something he hadn't experienced in the cold shower world of Cam Rahn Bay, he stopped at the front desk to make sure he was in the right room. The pretty, young local woman assured him it was correct. It was the only room left vacant last night, so he decided that it was time his luck had changed.

Bordeaux Street was bustling with activity. The name was left over from the French influence of the past several decades. The hodge-podge of storefronts seemed to run together as Patrick strolled along the stone sidewalk. It wasn't long before he recognized a familiar sight… the USO Club. Ducking in through large glass doors, he was hit with a blast of cool air unlike anything he had felt since leaving Seattle. Air conditioning… far out, he thought.

Patrick knew that the USO was the best place for information about his surroundings. Although staffed by civilian employees, they proved to be knowledgeable and forthright about the dangers that lurked beyond those doors. The maps and sightseeing highlights didn't show what the staff knew… there were dangers beyond anything Haney could have imagined. After schooling him on the life-threatening capabilities of the capitol city, the retired Army officer, now working for the USO told him about the various enterprises practiced by local con artists. Haney thanked him and strolled into the pool room just off the lobby.

It didn't take him long to get into a game with an outgoing New Yorker named Gus Blanco. The Army spec-5 had been in country for almost nine months and was awaiting his flight back to the States.

"I've been waiting for a ride back for four days… keep getting bumped by some officer every time I get on the flight manifest," the Little Italy native said. Even though they were completely different, the two hit it off, possibly due to their need for some sort of companionship. After a few hours of trading nine ball wins, they decided it was time to eat. Gus said,

"We can get something in the snack bar here, but I know a place we can get a great meal at half the price, but we'll have to change our script into local paper."

"Yeah," Patrick answered, "the guy at the front desk told me they had an exchange desk in the next room."

"Nooooooo," Gus replied. "We can get a lot more for our money on the street. Come on, I'll take care of it."

As the two headed for the door, Gus said, "How much you want to exchange?"

"I don't know," Patrick hesitated, "is twenty bucks enough?"

"Yeah," Gus answered, "but if we find a good rate, I'm going to do everything I got. I can always change it back and make a little on the deal."

Patrick spent the next fifteen minutes following his new friend, moving from local to local asking in perfect Vietnamese what their rate was. He sure seemed to know what he was doing, Patrick thought to himself. After a particularly heated exchange with a young teenager, they started walking away when the boy spoke in perfect English.

"OK, Joe, I know somebody who can give you that rate, he give me finder's fee."

Gus nodded, and they followed the boy around a corner to a worldly looking Filipino leaning up against the wall of a building. The boy said a few words to the man that Patrick had no clue about, but Gus seemed to know and started to converse with the money changer in Vietnamese. After another heated discussion, Gus grabbed the twenty from Patrick and added it to his own stack saying in English,

"One hundred, twenty OK?" The Filipino nodded and pulled out a wad of South Vietnamese dollars wound by a thick rubber band. Unrolling it, he counted it out and said, "Seven hundred seventy," as he came to the end of the stack.

The short, hairy man rolled the bills back together and pulled the rubber band back over the wad. The two men exchanged stacks, and Guy smiled as he pulled Patrick back to the main street.

"Man, seven to one, what a rate," he said. Patrick wasn't so sure. He asked Gus for his share but was rebuked on the grounds of being careful not to flash currency for the benefit of the pickpockets.

It was two blocks down before they arrived at the restaurant and took a seat just inside the open front window. Gus reached in and grabbed the money out of his pocket, unrolling what appeared to be the same wad the changer had shown him. As he opened the roll, it was obvious to both of them what had happened. Instead of a roll of twenties surrounding tens, inside the initial twenty was a stack of ones… fifty to be exact. Not only had they been taken but taken to an extreme. Seventy Viet dollars for 120 U.S. Gus jumped up and ran out the door, Patrick right behind him. The two blocks were covered in record time, but not quite fast enough. The street was crowded, but there were no Filipinos in sight. Neither was the young boy who had led them to the con man. A couple of MPs walking by noticed them looking bewildered and asked, "What's going on fellas?"

Patrick started to tell them when Gus pushed him away saying to the cops, "Nothing' man, just looking for chicks."

Being out of earshot gave Gus the opportunity to say, "Patrick, you can be arrested for changing in the streets, plus they'd just laugh at us. I'm sorry man, I thought I was watching his hands the entire time. He was quicker than I've ever seen. Here, take the 20, let's go get something to eat."

As they sat eating lunch, Patrick wondered what else was in store for him during his stay. He also thought that if a veteran like Gus could be taken that easily, he'd better be on his toes at all times.

*   *   *

After a short nap, the two new friends had made plans to meet in the ShowBar Lounge next to Patrick's hotel. It was already dark by the time they both showed up, so entering the bar wasn't as traumatic to their eyes as it could have been. Except for some low wattage red lamps on a few tables and the reading light over the cash register, the darkness engulfed them as they walked in. It still took a few seconds for them to adjust to the dark, and they decided to take the first available table so not to risk tripping over unseen obstacles.

They weren't sitting for ten seconds when the lights on the stage flashed as though someone had plugged in a set of those floodlights used with Motorola moving cameras. Adjusting to the stage lights was easier when they saw what was coming out to perform… two of the most voluptuous Asians that he had ever seen. Not knowing it was a strip joint, the two smiled at each other as they ordered cocktails from the topless waitress.

By the second piped-in song, it was apparent that this was no run of the mill strip show. The two women were joined on stage by a twenty-something male wearing only a patch of clothing similar to Tarzan's loin cloth. As one of the girls bent over and grabbed her ankles, the other reached under the loin cloth and grasped the man's penis and pulled him closer to her bending friend. Patrick and Gus couldn't believe what happened next. A live sex show. Patrick had heard of them but wasn't looking for one. Not only was the guy involved with one of the girls, the other female had her way with both of them.

The two Americans sat transfixed. Never had they imagined that their evening would start out like this. No sooner than the show ended, the lights went back down, but the two dark-haired beauties appeared in the chairs next to them, asking, "Buy me a drink, Joe?"

Already aroused by the performance, they were easily convinced to order another round of drinks including "champagne cocktails", knowing the three dollars per drink only bought apple juice. But they didn't care. They were out for female companionship, and they meant to succeed.

* * *

Patrick woke up in a plywood walled room on a lumpy mattress covered with a dingy, tea-colored sheet. A rickety fan in the corner was the only breeze blowing through the room that had one two-by-two window with broken glass on one wall. It wasn't until he heard a sigh coming from the other side of the room that he noticed the naked form bending over the makeshift crib. He thought he recognized her from the night before but couldn't swear it. She lifted the baby from the crib and returned to the bed with the suddenly shy Patrick grabbing for covers.

"You like my baby?" she said.

"Ah, yeah, I guess so," Patrick answered. "How old is he?" noticing the baby's sex since he wasn't wearing a diaper.

"He six months," she replied. "You stay with me today, maybe we go to PX later."

"No, I can't," Patrick murmured. "Where's my clothes?"

She pointed to a table with three legs leaning against a wall, and Haney suddenly felt the urge to check his pants pockets for his wallet. Relief was immediate when he saw all of what he estimated to be there.

"How much do I owe you?" Patrick asked.

"Ten dolla," she said quickly.

Patrick looked around as he dressed and opened the door to see a larger room outside of her quarters that was full of mothers in various stages of undress, some nursing babies seemingly the same age as his companion's child.

"We get bedroom if GI spend night with us," she offered. Patrick grabbed a twenty in US script from his wallet and handed it to her. Her eyes lit up and she blurted out, "You come back tonight, OK Joe?"

"We'll see," Patrick answered knowing full well that he wasn't coming back.

As he got to the bottom of the stairs in the three-story flop house, he saw Gus sitting on a bench, waiting for him. The two walked down the alleyway leading to Bordeaux Street and Patrick asked, "Is that typical of where they live?"

"Yeah," Gus answered, "There's probably 40 or 50 sluts living there with only half as many bedrooms, plus they all have kids."

"Who owns the place?" Haney asked.

"Probably some French guy who hires a mamasan to run the place for him," Gus continued. "The French still own most of the property in Saigon, thanks to a cozy relationship with the politicians."

Amazing these people live like this, Patrick thought to himself.

* * *

The next couple of days were very much like the first. Playing pool at the USO, a little sightseeing after a late lunch, a nap to be able to withstand the rigors of Saigon night life, and usually waking up in a strange place each morning. Gus had told him not to bring the women back to his hotel, they might cause more trouble than they were worth. He also advised him to sleep with his wallet on him, but Patrick didn't find it necessary… it was probably naïve on his part, but he got lucky and possibly found the only two honest pros in the city.

Day five brought Gus' departure. Patrick was sad to see him go but knew he would probably get more rest now that he was alone. Gus wished him well and wrote his Brooklyn address down encouraging him to come to the Big Apple so he could show Patrick his city. When his parents died, he couldn't afford to live in Manhattan so he had to move in with his older brother's family. But, Gus promised they would stay "in the city" if Patrick came. They gave a hearty "soul" handshake and Gus told him to stay safe. Given the circumstances, Patrick understood the smile on his friend's face.

That night Patrick had already made plans to have a nice dinner at the Australian Steak House just down the street from the hotel, and then turn in early… in his own room. Just as dusk fell, he entered the restaurant and was seated in a back booth big enough for six people. The hostess seating him was a sight for sore eyes… a blonde-haired, blue-eyed Australian named Suzie from Sydney. Standing at a good five feet eight inches, with reasonably high heels, she towered over the rest of the staff. She was wearing a colorful blue kimono that accented her eyes. Her body, outlined by the form fitting dress, was perfectly proportioned. A svelte 110 pounds that was quite obviously kept in shape through work outs. The slit down the front of her outfit was low enough that Patrick got an eyeful of her ample breasts. She noticed his attention and lingered long enough for him to see it all as she placed a menu in front of him.

She was the daughter of the owner, who was away on a purchasing trip to Taipei, and she was left in charge. Suzie immediately took a liking to the young man at least ten years her junior. But, she felt he had something she had missed since being in Vietnam; manners. Most of the clientele were loud-mouthed GIs with roaming hands. She had easily grown bored with their behavior and refused any and all advances thrown her way. She told the waiter tasked with serving Patrick to give him a drink on the house just for saying "thank you" for being seated.

Patrick was pleasantly surprised by the gesture and kept glancing at her as she went about her duties during his meal. While he knew she was older than him, it didn't stop him from wondering what it would be like to be with a non-Asian for a change. Nah, he thought, she's out of my league. A woman with her body and experience probably was dating an officer or some big shot businessman with money. Couldn't hurt to dream he decided.

The meal was great… a real steak cut from Japanese Kobe beef. That plus a few more drinks and cheesecake for dessert and he was set. With the check setting him back almost twelve dollars, he decided that an early night was just the thing his pocket could handle. As he was about to leave, he passed the hostess desk and the blonde beauty said, "Where you running off to, Joe?"

Turning, he said, "The name's Patrick, you must have been in country too long to be calling GIs Joe."

Standing she said, "Just pulling your chain, Yank. Name's Suzie, Suzie Brunson." She stuck out her hand and shook his vigorously. "Why don't you stay for a while? I'll be finished in an hour or so, I'll have a drink with you. "Without waiting for an answer she took his hand and led him into the bar that was full of Marines in jungle fatigues, celebrating a few days out of the jungle. She sat him down on a stool and told the bartender, "Ming, give him whatever he wants, I'll be back in a little while."

This stole the attention of the grunts from the jungle. As he placed his order with Ming, one of the Marines walked over and said, "What makes you so special, man, we been hittin' on that bitch for two days and can't get a peep outta her. What gives?"

Knowing not to give them any excuse, Patrick shrugged his shoulders and said, "Friend of the family… she used to live next door before moving back to Australia."

The group of humpers paused, looked at each other momentarily, and then went back to their conversation. Quick thinking, Patrick said to himself.

By the time she had finished her duties, the bouncer had already started the Marines out the door, threatening to call the MPs if they didn't move their party to the disco next door. Sitting next to Patrick, she ordered a shot and a Foster's for both of them. What the hell, Patrick thought. It wasn't his usual, but if it made moving in on her easier, he'd try it. Several rounds later, they both felt the effects of the eighty-proof alcohol and strong lager from her home country. Suzie suggested they retire to his room and gave some last minute instructions to the bouncer who would close up for her.

"I'd invite you to my place, but my Dad may come back tonight… bad form you know," she said as she grabbed and opened a bottle of Seagram's VO.

Patrick remembered what Gus had told him about bringing the girls back to his hotel. But, this was different. Suzie was a westerner. Different value system, he thought. So, he walked her back to his room and they set up shop in the living room. She went right to a cabinet by the window and opened the top, revealing a console stereo system he didn't even know was there. Tuning in the Armed Forces Vietnam station, the music was a welcome icebreaker to the room. With Led Zepplin playing 'Stairway to Heaven' in the background, she sat next to him on the couch and said, "How high do you want to get Patrick?"

"What do you have in mind?" he answered.

Reaching into her purse, she pulled out a little sheet of paper no larger than a memo pad. It was completely white except for little purple dots scattered across the side.

"What the hell is that?" he asked.

"Never seen window pane before, honey?" she answered.

He shook his head saying, "What is it?"

"A little acid, you game mate?"

Not wanting to appear as naïve as he looked, he told her, "Sure, but I've never seen it like that before," putting up an unconvincing front.

She tore off two squares and handed him one. "Just place it on your tongue… it's rice paper… it'll melt in your mouth like candy" she said.

He watched her follow her own directions and then did exactly as she had done, each of them taking a swig of the VO bottle to wash it down.

They settled back and started listening to the stereo playing a series of Motown hits and enjoying the moment. By the time Smokey Robinson's smooth soprano voice wafted through the room, smiles came across both their faces. She knew what was coming. He was in for the ride of his life.

* * *

Several more Motown hits and a few shots from the bottle later, Suzie got tired of waiting. She leaned over Patrick and started to gently kiss him as if on a first date. Seconds later, the sweet, sensual embrace turned into a lustful, hard and hungry battle. Every inch of his skin was ultra-sensitive and reacted to her every touch. It didn't take long for each of them to disrobe the other as they fell in unison to the wooden floor. The sex was like a rumbling earthquake. She was beautifully built, an athletic woman who knew so much more about sex than he did. The LSD had done its job, making them both cognizant of what the other one desired the most… pure pleasure.

After hours of writhing on the hard floor, she rose and grabbed his hand and her purse saying, "Grab the bottle, dear, the bed will be better." He obeyed and met her on the round bed, taking a drink before handing her the bottle. She took another swig and reached into her purse pulling out a joint and offering it to him.

"It'll keep the edge off the acid, and make the ride a lot smoother," she said.

"Nah, I'm kinda enjoying this," he countered.

She placed the stick next to the bed and climbed on top of him saying, "Now where did we leave off?"

Even though he was young, he didn't think he could rise to the occasion so quickly, but the acid helped… his penis was blue steel in a matter of seconds.

Several hours later, while resting between rounds, Patrick started to feel strange and uncomfortable. "What's that in the mirror up there?" he said pointing to the ceiling.

"What are you looking at honey?" she asked.

"Those bugs in the mirror…there…see them?" he insisted.

"Oh darling, take a toke of this joint, it'll help calm you down," she said handing him the lit dope. He puffed on the stick and immediately started to calm down, wondering what it was he had been looking at. The joint had cleared his head, and he started to feel sensual again. Just in time, Suzie was ready…again.

* * *

After finally falling asleep shortly before daybreak, the two were not out for very long when the knocking on the door startled them awake. Patrick stumbled to the door and opened it wide, wanting to see who in the world was bothering his much needed rest. The maid stood there, staring with wide-eyed amazement at Patrick. She shrieked and said almost inaudibly, "I come back, I come back," retreating back down the hall. It wasn't until she was out of sight that Patrick realized he was butt naked. Suzie was laughing so hard she could hardly get her clothes on.

"Where are you going?" he asked. "It's only 9 a.m."

"I've got a restaurant to run darling," she said as she completed donning her outfit. "Come by for lunch and we'll do something this afternoon," she called as she walked past him still standing in the doorway. She smiled and said, "Save that for later," looking down at his manhood sticking straight up.

He closed the door and fell into bed, wondering how she could possibly have the strength to get up for work now… after everything she drank and ingested last night… with only two hours of sleep. He didn't wonder long. Sleep got the better of him.

* * *

The banging on the door got louder and louder. Groggily, he stumbled to the door, stopping to grab a towel, a little embarrassed by his earlier encounter with the maid. Relief came when he opened the door to find Suzie, hands on hips, saying, "I knew you'd sleep right through."

"What time is it?" he asked as he dropped his towel and fell back on the bed.

"It's 3 p.m. and you've been sleeping enough, mister," she answered. Seeing him not move, she decided to wake him the best way she knew how. It worked. After showering, they spent the rest of the afternoon sightseeing. She showed him a side of Saigon that most GIs did not even know about… or couldn't find. Japanese Saki Bars, massage parlors catering to couples, and the last stop… an opium den hidden behind a camera storefront. Patrick was amazed how easily this woman could handle anything that life had to offer. He had never known a female that could drink like any guy he had been around, ingest any and all drugs she could get her hands on, and still have the desire to explore any sexual situation she could dream up.

Just before arriving back at his hotel, a light drizzle had started to saturate the steaming concrete and stone sidewalks. By the time they ducked into the lobby, it was a full-fledged monsoon. The lightning and thunder drowned out any conversation they tried to have, so they trudged up the steps to his top floor suite.

Patrick opened the door and allowed Suzie to enter first. Before he had a chance to react, something yanked her around the door as she screamed for help. Haney rushed through the entrance and was faced with his girlfriend being held from behind by an intruder holding a forty-five to her head. It took Patrick a few seconds to clear the drug-induced haze from his brain and recognize the man with a hand holding her head in place by her hair, and the other forcing the gun into her temple... it was Doctor Heath.

"I thought you were in the stockade," Patrick blurted.

"I've got too many friends to be caught because of you, asshole," Heath threatened. "But I promised them you wouldn't be a problem anymore, so.... Here I am!"

Patrick had no idea what to do. He wasn't trained in hand-to-hand combat, he couldn't outrun a forty-five, and he couldn't yell for help... no one would hear him over the storm raging outside. With all the corrugated tin roofing on the buildings, the noise from the hail storm that was coming down completely engulfed the room with a deafening roar. He needn't worry. Before he could move a muscle, Suzie took matters into her own hands... stomping on Heath's foot, she threw an elbow back into his face, squarely flattening his nose. Blood immediately flew out his nostrils as he dropped the gun, instinctively grabbing his face. Before either of the men could move, Suzie finished off her defense with a knee to his crotch, forcing him to his knees and then into a fetal position on the floor.

Patrick was still in shock as she grabbed the gun, pointed it at the helpless lump on the floor and said, "Who the fuck is this, love?"

"He's the scumbag I told you about that tried to kill me," Patrick answered.

"Well, he won't try anymore, that's for sure," she quipped. "You go and call the police, I'll keep him tidy right here."

Before he got down the first flight of stairs, the sound of the gun going off startled him and he raced back up the steps to the doorway of his room. Lying on the floor on her back was Suzie, all but covered by her assailant who was motionless. Quickly searching the floor for the gun, Patrick started to panic not being able to find it. His fears were immediately dismissed as his beautiful blond friend started to shove the lifeless body off of her.

"He lunged at me so I decided to end it," she offered breathlessly.

Looking into her eyes as he helped her up, he was amazed at how calm she seemed. He thanked his luck that she was on his side.

Although the Saigon authorities wanted to handle the case, the Military

Police had arrived, quickly identifying Heath as someone they had been searching for. The locals retreated and the MPs took their statements and had the body carted off to the base morgue. Before the investigators left, Colonel Bolden from Cam Rahn arrived via helicopter and entered the room. He took one look at the scene, quickly read the preliminary report and approached Patrick.

"You're one lucky SOB, son" he said.

"Why didn't you tell me he was on the loose?" Patrick insisted.

"Didn't want to worry you. Plus we didn't want to scare him off if he tried something stupid like this," the colonel answered.

Haney was dumbfounded. "You mean you used me as bait?" he asked.

"Something like that, son," Bolden answered. "We knew he was the one stealing the files out of Major Daly's office that night. Our investigator was tailing him. Your story had to be true... it fit in with the timing."

"How did you know to tail him?" Patrick queried.

"We knew we had a snitch for the black market in our office," Bolden replied. "Turned out it was a good customer of Heath's. He led us right to him."

Patting him on the back as he left, Bolden said, "Try to stay out of trouble in Thailand, son." Patrick nodded, and turned to Suzie to embrace her as though he never wanted to let her go.

The rest of his time in Saigon was a whirlwind of human pleasures... food, drugs, and sex. What more could he ask for. But all things DO come to an end, he thought, as he packed his bag and was driven to Bien Hoa by his voluptuous companion. She gave him her address and phone number at the restaurant and made his promise to come back on R&R as soon as he could. No worries, he thought. It would be his first priority after getting his new assignment in Korat. After all, he owed her his life.

Chapter 8
A New Setting: Thailand

May, 1972

As he stepped off the plane, he was reminded of his arrival in 'Nam several months earlier. The blast of hot, humid air was very familiar... and it was only 9 a.m. Checking in at Base Administration he was pleasantly surprised to find out he had been assigned to the Flight Safety Office instead of Social Actions. "I guess they thought I've had enough trouble," he said to no one in particular when the clerk handed him his written assignment.

He was delivered by Jeep to a concrete block building right on the flight line, which was surrounded by the usual corrugated tin hangars housing aircraft maintenance. As he entered, he was greeted by the cool, dry, unmistakable feeling of air conditioning. Following the signs, he walked through double-glass doors into a large room separated by partitions. He could feel and hear the activity going on in the other side of the room. As he presented his orders to a captain who approached him, he requested permission to ask, "Are all the admin buildings here air conditioned, Captain?"

"Are you kidding Sergeant?" the officer replied. "We're lucky enough to share the building with the Tactical Air commander. He and the base commander are the only ones with enough juice to score cool air. The rest of the base sweats it out like the barracks do."

It's about time my luck changed for the better, Patrick thought.

* * *

His duty assignment was routine. Responsibilities included accompanying the incident officer in charge in his investigation on any and all accidents occurring as a result of activity associated with aircraft... including planes crashing and being shot down during raids over Vietnam.

Sgt. Harris was happy to see him. Outside of an airman first class that didn't know his way into a filing cabinet, he had no help at all. The officer staff generated over thirty investigation reports each month, burdening Harris with staying late at night to finish compiling the information for the A1C to type the next day. Each day was filled with site visits with an officer to do their grunt work… measuring, marking and interviewing witnesses to the accident. Harris told Patrick that regulations dictated that each report was to be filed by a staff officer and at least an E-4 grade enlisted man certified in all Air Force safety measures.

"But I don't know squat about safety measures," Haney countered. "How did I get assigned here?"

"Don't sweat it young sergeant, we'll get you qualified in less than two weeks," Harris answered.

How effective could I possibly be in two weeks, he thought to himself. "Oh well, typical Air Force clusterfuck," he muttered to himself.

* * *

Ten days later, Harris was ecstatic when Patrick passed the safety exam and got his certificate.

"Now maybe we can put a dent in this backlog," he said as he slammed a stack of files a foot high on Haney's desk.

"Sarge, maybe this would be a good time to discuss some time off in the near future," Patrick asked.

"You just got here, man, don't you like my little empire," the sergeant insisted.

"Not that Sarge, just, I left a little unfinished business in Saigon, maybe you heard about the problem I had," Patrick pleaded.

The overweight, forty-two-year-old straightened up, paused for a moment and said, "Make you a deal… you help me clear this backlog and I'll let you go for a few days… as long as we don't get overloaded again. Is that a deal?" Patrick didn't hesitate, letting his boss know.

"Watch my dust, Sarge," he said, smiling as he opened the first file.

The next three weeks were spent mostly in their office. Going through every file, organizing the case, making notes, overseeing the typing, and forwarding up the chain of command. Every day they were bringing files for final review to the flight commander, knowing full well they would be bogging his office down with the backlog they were digging out of. Days started at 6 a.m. and usually didn't finish until after midnight… every night… seven days a week.

Not having much time to socialize, Patrick hadn't even met his roommate for the first three weeks. He knew he had one because the mamasan assigned to his cubicle in the barracks always had something to straighten out on the other bunk in the twenty-by-twenty cubicle he was assigned to, a castle compared to 'Nam, he thought. Finally, he happened to be retrieving Suzie's phone number at the restaurant after grabbing a bite in the chow hall, when he stumbled upon Aaron Cox, his roommate.

"I knew somebody was bunking here," Cox said, "your socks stink worse than mine," as he smiled and stuck out his hand. Patrick knew right off the bat he was kidding and was glad he'd be sharing his space with another southerner.

"Yeah, been a little busy since I got here," Patrick laughed. "But what about you, you're never here either."

"I run admin over at the radio station," Aaron offered. "It's usually twelve-hour days with an additional shift on the air, so I wind up crashing on the couch in the break room. Saves the time of having to walk back here. You off again?" he asked as he noticed Patrick starting to shuffle out of the room.

"Yeah, got a lot more to do," Patrick stopped long enough to answer. "I'll catch up as soon as I can. See ya'," and he was on his way back to the office.

As he walked back to work, he looked at his watch, confirming that he would be at his desk to accept the long distance call he had requested for 9 p.m. that evening. It wasn't like having a friend on the switchboard… his thoughts went back to Cam Rahn and his buddy, Chuck. He thought about him every day, hoping his family back in Minnesota was coping with the loss.

Right on time, the phone rang and the base operator was telling him he had three minutes and no more. He would be cut off no matter what. It didn't matter, a few seconds later he heard her voice answer, "Steak house, what 'cha want, mate?"

"Do you still want me to come back for a visit?" he asked, not even saying his name. The shriek in the phone answered his question.

"I thought you had forgotten about me," she said.

"That would be impossible, baby," he replied. "I'll be there on Friday if everything goes A-OK here… are you free for a few days?"

"I'll make sure I am," she answered. "What time's your flight?"

"If I don't get bumped, I should be there by 3 in the afternoon," he said.

"I'll meet you at the front gate, Bien Hoa, right?" she asked.

After a few more pleasantries, without warning, he heard a dial tone. Guess they weren't kidding about the three minutes, he thought.

* * *

Friday couldn't come soon enough. As soon as he walked in at 6, he reminded Harris that he would be leaving at noon to catch his flight. Harris just smiled and said, "Go ahead, you've earned it. The brass is so bogged down they've ordered no more accidents until they get caught up." They both laughed and started to finish up the last report before Patrick would be leaving for four days.

He had to beg, but he was the last to board the C130. Told there was no room, he promised to sit on the floor if he had to, but that he had to be on that plane. The duty sergeant couldn't figure out why anyone would be so anxious to get to 'Nam. Patrick didn't bother telling him the reason. He just made sure he could sell the guy on giving him a boarding pass. It worked. Being the last on, he did manage a seat… the jump seat right next to the hatch. It consisted of a canvas seat and the back was the fuselage of the plane. He didn't care, the two-hour flight would be worth it.

* * *

Patrick arrived at the outer gate to Bien Hoa at 3:30. Had he missed her? He asked the MPs if they had seen a beautiful blonde waiting at the gate.

"No man, we would've noticed something like that," one of them answered. He decided to sit on his carry bag and wait.

By 5 p.m. he had grown overly irritated and started walking toward the bus stop about 100 yards away.

"If she was too busy to get away, she should have sent word," he said to himself. Luckily, the bus came immediately and had plenty of room to sit, an unusual occurrence on the Mercedes-made transit buses. He had calmed down completely by the time he stepped off the tram near the U.S. Embassy. It was just a three-block walk from there to the restaurant, so he decided to take in the springtime that had arrived in South

Vietnam with the cherry blossoms that bloomed along Burgundy Avenue. It was going to be a great long weekend, he thought as he stepped up into the doorway of the restaurant.

He glanced around, looking for the reason he had come all that way. There were only a few tables with customers, but no employees were in sight. He stood there, waiting for her to come popping out of the kitchen, profusely apologizing for not being able to get away to "fetch him," as she would say. Instead, a familiar figure came out of the darkness of the bar area. Colonel Bolden, flanked by two SPs. Patrick was dumbfounded. Instinctively snapping to attention, the look on Patrick's face told the colonel he had no idea what was coming.

"Sit down, Sergeant. I've got some bad news for you," the officer said grimly. After making sure he was seated, the colonel continued, "Your girlfriend was murdered this morning. Her body was found about 11 a.m. in her apartment. She hadn't shown up, so the staff went to check on her. The door was broken open... her body was found in bed... she was probably killed during the night."

The words struck Patrick like a bolt of lightning. He felt the air being sucked out of his lungs. The pulse in his temples kept growing until he felt consciousness leaving him. The colonel saw him in obvious distress and ordered the SPs to get him a cold towel and something to drink. It took a few minutes for Haney to exhibit some sense of order in his mental state before he could ask anything. "Who did it?" he asked softly. "Why... how...?"

"The Saigon police don't have any suspects yet, but they called us in when they found the body... there was a black piece of cloth stuffed in her mouth... they knew we would be interested," the colonel said.

"That's how she died?" Patrick asked. "A rag in her mouth?"

"You sure you want to hear this, Sergeant?" Bolden asked.

Nodding in the affirmative, Patrick was now clear-headed and wanted to hear how this could happen.

"The black cloth is symbolic of someone being silenced by the underground market," the Colonel continued. "She was shot in the forehead... probably in her sleep."

The thought of her not being able to help herself... being at the mercy of these animals brought a rage out of him. "Why would the black market hurt her?" Patrick asked.

"Probably has something to do with your friend, Doctor Heath," Bolden answered.

"It was strictly a payback for cancelling their conduit to the drugs Heath was siphoning off."

Patrick thought carefully for a second before asking, "Did you have any clue this could happen, Colonel?" Pausing, the colonel measured his answer carefully, "There's always a chance something like this could happen, but you can't predict how this cartel will react. Heath was just a supplier, we have to find the head of the serpent and cut if off. Then, we'll see some results."

As the colonel and his troops walked out the restaurant, Patrick pondered the colonel's comments and blurted out before they left the building, "Colonel, excuse me… do you have any idea who's in charge?"

Patrick wasn't totally sure he wanted to know the answer, but his deep feelings for Suzie compelled him to. "We have some clues," the colonel stopped to answer. "We're following all leads… we'll get him. You try to stay out of trouble, Sergeant." He hesitated before heading out the door, "I seem to be saying that to you a lot lately."

Patrick thought, he's right, but he hoped this would be his last contact with the Colonel. But it wouldn't be.

* * *

Patrick had decided to check into a small hotel. He needed the rest. There was no need to get back right away. The nearly solid month of eighteen-hour days had taken its toll. After dropping his bag on the floor of the sparsely decorated closet they called a room, he fell fast asleep even though rush hour was just outside his window. It didn't matter. He slept through to the next morning.

After contacting the flight line about availability for his return, he decided to make a stop before leaving for the base. Although there was a black silk garment hanging from the door jam, the restaurant was open for business. Some of the staff recognized him, and just lowered their eyes and bowed briskly toward him, showing their respect and sympathy. He struck up the nerve to ask his waitress if Suzie's father was in. She nodded politely and retreated toward the kitchen. Shortly, a tall, blond-haired, rugged looking man appeared through the swinging metal doors. He looked like he had just stepped out of a Marlboro ad.

"You wanted to see me, young man," the man asked. Standing and extending his hand, Patrick introduced himself and offered his sympathy. The man looked stunned at first, hesitating as Haney's hand remained in shake position. Starting to feel embarrassed and like he wanted to shrink out the room under the door, Patrick began to retrieve his hand but was stopped when the grieving father grabbed his hand and threw his arms around him, embracing him like he had known him forever. Patrick thought how tall this man was, given the fact that his face was buried into the man's shoulder. After a few awkward seconds, the man released him and urged him to take his seat.

"I'm sorry for my outburst, Patrick," he said in a heavy Aussie accent, "but I feel like I've already met you. My Suzie told me so much about you. You know she thought she was in love with you, mate." The words were calming to Patrick. It gave him a sense of relief he hadn't experienced in some time.

"Thanks for saying that Mr. Brunson," Patrick started, "she told me a lot about you, too."

They spent the next few minutes talking about how they had met and shared a short, but intense time together. Mr. Brunson seemed to be proud when Patrick told him of the details of their climactic meeting with Heath.

"Since her mother died when she was young," Brunson said, "she always found a way to diffuse volatile situations, but certainly could defend herself with the drunks in our bars." The proud father suddenly stopped, thinking about the reason for her death, and became visibly angry. "Those bastards," he spoke with a forceful anger. "They're nothing more than cheap imitations of the Mafia back in the States. I've been fighting them off ever since I opened up here. They want to offer their 'protection' from the VC insurgents. Yeah, right, like I need their help."

"When and where is there going to be a funeral, Mr. Brunson?" Patrick asked.

"Don't know, son," the man answered. "But please call me Paul. The police won't release the body yet. I've got the Aussie Consulate working on it. But, it may take a while. Leave your contact info with me, and I'll let you know as soon as I hear something, OK son?"

"Yes sir, Paul," Patrick answered obediently. As he rose to head to the base, Brunson grabbed his hand and shook it firmly, saying, "Patrick, these guys can be dangerous. Call me if you need help with something… or someone. I have my sources." Patrick took his leave and felt a certain sense of thankfulness his new friend exhibited the moxie to stand up to this group of terrorists.

* * *

Arriving back in his barracks cubicle, he was surprised to see his roommate lying in his bunk, reading a six-month-old Sports Illustrated. Roberto Clemente was on the cover, posthumously.

Aaron popped up and said, "Good, you're back early. Now maybe we can do something."

"What are you doing off?" Patrick asked. "I thought you worked every day." Rising to shake his hand he answered, "They insist I take a full day off every two weeks. I told them I don't need it, but they insist."

"What'd you have in mind," Patrick responded.

Dropping his bag on his bunk, he followed his roommate down the gravel path from the barracks to the mess hall… evidently the highlight of the day for Aaron. Patrick hadn't seen such a skinny guy put away so much food. While it was much better than 'Nam, it still wasn't anything to write home about. He didn't get the attraction.

A short walk over to the USO club and a visit to what Aaron said was one of his vices… a banana split. Being full from the almost palatable grub, Patrick decided on a small cone… after all, he hadn't had ice cream since the States.

"What's next?" he asked Aaron when he saw the last drop of chocolate syrup drained from the boat-shaped bowl.

"I assume you're cool," Cox answered, "so we'll go meet the boys at the tree."

"The tree?" he asked. "What are you talking about?"

"You'll see," Aaron answered.

It was a ten-minute walk toward the airfield. As they neared a large banyan tree sitting in the middle of a field halfway between a road and the main runway, Patrick could see figures sitting under the expansive shadow cast by the giant banyan. As they approached, one of the guys stood and strained to see who was coming. He sat when he recognized Aaron, figuring the stranger was OK if he was with him. Before they entered the canopy area, Patrick could smell the unmistakable odor that he hadn't experienced since his time with Suzie in Saigon. He felt a sadness as he reminded himself of what he had lost less than two days ago.

"Who's the geek, Aaron?" asked one of the five sitting in a circle on the exposed roots of the banyan tree. It shook Patrick out of his thoughts and back into the moment. Aaron did the formalities as each group member rose and gave Patrick a hearty soul shake before offering him a hit on the joint going around the ring. As he sat on a root that seemed to be grooved out for a seat, he took a long, deep drag on the dope, passing it over as he held it in his lungs. Immediately he started to feel a welcome warmth that seemed to settle the initial fear he had felt being out in the open like they were.

"Aren't you guys worried somebody might see us out here?" Patrick asked no one in particular.

"Nah, they really don't care as long as we're not causing trouble," Richard Frost, the tallest of the group, answered.

"The SPs came out here once, but by the time they got to us, we had disposed of the evidence, so they don't bother us anymore. We just make sure we don't have any stash on us, that's all." They nodded and proceeded to indulge as the joints seemed to keep going around without any gap between tokes.

Darkness fell as Aaron and Patrick started back to the barracks. Joining them, Richard said, "I'm in the cube next to you and Aaron." As they took the fifteen-minute walk back, Patrick found out that Richard was from Hyde Park, New York. He had been in Korat for eight months and was already counting the days until he could get back to the States. Patrick had to look up to him, figuring him to be about six foot six or seven, but he only weighed about 170 pounds or so. You could tell who the boozers were and who the dopers were, he thought to himself.

Aaron went straight to his bunk and was immediately snoring, so Richard waved for Patrick to follow him down the hall to a dayroom that he didn't know even existed. Although it was only 8 p.m., the room was empty, but the television was on and blaring the introduction theme to "Sanford and Son", with Redd Foxx blinking in black and white on the screen. They plopped down on the fake leather armchairs and proceeded to stare at the screen. Patrick's mind quickly went numb when he realized that he had seen this episode last year back home. The next thing he knew, Richard was shaking him and motioning to go outside. As they left the room, Patrick could hear the unmistakable sounds of the beginning of "The Twilight Zone" on TV. Nothing but reruns, he thought. He led Haney to a row of bushes just next to the side of the barracks and lit a joint. Patrick thought it must be OK, he seems to have done this before. Every time they heard someone approaching, Frost would put the cigarette close to the sole of his shoe, ready to stomp it out before they were caught. They needn't worry. No one coming into the barracks this time of night would even care, much less turn them in.

Being satisfied with the level of high they had achieved, Richard looked at his watch and said, "It's almost 11, let's go to the club and get something to eat before they close."

He hadn't realized it, but he was hungry. The dope had had its usual effect on him. The NCO club closed at midnight every night. Patrick hadn't expected to see many people there, being a Sunday night and all. Boy, was he wrong. While the bar only had a few older lifers nursing their drinks, the dining room was packed with fatigue-clad young guys, all sporting the same glazed look in their eyes that Patrick and his new friend had. Although no one had the guts to light one up in there, the air was filled with the odor of the dope they had been smoking only moments before. Patrick knew the room was jammed with other "heads" just like the two of them.

* * *

Patrick had made plans to meet Richard back at the barracks the next evening and they would go to the tree together. As he walked toward his work place near the flight line, he thought that maybe his time there wouldn't be too bad. He had no idea what was waiting for him as he walked through the Safety Office door.

The look on Sergeant Harris' face told Patrick that something wasn't right.

"Sit down and clean out your desk, Haney," his boss said.

"What do you mean Sarge?" Patrick asked obviously taken by surprise.

"Don't play coy with me, boy," the Sergeant said indignantly. "I know you must've asked for a transfer outa here."

Patrick pleaded his case, "I have no idea what you're talking about

Sarge."

"All I know is I got orders on Saturday for you to report across the street to building 65 this morning," the sergeant answered. "I've already talked to the colonel, there's nothing he can do… you're gone."

Standing silent for a minute, Patrick wondered what was happening. The Air Force had taken the time to train him to do this job and now were sending him somewhere else. It didn't make sense.

"Where am I going, Sarge?" he asked.

The older man looked at him and realized he probably didn't have anything to do with the transfer, answering, "Social Actions Office, they're just starting to set up their office. You're needed right away."

Patrick stuck his picture and postcards from home that were under the plastic covering his desk in an envelope. He assured the sergeant he was sorry this was happening and proceeded to take the short walk outside and across to building 65. As he walked up the steps to the elevated hut, he noticed a handwritten piece of cardboard saying: Social Actions/ Race Relations/Drug Abuse.

Chapter 9
Testing and Crashes

June/July, 1972

The office was an oven. After spending the last six weeks in the air-conditioned peace of a real, concrete building, the hut that was numbered building 65 felt like hell on earth. It was only 9 a.m., the outside temperature was already over 90. With nothing but a plywood roof topped by tin, the heat radiated through to raise the thermometer to nearly 100.

Patrick walked in carrying his orders and envelope of pictures and, without seeing anyone, yelled out hello. From around the corner came an officer in fatigues covered in dust and grease. Haney snapped to attention, saluted and handed his orders to the captain.

"At ease, Sergeant," the officer told him. "You must be Haney. Forgive my appearance, but I've been clearing a space to work in since I got here this morning." Wiping his hands on a rag, he said, "Sorry, I'm Lyle Wixon. I requested you be transferred here. Figure you could help get me acclimated a little faster, already knowing the ropes as you do."

Haney countered, "But I was only in Social Actions for a few months, I'm not sure I can be that much help to you."

"Nonsense," Wixon replied, "Any experience is a head start. Now come on in and give me a hand. We've got a commanding officer coming in this afternoon to take over. I'd like to have his office ready to go." The place was a disaster, Patrick thought to himself. Wixon told him it had been used for aircraft parts storage, so cleaning wasn't high on the priority list... until now.

* * *

Lieutenant Colonel Brad Waggoner was a career officer. Early 40s, married with three kids back in Virginia. He had been in Thailand only two weeks but was doing the same thing he had done from Bien Hoa before he came... flying a B-66 in radar cover for the B-52 bombing runs over North Vietnam. Every flight officer was required to work in support services when they weren't in the air. Waggoner felt slighted that he had a "real" office to run. He didn't know anything about Social Actions except what he read in the Pentagon Directive outlining his duties. He didn't try to hide his distaste for having to be there to Wixon and Haney.

"Captain," he said, "you'll be in charge of the day to day here. Just keep me posted on progress. Have you set up the testing procedures yet?"

"No sir," Wixon answered. "I just arrived on Saturday and haven't had the chance to yet. But it is first on the priority list."

"Very well," the colonel continued, "let me know as soon as you have it worked out. I've got a flight this evening. I'm going to get some rest. Carry on."

Haney looked at Wixon after the colonel left. "Testing?" he asked.

"New directive just in from the States," the captain said. "We have to set up a random testing procedure for everyone on the base. We'll handle the selection with the help of personnel computers, but the hospital will administer the test. It's new technology. Supposed to detect drugs in the system of the testee. Data says it'll detect anything in their system within three days of ingestions, including marijuana."

Patrick was stunned. He hadn't hear of this before. He asked, "Testing? How do they do it?"

"Urine samples," the captain responded. "You'll be responsible for notifying the commanding officer of the subjects' test day and make sure they show up at the appointed time with the clinic." Haney's brain was already going through the possible scenarios this could bring.

Before they could say anything else, the captain ordered, "Contact base personnel, I need to request the transfer of a lieutenant to handle the Race Relations Course we have to institute, and to schedule the computer time for the testing selection."

"Yes sir," Patrick responded and immediately got the personnel office on the phone.

* * *

Captain Lyle Wixon was as straight an arrow as Patrick had ever encountered. Extremely personable, maybe to a fault. He was a former all-American halfback from the University of Michigan. A hometown hero of Ann Arbor, he passed on the chance to try the pros, and instead followed his dream of flying for the Air Force. A late season knee injury in his senior year not only hurt his chances to further his football career, but also caused him to wash out of flight school when the knee required further surgery, forcing him out of the flight program. He was constantly talking to Patrick about his wife and two young children living back in Michigan. Haney just knew from the glowing descriptions Wixon gave him about his family that he would be the last guy to stray from his marriage vows... something that was common, almost expected, in this part of the world. The one time Patrick invited him to have a drink at the NCO club after hours, Wixon sipped nothing stronger than cola.

Even though he knew not to talk much about his extracurricular activities with his new supervisor, Patrick also knew he was someone that could be trusted. The kind of guy you could count on not to turn his back when you needed him. He was also a great boss. Someone who pitched in to get a task done, no matter how menial it may have been.

The transfer of Lieutenant Walter Weaton to handle the race relations course was a godsend for Wixon. The guy walked in with a clear idea of how to start the program and what it would consist of. Being black and from Chicago gave him a head start on understanding the problems that prejudice created in the military. Even though he was an officer, every day brought reminders of where he came from and who he was. His gung-ho attitude allowed Wixon to totally concentrate on implementing the drug testing that Patrick would operate.

Guidelines were clear: base personnel computers would randomly select eight names from the list of assignees. Haney or Wixon would be the only two authorized to pull the list off the computer. From there, the squadron commander of each person would be notified along with written orders handed to the individuals themselves. This was only done the day before the test was given to make sure the testee would not be able to flush out their system. Officers were included in the procedure. Failure to show for testing was a court martial offense punishable by six months in the stockade and a reduction in rank. The Air Force was serious about cracking down, or so it seemed.

* * *

Testing went smoothly the first week. Several people tested positive and were immediately retested to confirm the results. After confirmation, they were immediately placed in protective custody in the prison ward of the base hospital. Seven days of detox were followed by enrollment in the drug counseling program set up by Social Actions. Weekly testing was mandatory for the next six months. Another misstep and they would be automatically dishonorably discharged, something that could haunt them the rest of their lives.

When the first few days turned up several pilots testing positive, the flight commanders started rumbling to the big brass. The end of the first week brought an addendum to the testing orders: squadron commanders were to be notified three days in advance for their junior officers to be tested. The reason: flight scheduling. They cried hardship when officers didn't know they would miss a scheduled sortie on testing day.

"Do you believe this?" Patrick asked Wixon. "What good does the system do if they can circumvent it like this?" he continued. "Patrick, I understand your concerns," Wixon answered. "But we follow orders without question. Is that understood?" Haney nodded, saying, "Yes sir, no problem." But Patrick knew that the only people testing positive from now on would be the enlisted men.

Haney had been expecting a phone call from Paul Brunson earlier. When it finally routed to his office, he questioned Paul on what had been happened.

"Mate, it's been a nightmare," Paul started. "Not only did they just today release her body, but I've been ordered to close my restaurant immediately and leave the country. It seems things are getting dicey here and the government can't guarantee our safety anymore. There are bombings of foreign-owned businesses every day."

Patrick was stunned it was happening so quickly. "What are you going to do Paul?" he asked.

"I'm lucky," Paul responded. "I'll be able to sell my place for ten cents on the dollar to my chef and head waiter. Be honest lad, I don't have the heart for it after Suzie. I just don't belong here."

"I understand," Patrick said, "So what's the plan?"

"I'm leaving tomorrow," Paul answered, "taking Suzie and going home. Just wanted you to know."

"Thank you, Paul," he said. "Let's keep in touch. Maybe I can come visit you in Sydney someday."

"I'd like that mate," Paul said. "I'd like that, indeed".

* * *

The next few weeks were routine. Patrick spent his mornings retrieving the list from personnel and then notifying the squadron commanders. Afternoons were filled with the actual tests conducted at the hospital, and results being typed up and delivered to the appropriate authority.

Evenings were always started with a visit to the tree after chow and finding the group already there. Richard would usually get there about the same time as Patrick, so they had the same amount of catching up to do.

When the others realized the scope of Patrick's job, they seemed to treat him especially nice. But, he wasn't fooled.

"You guys think I'm going to risk jail time for you?" he said. "You're more nuts than I thought you were. I only know three days in advance anyway. There'd still be a chance to test positive, depending on what you were taking."

Craig from Dallas asked, "What do you mean… what could possibly be missed after three days?"

"Well," Patrick answered, "smoke probably would be clear, but anything else would have a good chance of still being in your system. But ya know, there is a way to beat the test, no matter what." This caught everyone's attention. They stopped passing the joints around to hear his explanation. "All you do is stay clean for four or five days, pee in a jar, and save it for your own test," he explained.

"How in the world would that help?" Richard asked.

"Simple," Patrick answered. "You take the cup they give you, go to the urinal, while you pretend to piss, pour the sample into the cup they gave you. They don't follow you to the pisser." They all looked around the circle, smiling as the realization came over them.

"Brilliant, man," Richard said.

The nights ended the same for Patrick and Richard every time. A few old TV shows, more smoking, then a late night meal before hitting the sack. Patrick did get Richard to promise not to tell the other guys when he let him know the time came for Richard's test. He knew Richard could pass… smoke was the only thing he did.

They became close over the next few weeks. Richard confided in Patrick his privileged background. After his grandfather, Robert Frost, made his fortune as a writer, the rest of the family was set, as long as the investment held out.

"Why did you enlist?" Patrick asked. "You could have used connections to stay out of the draft."

"I was getting bored," he answered. "My family wanted me to go to law school, but I couldn't see myself doing that, so I quit Yale in my junior year."

"Yale… you went to Yale?" Patrick said, not believing what he was hearing. "How rich are you?"

"It's not me," Richard answered, "It's my family… something in the neighborhood of thirty million plus real estate."

"And you left that!" Patrick said incredulously.

"Yeah, kinda crazy, huh?" Richard said realizing how nuts it sounded. "I couldn't get used to being broke all the time," he continued. "So my mom sends me a little stipend every month to ease the rough spots."

"Stipend?" Patrick asked. "How much are we talking about… just curious."

"Thousand a month, that's all," he answered nonchalantly.

Patrick nearly choked on his grilled cheese. "What the hell do you do with it?" he asked.

"Who do you think pays for all the dope?" Richard responded. "Tell you what," he continued. "Tomorrow is Saturday, we can hit the town, my treat."

"Great," Patrick said, "It'll be my first trip down there."

* * *

Even though there was a bus service every hour to downtown Korat, Richard insisted on taking a taxi, gladly springing for the extra 50 baht for the air conditioned ride. It was a five-mile trip that took forty-five minutes due to all the traffic headed into town for the biggest night of the week.

First stop was the American Bar. It looked like the inside of a warehouse with tin walls and ceiling. Ceiling fans kept the smoke moving and air a little less humid than the night outside allowed. They found two seats at the crowded bar, and Richard ordered two of the local beers. Patrick was surprised by the size of the drinks. They looked like the milk bottles delivered to his door back home, except with smaller necks. Clinking bottles in a silent toast, they both took long, quick swallows. Patrick nearly spit the golden brown brew out, but caught himself at the last second. His eyes started watering and his throat was burning. When he regained his composure, he asked, "What's in this stuff?"

Richard laughed and said, "All we know is there's plenty of alcohol in there. It's not known how much, and what else they put in for flavor. Every time you drink one, it'll taste different. But, we do know one thing… they use formaldehyde as the preservative. Trouble is, there's no measurement for that either."

Patrick shook his head in disbelief as Richard continued, "There have been some deaths attributed to it… so the key is… if your throat burns too much… don't drink it!" Patrick's eyes got much bigger. Richard finished by saying, "Don't worry, most people can't drink more than two of these. The deaths were some old lifers who drank for a living. One of them was supposed to have downed eight of these."

After the second one Richard suggested moving on to a place just down the main drag. The Gold Bar was a much smaller place, but with the bright lights and stage for dancers that Patrick had come to expect in Southeast Asia. Even though the beers were only five baht, Richard shelled out 50 each for a couple of Jack Daniels. No sooner were their drinks in front of them than two of the house girls sat on either side of them. I guess things are the same all over, Patrick thought to himself, remembering every bar in Saigon was a carbon copy of this one.

Several rounds of Black Jack's and champagne cocktails later, Richard handed the bartender a ten-dollar bill, and herded the girls and Patrick out to the street and went next door to the Ambassador Hotel. Patrick pulled Richard aside before getting to the front desk and told him of the warning he had received in Saigon about never taking them to your place. Richard shrugged it off and said, "Don't worry, the girls here are honest… the 10 I gave their pimp will make sure of it." Patrick decided to trust his friend… after all, it was his dime anyway.

* * *

She wasn't anything to write home about. Patrick thought all he wanted to do was get rid of her after he had her. He gave her the 10 bucks Richard had given him. She immediately started yelling at him in Thai and swinging her fists. At first he was frozen with surprise and took a few blows to the chest. Gaining the upper hand, he grabbed her purse, shoved it in her arms to occupy her, and pushed her out the hotel door. He immediately locked the door when she must have regained her balance as she started banging on it. Patrick picked up the phone and rang Richard's room down the hall. The banging and yelling continued as Patrick told him what happened and held out the phone so Richard could hear it.

"I'll be right down," Richard said. At the same time the pounding had stopped. A few seconds later Patrick noticed smoke coming under the door. He ran over and grabbed the doorknob, jerking his hand away when the metal burned it. By the time he had retrieved a towel from the bathroom to open the door, he heard a swooshing sound just outside. Using the rag to turn the knob, he opened it to find Richard standing there with a fire extinguisher in his hands.

"That bitch must be crazy, man!" he said to Patrick.

By this time the other guests had been disturbed enough to have called hotel security. Two men in blue jackets and ties appeared. The bulges on the side of their coats told the two friends not to mess around with them. Thankfully, the next-door guest had witnessed everything and spoke in Thai with the security officers, explaining the situation. They listened intently, and when he was finished, they uttered a few sentences and retreated to the lobby. Even though the guest was Korean, he spoke fluent Thai, was dressed in a flowery silk robe, and had a scantily-clad guest of his own. It wasn't until Patrick stopped staring at the nearly naked girl did he realize his interpreter was someone he knew... John, the Stars & Stripes distributor from Cam Rahn Bay.

* * *

The lobby bar of the hotel was typical of a business traveler's lodge. Sedate compared to its competition on the street. But it was a good place for Patrick to catch up with his friend. It turned out John was just awarded the franchise for the paper in Korat. He hadn't been in town but a few days and wasn't able to find a place to rent yet, trying to get the distributorship straightened out.

"Where's James?" Patrick asked.

Without hesitation, John answered, "He's back in Korea. Got into trouble with the Army... The Korean Army. They took over base security after you left. Things got kind of hairy until they were in charge."

"What kind of trouble is he in?" Patrick inquired.

"Drugs... seems he had a sideline going on with the black market," John replied. "He was dealing in heroin. Our country takes that seriously. He's already been sentenced to life."

Patrick was tongue-tied. He had no idea his friend had been involved. He privately wondered if he had been conspiring with Heath. Had to be, he thought. One thing he knew... the underground was organized.

* * *

Even though the night was marred by a crazed call girl, Patrick was glad to have gotten out for a change. So much so, he and Richard started meeting John at the American bar just about every night. Although they weren't smoking as much anymore, the alcohol took an even greater toll on their bodies. The mornings got harder to get to the office on time. Hangovers were the norm. Wixon was forgiving but getting more irritated with each tardy day.

The second week of meeting at the bar, the two were introduced to some of the office workers who worked with John. Just like Vietnam, they were all women. But, unlike their counterparts, these women were not demure. Just the contrary. They were bold, sexy and fun-loving. They drank tequila shots like they had been doing it all their lives. Plus, they put the bar girls to shame with their bodies and the way they moved them on the dance floor. Patrick and Richard took turns among them as dance partners. Especially enjoying the slow numbers. The girls could grind with the best of them. It reminded Patrick of his only girlfriend back in high school. The first time they danced as sophomores, she rubbed her pelvis into him and made his head swim.

Several nights of meeting John and his groupies were starting to take its toll on Patrick. By the time Saturday rolled around, he had decided to take a break and get some rest. Monday morning would come soon enough, he thought. But Richard had other ideas.

"C'mon, man," he said. "The chicks won't have anything to do with me if you're not there. Get dressed, you're coming." Patrick knew it was an argument he couldn't win.

As soon as they entered the bar, Patrick noticed something different about the S&S group. There was a new member. An even more beautiful specimen that any of the others. John introduced her as Noy Rodrigues. Clearly she's Thai, so what's with the Spanish name Patrick asked. No, she wasn't married, but she did have a child from one of her former boyfriends… a GI who had gone home a few months ago, leaving his child and her mother behind. Noy had taken his last name, hoping that he would at least send for them after he got settled back in the States.

Noy and Patrick connected instantly. While Richard took turns with each girl at the table, Patrick never left Noy's side. He quickly learned that she could only get out on Saturdays when her mother would come stay with her and was able to babysit.

Being the last left at the table, the two of them didn't want the night to end. When she invited him back to her house, he didn't hesitate. The taxi ride was only a few minutes away. The house was in a suburban section of town, raised off the ground by stilts as most of the nice ones were. As they climbed the stairs and entered the main floor, she turned on the lights and Patrick saw a very modern home by Thai standards. One with conveniences that most didn't have. A refrigerator, stove, kitchen table, separate bedroom and a western-style bathroom.

"Where's your mother and child?" he asked.

"Oh, they stay downstairs," she explained.

He noticed the pilings underneath had been bordered by screening but was exposed to the elements.

"Don' worry," she said in broken English, "they very comfortable there."

The first thing he was thankful for was that Noy would kiss him, unlike all the other girls he had been with since being in Southeast Asia, except for Suzie, and she certainly knew how. Although she had a baby less than a year ago, her body was immaculate. She looked like a teenager even though she admitted to being 28. Unlike most of the Thai women, Noy had breasts that would make any movie starlet green with envy. With a perfectly proportioned bottom, she was built for pleasure. It was the best sex since… Suzie.

Morning brought a smile and a plate of real eggs and rice. Although he knew they were down below, Patrick never saw the mother and Noy's child the whole day. Instead, they lay in bed, watching kick-boxing on the small black and white TV in between rounds of beautiful sex. One thing Richard had told him that Thai women never did was have oral sex… but he had never met Noy.

He started back to the base that evening, but not before he made plans for the next night. Since her mother would be gone, he would come back and she would cook him a traditional Thai dinner. Although he was sorry to be going, he was glad to be getting to his bunk at a decent hour. Tomorrow evening would be there soon enough.

* * *

The walk to the office the next morning was just like all the others... so hot and humid he was sweating before he even had the hut in his sights.

"Jesus," he thought, "it's not even 7:30 yet." Before he barely had finished the thought, a loud, piercing siren jolted his thoughts to attention. He had only heard it during practice emergency drills. It was the base alert system used to signal an incoming danger. Back in 'Nam, he'd be diving into the ditch next to the road. But this was Korat. The only danger was supposedly outside the gates in the form of con artists and muggers.

As he tried to get his bearings on what the trouble could be, he was drawn to additional sirens moving in the distance. The multitude of fire trucks, ambulances and crash vehicles were racing down the runway obviously anticipating a flight in trouble. Patrick stood there and strained to make out a small dot on the horizon that seemed to be trailing something. As it got closer, he could tell the trail was smoke coming from a plane... a B-66. They usually took off in the middle of the night to rendezvous with B-52's out of U-Tapao, 60 miles north of Korat. Their job was to escort the bombers on their runs over Vietnam, jamming the radar of the surface to air missiles, and generally distracting the enemy on the ground. It was unusual for one of them to get hit because the SAMs were mostly aiming at the bombers. "Bastards must be unlucky," Patrick said out loud as the plane inched closer to touchdown and the safety awaiting.

Patrick had moved closer to the flight line by positioning himself just across the road from the safety office, his first assignment in Korat. As the plane got closer, it seemed to steady and prepare for the landing, even though smoke poured out of it. His pulse rate started to slow anticipating a happy conclusion to the emergency when things went terribly wrong. About 100 feet off the ground the plane suddenly lurched upward and on its left side, forcing it to veer to the left... toward the buildings lining the landing strip. Patrick was frozen in his tracks. The plane continued to turn until it was completely upside down and continuing towards the ground. It disappeared under the roof lines and almost immediately, the explosion shook the earth and sent a fireball rolling into the sky. A wall of fire resulted as the remains of the plane kept moving toward the row of one-story buildings directly in front of him. As the plane continued forward, Patrick knew he had to act quickly. Without hesitation, he dove into the drainage ditch just in front of his old office building. He heard the second explosion and knew immediately the plane had struck, sending debris flying over his head. The force of the blast lifted him off the bottom of the ditch and crumbled the sides of his protection.

He didn't know how much time had passed. The continuing sirens and clamor of frantic rescue workers jolted him back to consciousness. Rolling over onto his back, he felt pieces of wood falling off as he tried to sit up. Before he could completely sit up, the pressure in his head forced him back down on his back.

"There's one over here," a voice cried out. The medic immediately started to calm Patrick down and said, "Take it easy man, we'll take care of you… stretcher!"

* * *

Déjà vu, Patrick thought as he slowly opened his eyes and focused on his surroundings. The hospital, again! The doctor taking his vital signs said, "You're lucky to have found that ditch. Was it by design or were you blown in there?" Patrick answered, "Design." It was all he could get out. The pain in his head was excruciating. He instinctively reached up and felt a bandage wrapped around it. "Don't worry," the doctor said, "it's just a concussion and some superficial cuts. We'll have you out of here tomorrow."

The doctor left and was immediately replaced by Captain Wixon.

"How ya feeling Patrick?" he asked.

"I've been better," he answered. Something was wrong, Patrick thought. Wixon usually had a smile on his face. Now he looked like he had seen a ghost. "What's wrong, Captain?" he asked weakly.

Wixon hesitated, not wanting to upset the young man. But, he knew he would have to tell him. "That plane…" he started. "The pilot… it was Colonel Waggoner. He's dead."

Although they weren't close, Patrick still felt the pain that was becoming all too familiar to him. Someone else he knew had died. When would it end, he thought.

"What happened?" he asked his boss.

"They took some ground fire over Laos, on their way back," Wixon answered. "Scuttlebutt has it everything was A-OK until just before landing. The plane must have lost hydraulics. Flipped out of control and slammed into your old office. They're still searching for bodies in the wreckage."

Patrick already knew. Given his workaholic attitude, he already knew his old boss and friend Sergeant Harris would be found in the debris.

* * *

Given a few days off by Wixon, Patrick took the opportunity to relax at Noy's house, resting during the day and enjoying her company at night. She was a great cook and enjoyed taking care of Patrick during his convalescence. Noy had just hired a neighbor's teenager to come over in the evenings and babysit for her child, conveniently allowing them time alone. Patrick enjoyed her son but was definitely not ready for full-time parental status.

Before leaving to catch a bus back to the base the morning of the third day, Noy asked him to move in with her. Although it caught him off-guard, he immediately said yes, and promised to bring some clothes that evening. On the bus, he ran into a guy from his barracks on his way back from a night on the town. When Patrick told him about Noy's offer, he said, "Man, you lucky bastard, you gotta tee loc!"

"A what?" Patrick asked.

"A tee loc... you know, a live-in," his friend answered.

"What does that mean?" Patrick countered.

"Well, you provide the dough, and she'll provide the food, house and sex," he said, "not a bad deal."

When he arrived at the office, Wixon and Lieutenant Wheaton were in his office reading over a memo. Without saying anything else, Wixon threw the paper on the desk and said, "Another do-nothing coming in... like we need that kind of help." Seeing Patrick in the doorway, Wheaton cleared his throat to warn Wixon against saying anything else.

"What's up, Cap?" he asked deciding to ignore what he had heard.

"New commander being assigned next week to take Waggoner's place," the Captain responded. "A Major Murphy, coming in from the Philippines… has Social Actions experience there."

"Well, maybe he'll be able to help a little more sir," Patrick tried to offer. The two officers shrugged and went back to their own offices. Patrick looked at the pile of paper in his in-basket and wished he'd have some help coming in.

Chapter 10
A Little Slice of Home

Major Thomas Murphy had seen it all. A former helicopter pilot who fished more than his share of GIs out of the bush in Vietnam, he was grounded when he developed vertigo three years ago. Although the disease had disappeared as mysteriously as it had struck, he did not want to retire early, so he became a full-time desk jockey, taking on the position offered by the new Social Actions directive. Although he knew that accepting the job in Thailand would mean leaving his wife and family behind in the Philippines, he felt he had to take the challenge given the fact that Thailand was the mecca for drug and alcohol abuse in the Air Force.

He wasn't in his new office ten minutes before he had Patrick summon all assigned personnel to a meeting in the classroom housing the race relations course. Luckily, everyone was in the office that morning, anticipating his arrival. Normally, only Patrick, Wixon and Wheaton would be there. But today, the two volunteer counselors were also in attendance.

Murphy started by saying, "I know your former commander didn't spend much time here and, consequently, did not give you much direction." His casual demeanor put everyone at ease immediately. Continuing he said, "But things will be different from now on. I'll meet with each of the officers individually to discuss my expectations, but, for now, just know I'll be here every day…all day… and nights for the counseling sessions. Having said that, I'm bringing in a few people with plenty of experience in dealing with addictions. I've worked with them before and have the utmost confidence in their abilities. They'll be arriving later this week. I'll be placing Sergeant Lyman, the lead counselor of the group, in charge of all counseling. You volunteers will take direction and training straight from him. Captain Wixon will still run the testing procedures with Sergeant Haney's assistance, but Lyman will report directly to me. I know you people have done a good job up to this point, but it's time to raise the bar and become more proactive in our work. Any questions? Good… dismissed gentlemen."

Patrick knew that Captain Wixon's head was spinning. His workload was just cut in half. But, he also knew that the captain wouldn't be pleased. Patrick had already pegged him as a workaholic, and this shifting of duties would leave him searching for things to do. But he was too much of a by-the-book officer to let any displeasure show. The comment Patrick had overhead from the captain was something he had not witnessed before. He knew he wouldn't hear anything remotely considered insubordination in the future.

After his private meeting with the major, Captain Wixon emerged from the office and forced a smile for Patrick's benefit. He's not a very good actor, Patrick thought to himself.

The captain approached Patrick and said, "The major thinks it will be a good idea to put on a rock concert to promote an anti-drug message and get the word out that we can help anyone with a problem. He says that Sgt. Lyman has experience doing this, so he wants you to do the preliminary legwork with the base commander's office on the protocol. We'll meet with Sergeant Lyman on Thursday to discuss details so have the information ready by then."

Stunned, Patrick said, "Yes, sir." Although he knew he was not very convincing.

* * *

Chip Lyman was a sight to behold. He didn't arrive wearing his uniform. Instead, he was dressed like the thirty-year-old hippie from California that he once was. A faded pair of orange and brown checked bell bottoms with a light blue tuxedo shirt topped by an American flag suede vest with red, white and blue tassels that hung down at least two feet, almost reaching his knees. It was quite a sight to the office, given the fact that he was six feet four with bright red hair that was wrapped behind his ears to try and usurp grooming regulations.

He was accompanied by two burly looking linebackers posing as buck sergeants. They were the exact opposite in appearance from Lyman. Both had jungle fatigues that were pressed and starched, shined boots and closely cropped hair. They were introduced as Craig White, a black twenty-year-old, and Steve Forrest, white and also about twenty. They both were from New York City.

The three of them sat down in Patrick's office and were joined by Captain Wixon. The conversation quickly centered on the proposed rock concert. Lyman punctuated every sentence with "man" and "right on" as he relayed an overview of the concert he put on in the Philippines. Patrick offered to help secure local bands thorough his friend, John Na.

He still had connections with all the Korean bands traveling the Southeast Asia circuit.

Base administration had already given approval for the concert for the last Sunday in August. Given the expected heat on a typical August afternoon, Patrick had arranged for the communications squadron to use their cherry pickers and install parachutes over the audience area in front of the outdoor stage already in place. "Man, that's far out dude," Lyman exclaimed.

"It's going to be great working with ya'." Patrick just nodded and stole a glance at Wixon, who was rolling his eyes in response to Lyman's behavior. They both thought this guy was stoned out of his gourd and looked the part with glassy eyes and his lazy speech patterns.

When the meeting was over, the three new people left and Wixon said to Patrick, "Watch yourself with these guys, Patrick." He left before Patrick could ask him why.

* * *

Patrick enlisted the help of Richard and the rest of the group from his barracks to help set up for the concert. Midway through the day, the boys took a break behind the stage and started passing around a joint. Patrick abstained, afraid of all the activity surrounding the concert area. He decided to work on making signs directing the concertgoers to food and facilities. As he drew on the poster board, he noticed Lyman coming toward the group, so he signaled Richard. Lyman made a beeline toward the group swishing his now trademark flag vest as he was followed by his constant companions… White and Forest. There had been rumors flying about that anyone who crossed Lyman would receive a visit from his goons, who had been re-named "Black Forest". While no physical violence was reported, the threats were not mistaken.

As Lyman reached the group he said, "Come on man, share the wealth," as he snapped his fingers looking for the joint. Richard handed it over and watched as the red-headed hippie took a long, experienced drag on the dope.

"What about them?" Richard asked as he pointed to the two goons.

"They don't partake," Lyman answered. "They just watch my back."

Before the joint was finished making its rounds, Lyman had pulled out a metal cigarette case and passed out several hand-rolled doobies. The group smiled in unison and proceeded to light up. Luckily, most of the work was done, Patrick thought. He was right. His friends weren't much help the rest of the day.

Patrick joined his friends that evening after chow at the tree. As a few joints were passed around, Patrick confessed to being run down, owing to the long hours he had put in the previous two weeks. Noy had given him grief because his fatigue had interfered with their sex and social life.

"Got just what you need, Patrick," Craig offered. He handed him a white pill that looked just like aspirin, except it had two lines engraved on one side forming a cross.

"What is it?" Patrick asked.

"It's a white cross," Richard answered. "You know… speed. It'll perk you up for a few hours. Go ahead, it won't hurt."

Trusting his friend, he downed the pill with a beer someone had brought.

At midnight, Patrick accompanied his closest friend to the club for a late night meal. Richard ordered his usual triple stack of pancakes, but Patrick only ordered a beer.

"Not hungry or tired," Patrick offered.

"I'll join you after I eat," Richard said. "I've got plenty more of the crosses." He wasn't kidding. Back at his cubicle, Richard produced a large bottle of the little white "pocket rockets". Evidently, Richard had gone beyond just smoking dope.

"Only paid a nickel a piece for these," he said. "I'm sending them back a few at a time to my cousin. Taping 'em to the flap of an envelope. I can get eight on a regular size envelope."

"Are you selling them back in the world?" Patrick asked.

"Naw, personal stock only," Richard answered. "Splitting with my cousin."

Patrick decided to join his friend with another dose, knowing full well they both would be up all night. What the hell, he thought. I'll just take more to get through the day. He was right on both counts. Just as they were both tiring, it was time to meet the whole crew at the concert venue. Another dose and they were off.

* * *

Just before the concert started, Noy approached Patrick, seething. He hadn't spent much time with her the past few days and she was growing tired of being ignored. She was ready to light into him when Major Murphy started to welcome the crowd. After promoting the Social Actions Office and what it had to offer, he warned the crowd that drug use would not be tolerated during the concert. To punctuate his point, he showcased the security police detail that would be roaming through the crowd, estimated to be in excess of 2,000.

Patrick kissed Noy, and apologized, saying he would see her that evening at home. He promised he would spend the next two days with her, given the time off by Captain Wixon. With that, he was off to make sure things ran smoothly backstage.

The concert was running smoothly. There were six bands split between locals and the much better Koreans who John had arranged for Patrick. After helping to set up the final act, a headliner that mimicked Led Zeppelin, Patrick decided to make a toilet run to the port-a-potty behind the stage. Unfortunately, the line was full of band members who had already finished their set. Deciding he couldn't wait, he ducked behind a truck parked for transporting the bands. As he turned the corner of the canvas-colored back of the truck he ran directly into Lyman, whose eyes were glazed over as he pulled a needle out of his arm, releasing the rubber tourniquet at the same time. Before he could utter a word, Patrick felt his body raise off the ground and up against the truck. It was Black Forest, protecting their leader. Just as White reared back to deliver a blow to Patrick's face, Lyman grabbed his fist and said, "No... he's OK. Leave him alone." Patrick knew that two goons were hoping to satisfy their aggressive nature and showed their disdain for being restrained. Lyman shoved them both away and put his arm around Patrick.

Raising his finger to his lips, he said, "We're not going to say anything, are we?" Patrick knew any other answer would mean releasing the goons to take out their frustrations on his face.

"No, man, I don't care what you do."

Slapping his back, Lyman said, "Good boy, I knew we'd get along."

Given the fact that there were arrests made at the concert, Patrick wondered how big Lyman's balls were to be doing that close to all the activities. To each his own, he said to himself. He thought about the irony of the lead drug counselor being hooked on drugs. Should he tell somebody? He knew he would risk the wrath of Lyman's bodyguards. What about those two? He had never seen them counseling anyone. When Lyman was meeting with a patient, those two occupied their time reading the old magazines in the waiting room. Besides protecting Lyman, what job did they serve? Did Major Murphy know what they did… or didn't do? Too many questions, he thought. He boarded the bus to the town, looking forward to a few days of rest and sex… two things he hadn't had much of lately.

* * *

He slept until noon. Noy had arranged to take off that afternoon. She said there was something they needed to discuss. After a late lunch downtown, they strolled along the street housing all the bars that seemed docile compared to what it looked like after dark.

"I heard from the baby's father," she started.

"OK," he said pensively, "What does that mean?"

"He says he miss us and want us to come live with him in States," she answered. "He send enough money for us to fly over there."

He didn't know what to say. He hadn't realized she still kept in touch with him. She told him the father, James Rodrigues, lived in Palo Alto, California, and worked as a mechanic at the same place he worked before he enlisted. Although he still lived with his mother, she was all for the idea, wanting a grandchild at all costs.

"Rodrigues?" he exclaimed. "Are you two married?"

"No, no," she insisted. "I just use his name for baby's sake. But he say we get married if I come."

"So, what are you asking me?" he said.

"I no go if you take us back to States with you," she said matter-of-factly. Another stunner for him. Although he had grown very fond of her, he wasn't ready for an instant family, especially one with a woman he hadn't known that long and sure wasn't in love with.

As they continued walking, he said the only thing he could. "I can't promise you that, Noy." She stopped and angrily spun him around saying, "You realize what you giving up? I take good care of you… I cook for you… keep clean house… give you all sex you want… including head... you can't find anybody do all that."

For a moment he thought the anger in her eyes would lead to an embarrassing street scene, one he had seen many times before with the hot-blooded Thai women. He grabbed her shoulders and stared straight into her eyes, saying, "Look, you need to take his offer. I'm sure he'll provide a good home and be a good husband. Sounds like his mother will help take care of the baby so you can get a job if you want. I can't offer those things to you. I don't even know what I'll be doing when I get back home."

She seemed to calm down as they continued walking. After a short, friction-filled moment, he blurted out, "Tell you what, I'll give you my phone number in New Orleans. If things don't work out or you need help with something, you can call me, OK?" She nodded approvingly.

Heading back to the bungalow, he started to mentally kick himself for promising what he did. He could just imagine his mother's reaction when he told her a Thai girl was coming to live with them... and oh, by the way... she had a baby... but don't worry... it wasn't his. Yeah, right, she'd be real happy with that one.

* * *

He had until Saturday. Noy was leaving from Bangkok with the baby and he'd promised to charter a taxi to bring her. It would be a sixty-dollar trip, but it was the least he could do, feeling as guilty as he did.

Although he promised her to come right home every night until she left, on Thursday the base computers went down and he had to call her office to tell her he would have to hang around until they were up and running to retrieve the drug test list for the next day. She wasn't happy but made him promise to catch a taxi no matter what.

Just before 6, they got the computers running again and it took another hour before the list was spit out. He knew he had to get the names typed up back at the office and deliver the orders to each squadron commander's office. It would be easier knowing he could use the office Jeep, which was sure to be there.

He finally reached the office around 7:30 and was surprised to see a hospital truck parked outside next to the Jeep. He jiggled the door handle to the office and realized it was locked. Strange, he thought, it looks like someone is here with those lights shining through the windows. He unlocked the door and immediately heard loud voices. Waiting to see if he could make out what they were saying, he started down the hallway to the counseling rooms where the commotion originated. Moving as quietly as possible, he felt that he could find out what was going on quicker if whoever it was didn't know he was in the building.

As he snuck up to the doorway, he saw it was ajar just enough for him to see in the room through the hinged side. The first thing he saw was the familiar flag vest that Lyman wore everywhere, accompanied by his two burly bodyguards. Across the table from Lyman were two enlisted men Patrick had never seen before. But he did recognize the medical insignia on their collars.

The animated conversation finally calmed enough for Patrick to realize they were talking about the two clear plastic bags on the table in front of them. Although they never said the word, Patrick knew the bags were filled with heroin… probably ten pounds in each bag. He obviously was catching the tail end of the argument, because almost immediately after the shouting stopped a large manila envelope was dropped on the table. Spilling out of the top were stacks of fresh, green American currency. Patrick's eyes popped open. It was more than he had ever seen. It was also more than he had wanted to see.

He retraced his steps back out the door, making sure he didn't alert the group down the hall. Outside he started to walk away. But, he stopped, thinking that maybe he needed to protect himself with more information… just in case. He hopped into the Jeep and found the keys under the seat where he knew they would be, pulling the vehicle across the street to the parking lot of the former safety office. Turning off the lights, he left the engine running and waited.

It only took a few minutes. The two medical GIs left the building carrying a box that Patrick certainly knew what the contents were. As the truck pulled out, he turned the lights on and followed at a safe distance. He was surprised when they went straight to the hospital and backed into the area where the doors were marked 'emergency'. Parking across the lot, he waited until they had started to enter the building before he followed. In the hospital, although there weren't many people around, Patrick could more easily follow his prey without detection.

Going straight through the ER, the two entered double doors with a sign above them clearly marking the morgue. Watching them through the single-pane safety view glass, Patrick saw them enter a second set of doors that undoubtedly led to the room with the bodies. He entered the outer room and silently tried to open one of the doors leading to the 'cool room,' as it was marked. Unfortunately, the mystery men had locked them from the inside. Patrick hastily retreated to the ER waiting room and sat with a magazine in his hands waiting for them to reappear.

Ten minutes later, the two mysterious soldiers reappeared… without the box. As they walked past him, Patrick buried his head deeper into the magazine, hoping they wouldn't notice. After the hallway cleared, he stood up and watched them get back into their truck and drive off. Glancing around and seeing no one else in the area, he walked back to the morgue and found the two inner doors unlocked. Not knowing what to expect, he opened the doors and felt the wall for the light switch. The fluorescent bulbs flickered on as he got his bearings for the room. Three stainless steel tables in the middle. One wall had a counter attached to it with no cabinets. The other had a bank of doors he had seen in enough movies to know what they were… holding drawers for the bodies.

Just as he was about to strike up the nerve to start inspecting, a loud, whispery voice yelled to him, "What are you doing in here?" He turned suddenly to find a young nurse lieutenant scolding him for being in the wrong place. "Sorry," he said. "I was trying to find my way out," he explained as he brushed past her. Glancing back, he saw the disbelieving look on her face. He knew he couldn't explain why he was really there.

Chapter 11
Ninety and a Wake Up

The Saturday trip to Bangkok was long, hot and sad. The air conditioning didn't work in the Mercedes he had hired, and Noy cried practically the whole time. She begged him to reconsider, offering to cash in the plane tickets and stay with him until he went back stateside. Although he would miss her, he couldn't wait to make sure she was on the plane. He kept thinking what his life would be like back home with a Thai wife and child. The Irish Channel was ultra-conservative and had already lost many sons to the war. The backlash may have been overwhelming.

On the way back, the driver kept looking at him in the rearview mirror and shaking his head. Patrick wasn't sure if he could understand English or not. But he didn't get the head shaking. He was just glad to get back to the base. His ninety-day mark was coming up. It was something he had been looking forward to for a long time. He could finally show less than triple digits on the countdown calendar above his desk.

The rest of the weekend was spent with Richard and the boys, mostly under the tree. Patrick had thought about telling Richard of his findings but decided it best to not involve him. But he knew he would have to confide in someone, if for no other reason than to protect himself.

* * *

Monday morning brought some degree of normalcy back to his life. With eighty-eight days to go, he just wanted to do his time and get back to the world. But, it wouldn't be long before his personal peace was shattered, and he was thrown into a living nightmare.

The testing notification routine got back on track, so Captain Wixon told Patrick they would take over the race relations course notification. Patrick didn't see that as a problem since the course was once per week for three days. It would only take him a few hours a week to do the job, but it would help Lieutenant Wheaton tremendously, freeing him up to concentrate on making the course better each time.

His routine was the same every day. Work until about 5 p.m., meet Richard and the boys at the chow hall, then proceed to the tree for a few hours of relaxation passing joints and shootin' the shit, as Richard like to call it. The two of them always ended the night with a snack at the NCO Club. But, things would change again… for no other reason than Richard was going home.

The night before he was to leave, the boys decided to give him a send-off at the Club. Instead of dallying around the tree, they adjourned to the bar and started buying rounds. Since none of them were used to the alcohol, it didn't take long for them to drop off, one by one, until it was just Richard and Patrick left to fend for themselves. They continued to drink, talking about Richard's plans after he did one more year stateside at Wright-Patterson in Ohio. He had decided to follow in the writing steps of his grandfather, but in the literary vein, instead of poetry. Since he was already wealthy, he could afford to wait until he wrote the great American novel.

With the alcohol blurring his judgement, Patrick's defense mechanisms were down and he started telling Richard about some of the things he had witnessed at the Social Actions Office.

"Man, this guy Lyman is a piece of work," he started. "Murphy gives him the run of the place, since he reports directly to him. He'll pull shit like studying the drug test list and pulling his friends' names off to avoid the test. He doesn't think I know about it, but it doesn't take a mental giant to see it."

Richard asked, "Doesn't Wixon say anything about it?"

"Nah, he trusts me to take care of things," Patrick responded. "Besides, I'm not sure he would rock the boat. He knows how much pull Lyman has with Murphy."

Defenses being compromised, Patrick didn't notice the guy sitting two stools down from him at the bar. Since his back was turned, he didn't notice the airman leaning in when he heard names he was familiar with. He also couldn't have noticed the medical insignia on his collar.

Patrick continued, "But, there's something else… something I wish I wouldn't have seen."

"What are you talking about Patrick?" Richard asked.

After Patrick told him the story of witnessing a drug buy in the office and following the two buyers to the morgue, Richard exclaimed, "Wow, what a story that would make!"

"Come on, Richard!" Patrick pleaded. "I need some advice on this."

Without hesitation Richard said, "You gotta tell somebody, man. You're fooling with dangerous stuff here. I'm talking hard time at Leavenworth."

"I know, but who do I go to?" he asked.

Richard thought for a moment, then responded, "Wixon first, then he can go with you to the SPs."

Patrick knew he was right. He mentally decided to see Wixon first thing in the morning. He may have thought twice about it if he had noticed the guy two stools down leaving immediately after their conversation ended.

* * *

Although he was a few minutes late, Wixon wasn't there yet either. Patrick stopped Lieutenant Wheaton in the hall on the way to his class and was told the captain reported to sick call that morning, and that he probably wouldn't be in that day. No problem, Patrick thought. I've hidden it this long, one more day won't hurt.

Just before lunch, he left to meet Richard at the departure gate to say his goodbyes. He looked as bad as he felt. Baggy eyes, drooping shoulders and reeking of alcohol. They hugged and shook hands and promised to keep in touch. Patrick felt he was losing his only friend, but figured with a couple of months left, he could grin and bear it. There was always Aaron, his roommate and the rest of the boys. But it wouldn't be quite the same. Richard and he were of like minds. They knew not to fool around with the hard stuff, unlike some of the boys under the tree who would try anything without worrying about the consequences. Aaron was unfortunately working all the time, so Patrick knew he would be left to his own devices.

He did join the boys under the tree that evening, and the conversation centered on what a good guy Richard was and how much he'd be missed. Patrick knew he would miss him more than the others realized. It showed when the late-night snack was missed because Patrick didn't feel like going on his own. So, it was straight to bed at a decent hour for a change. He fell fast asleep, not knowing his slumber would be broken when he least expected it.

The flashlight shining in his eyes was the catalyst for him to jump from his bunk to a sitting position. He looked at the luminescent face of the alarm clock as it approached 2 a.m. He turned his lamp on to see four men in his room as though they expected him to know why they were there. The officer among them said, "Get up, Sergeant and open your locker, now!" Apparently not moving quickly enough, he was helped to his feet by the two SPs standing over him. He shuffled over to his locker and started to open the combination lock.

"Why am I doing this?" he asked the Lieutenant.

"It's either you do it, or we do it," he said as he pointed to the third SP, who was holding a large pair of wire cutters which could have easily made mincemeat of the lock.

As he pulled the lock from the hasp, the Lieutenant shoved him aside and opened the locker. Sitting right in front of the top shelf at eye level was a small plastic bag with a fine white powder.

The officer picked it up and held it in front of Patrick's face, saying, "Care to explain this son."

Patrick's puzzled look did nothing to convince the Lieutenant of his innocence. He was handcuffed behind his back and read the military version of his Miranda rights. In a blink of an eye, he was sitting in a jail cell, on a shelf with a one-inch mattress on it. The only other thing in the cell was a toilet with no seat. The jailer told him to ask for paper if he needed to go. That was the extent of his instruction for the evening.

* * *

Questioning took place in the office of the SP commander. He told his story, and how he must have been set up by someone.

"But how did they find out you knew," the colonel asked.

Patrick couldn't answer that one. He was sent back to his cell and told he would be held until they checked out his story of the heroin finding its way to the morgue. Patrick asked for a lawyer and was told one would be assigned to him that morning. He sat down on the bunk in his cell and wondered how this could have happened.

A few hours later he was delivered to an interrogation room that had a small table and two chairs sitting on opposite sides. As he walked in, a young blond-haired Captain stood and introduced himself as Christian Robbins, his attorney. They sat down and Robbins asked him what happened. Patrick shared the same information he had given the SP Colonel earlier that day. The young Captain made notes on a yellow legal pad and never looked up until Patrick had finished.

"So, the bag in your locker wasn't yours?" the lawyer asked.

"No sir," Patrick answered, "I've never seen it before." Pausing to gather his thoughts, the Captain continued his questioning.

"Did you at any time handle the bag?" Again answering in the negative, Patrick started to feel some hope for his situation.

"What about the morgue?" the officer continued. "Did you see what they did with the heroin?"

When he said no, the lawyer shook his head and wrote on the pad, giving Patrick that sinking feeling again.

After he finished his questioning, the lawyer stood and started to pack his things away in his briefcase.

"What's next?" Patrick asked.

"You will be kept here until a hearing to determine the merits of your case the day after tomorrow," Robbins answered. "In the meantime, I'll have your locker and the bag dusted for prints, and if possible, inspect the morgue for residue. I'll let you know what I find." He shook Patrick's hand and told him to keep his head up, he would help him get through it.

Patrick felt a slight ray of hope as he was led back to his cell.

* * *

Wixon was very upset at first. He said he had trusted Patrick, and now he didn't know what to think. His facial expression slowly began to change as Patrick relayed the story to him.

"Why didn't you tell me when you found out what was going on?" Wixon asked.

"I was afraid to tell anyone," he answered. "I didn't have any proof and after my experiences in 'Nam I didn't know who I could trust."

"Don't worry, Patrick," the captain continued. "I'll go see Major Murphy. I've already spoken to your attorney, he says he's getting opposition to searching the morgue, but he doesn't know why."

Social Actions: A Vietnam Story

"Captain, get to Robbins," Patrick said. "Have Lyman and his henchmen's quarters searched. That may come up with something. That money may still be around."

Wixon assured Patrick he would and told him he'd be at the hearing in the morning.

"Captain," Patrick said, stopping just before he was led out. "Thanks… for believing me."

Wixon waved him off as if to say it was nothing. But Patrick knew it took a lot of courage for an officer to side with him at this juncture before all the evidence was in. The evidence… he hoped it would help prove his story.

* * *

The hearing took place in the courtroom with three flight officers assigned to listen to the arguments and then determine if a court martial should move forward.

The prosecutor presented its case and asked that Sergeant Haney be tried for possession of one ounce of pure heroin. Although, he said, he could ask for a distribution charge, given the pureness of the drug… he felt that the possibility of ten years of hard labor was sufficient punishment. What a nice guy, Patrick thought.

Captain Robbins did not dispute the fact a bag of heroin was found in Patrick's locker. He did however present a detailed report from the SP investigators stating that although his fingerprints were all over the locker and its contents… no prints whatsoever were found on the bag.

"NONE, at all," he emphasized. "So, the question is how it got there if there were no prints on it. I submit to the panel that the only way was by someone who placed it knowing it would be found."

The attorney next called the SP commander as a witness. The colonel swore under oath that they had received an anonymous phone tip about drugs being in Haney's locker.

"The caller specifically gave Haney's name and no others," the colonel offered.

When the questioning was finished, Robbins then called the physician from the hospital that also was responsible for the drug testing, Dr. Fielding. Under oath, he testified that when Robbins came to him asking about Patrick's character, he mentioned to Robbins that he could help him search the morgue for residue.

"The only catch was having to get the hospital administrator's approval for the search," the Doctor said.

"And what did your commander say?" Robbins asked.

"He refused," Fielding answered curtly.

"Did he give you a reason, Doctor?" the lawyer continued.

"Yes, he said there was no evidence to warrant a search," he answered.

"What did you do then, doctor?" Robbins asked.

"I went with you to the base commander's office to request authorization for the search," he answered.

"Did you fully understand the ramifications of going with me over your boss's head?" the lawyer asked.

"Yes, I did," he answered.

"Why did you do that?" Robbins continued.

"I've come to know Sergeant Haney," the doctor continued. "And I find him to be someone of character. Someone I could trust to run the drug testing program with integrity. If he said it happened... I believe him."

"Thank you, Doctor," Robbins continued. "Do you recognize this?" he questioned as he held up a plastic bag containing a small particle of another piece of plastic.

"Yes, I do," answered the Doctor. "It's the piece of plastic we found when we searched the morgue. It was in one of the holding drawers where the bodies are kept."

"And you searched all the drawers, is that right?" the lawyer continued.

"Yes, but that was all we found," Fielding answered.

"And what's so important about this piece of plastic, Doctor?" he asked.

"It contains residue of pure, 100 percent heroin," the physician answered. "It probably was part of a plastic bag holding a larger amount of the drug."

"How can you be sure it wasn't something else?" Robbins asked.

"Because the only thing that goes in those drawers is dead bodies in body bags," the doctor answered.

"Could it be part of the body bag?"

"No, sir," the doctor said matter-of-factly.

"The body bags are all black. This piece of plastic is clear. How do you explain this phenomenon, Doctor?"

"I suspect someone used the drawer as a holding place and a part of the bag was ripped off by the sliding drawer," he answered.

"No more questions," Robbins concluded.

The prosecutor stood and asked one question of the doctor.

"Could that plastic have come from any other place?"

"I'm sure it could have, sir," he answered. "But that still doesn't explain why there was heroin attached to it."

Captain Robbins gave his summary based upon two questions: how did the bag of dope appear in the locker with no prints, and how did the residue and plastic show up in the morgue. The three officers adjourned to a back office and only took twenty minutes to come back and render their decision.

"We find that although there were drugs found in Sergeant Haney's locker, there is enough of a question to cast doubt upon whether he was set up or not, especially since the security police have never before received an anonymous tip," the lead officer announced. "That coupled with his story of the heroin being brought to the morgue, and the residue being found… we find there is sufficient doubt cast that does not warrant a court-martial. We further find that there is enough evidence of wrong-doing at the hospital that the security police immediately begin an investigation on the activities surrounding the morgue."

Robbins stood and held out his hand to Patrick. Haney jumped out of his chair and bear-hugged the captain, unable to contain his joy.

"What happens now?" he asked his lawyer.

"Well," the attorney said, "we didn't find anything in the quarters of Lyman and his goons, but we did find evidence that he had a bungalow downtown and requested Police Chief Mendez to accompany us on a search of the property. We found one hundred-and-eighty-thousand in U.S. dollars along with thirty pounds of pure heroin. They're in custody now, being questioned as we speak."

"What about the hospital?" Patrick asked.

"The base commander was interested in why the administrator wouldn't allow a search," he answered. "So the investigation started immediately. The commander wants to meet you and thank you personally."

As Patrick walked back to his barracks, he thought back on the roller coaster of emotions of the past few days. After his close calls in both Vietnam and Korat, he wondered if he could serve out his tour in relative peace.

Chapter 12
Implications and Eradications

The next day, Patrick tried to get back to normal. As soon as Captain Wixon sat down with him, he knew normal was not going to be possible.

"Patrick," he started, "the SP commander is sending over an investigator to ask you some questions."

"Now what, Captain?" Haney asked.

"They're starting a deep investigation of what's going on over at the base hospital," he answered. "Don't worry, after your lawyer's unselfish digging, they're on your side now."

Patrick thought for a moment. Then the words jogged his consciousness... unselfish digging... what did that mean? Wixon's answer was simple and direct.

"He went over the head of the hospital commander and his own JAG superior. If he hadn't found anything, he could have been court martialed and lost his law career."

Patrick knew he owed the young attorney a great deal, but he hadn't realized how much until this moment.

* * *

Questions from the investigator were only about Patrick's tailing the two enlisted men into the holding room at the morgue. After assuring him that he had no idea what the men did with the package, he asked, "What does your office think happened to the contents?"

Standing, signaling the interview was over, he answered, "I'm not permitted to talk about an ongoing investigation, Sergeant."

Patrick stood quickly, asserting, "Don't you think I have a right to know? I mean, if Lyman's boss is still on the loose, he could come after me." The officer turned to walk away without answering but stopped just short of the door.

Turning to face Patrick he said, "You're right, you could be in danger. I'll post a guard to protect you. He'll be parked outside during your duty hours and stay with you all day. At least until we get to the bottom of this."

A bodyguard, Patrick thought. What in the world have I gotten myself into?

The next few days were spent doing the routine, except for one big change. He had a shadow 24 hours a day. The guard would eat chow with him and another would be posted outside his door at the barracks. The boys in his building shied away from him completely, not wanting to be associated with the investigation. Everybody on base knew what happened. The grapevine was always reliable, and this time it was right on the money. Patrick's roommate was even ordered to stay in the break room at his office, only coming to pick up essentials from time to time.

The investigation of the hospital found that the administrator was involved in a smuggling scheme with drugs going to the States. But, they couldn't unearth who he was in cahoots with, both there and back in the States. Small consolation to Patrick. He lived his life under the watchful eye of his protectors. There was no social life since nobody wanted to get near him.

After a week of this, Haney was suffering from cabin fever. The others working in the office could sense it was getting to him, but they knew not to get involved. Which made Major Murphy's offer of getting a drink after work sound great. Although he had never wanted to socialize before, Patrick chalked it up to his affable nature and possibly feeling a little sorry for him.

Riding over to the NCO Club in the office Jeep allowed Haney to talk to someone besides his constant watcher. Although he could see him following close behind in the rear view mirror. Major Murphy had started to pull into the Officer's Club, but Patrick reminded him that enlisted are never allowed in, so they agreed on the NCO Club. Slapping a twenty on the bar, the officer told the bartender to keep 'em coming, because his guest deserved a night out.

After a couple of hours and many V.O. and sevens, the officer whispered something to the bartender who returned with the smoky brown bottle that had been their source of relaxation. He thanked the bartender and grabbed the blue and yellow ribbon that comes on every bottle of V.O. tearing it off, he asked Patrick to stand and said, "It is my honor sir, to pin the official short-timers ribbon on your uniform."

With all that had been going on, Patrick had forgotten about the traditional insignia worn by those under ninety days of returning to "the world".

"Thank you, Major," he barely got out. The alcohol starting to take its toll.

No sooner had they sat back down, the SP who had been sitting outside the Club standing watch burst in and told Patrick, "Sorry man, I gotta go. Something is happening over at the flight line. They're calling everybody on duty out there. Major, can you watch him until we can get someone back here?"

"No problem, Airman," the major responded. "I'll take good care of him."

With that, they were left alone at the bar, the only customers left. A new round of drinks were set in front of them and Patrick excused himself to go make more room for the fresh libation. He wasn't gone but a couple of minutes when he returned to find the major gone.

"What happened to my drinking buddy?" he asked the bartender.

"Dunno," he answered. "Just finished his drink and left."

Although he thought it to be a little strange, the alcohol had allowed him to not be too concerned. So, he sat down to finish his last drink for the night, thinking he didn't know when he would get a chance to do this again.

Halfway through his drink he started to feel woozy. He figured it was probably due to not being used to drinking so much. A couple of more sips and the room began to spin for him. Trying to stand and get back to his bunk across the street, he felt his legs give out from under him, and crashed to the floor. The bartender started to come around the bar to lend assistance but was beaten to the punch by two sergeants who had come in a few minutes earlier.

"That's okay, Mac," said one of them. "We know where his barracks are. We'll get him there."

With an arm over each of their shoulders, Patrick was dragged out of the club with the bartender thinking he was going back to sleep it off.

* * *

The muffled sound of voices slowly started to wipe the cobwebs from his brain. He suddenly felt that his arms and hands were tied and wouldn't allow him to stand up from the chair he had been attached to for the last several hours. The first figure he recognized was Major Murphy. He couldn't tell who the other two were, but they were in uniform and looked vaguely familiar to him. Next, he realized he was in the outer room of Murphy's office. Looking his way, Murphy said, "It appears our problem child has perked up. Welcome back, Sergeant."

Groggily, Patrick asked, "What happened to me... what did you do?"

Laughing, Murphy answered, "A little old fashioned mickey. Put it in your drink when you went pee." The three of them started laughing. It was then that Patrick recognized them. The two who delivered the package to the morgue after dealing with Lyman. Haney saw Murphy speaking to one of his henchmen, and the muscle-bound enlisted man walked out.

"Why are you doing this, Major?" Patrick asked.

"What did I do to you?" The major smiled as he decided to divulge the plan. "Anybody about to die deserves to know why," he answered. "It seems you've already been responsible for a disruption in the supply line. My connections don't take kindly to someone fucking with their livelihood. Neither do I."

Patrick, fully awake by now, realized he had to keep him talking while he thought of something... anything.

"You can't think you'll get away with this," he countered. "People saw you with me tonight. You'll be the first place they turn to."

"Don't worry son," Murphy sneered. "You'll just be another dead junkie to them. A needle stuck in your arm. A lethal dose of heroin in your body. It's too easy. As soon as my colleague gets back you'll find that the initial rush from the drug will be ecstasy. You'll pass out before any pain will set in. You should thank me. These boys wanted me to put a .45 in your brain and dump you downtown. An unfortunate victim of a mugging. Happens all the time."

As soon as he got the words out of his mouth, something heavy hit him in the back of the head and he went immediately to the floor. The force of the blow pushing Murphy over succeeding in tumbling the goon next to him to the floor. Patrick was frozen. It had happened so quickly he didn't have time to see who his benefactor was. As the shattered wooden chair lay on the floor in pieces, the attacker lifted his head and said,

"You OK Patrick?" It wasn't until then that Haney realized that Captain Wixon had just saved his life. Suddenly the goon started to struggle to his feet, but he never had a chance. The former all-American athlete showed he still had speed as he grabbed a chair leg and gave one vicious shot to the side of his head. Back to the floor the goon went and obviously for good this time. A noise by the doorway drew the attention of both of them. The second goon was standing there with a needle in his hand. His jaw was dropped down as low as it could go. Wixon acted quickly again, jumping to his feet, ready to defend himself once more. The much younger man didn't want any part of it and ran out the front door of the building. Wixon looked at Patrick and said, "Let him go, the SPs will find him easily enough."

* * *

The security police had handcuffed the remaining goon while the medical team worked on Murphy. Wixon had called as soon as he was sure the fleeing henchman wouldn't double back. Although the bleeding from the major's head wasn't that bad, the medics pronounced him dead. Speculation was a snapped spinal cord; the autopsy would confirm that.

Next to show up was Captain Robbins with the SP commander. While the medics worked on Haney, he noticed a smile cross the face of his lawyer.

"You don't know how lucky you are, Patrick," he said. "We've already gotten a confession out of the hospital administrator about his part in the supply line, and he had just given us Murphy's name this afternoon. We had already put out an arrest warrant for him."

Looking over to Wixon, Robbins asked, "How did you wind up in this?"

Wixon answered, "Just happenstance. I was coming in early to do some paperwork this morning. Noticed the door was unlocked and then heard Murphy confess his involvement and his plans for Patrick here."

"How did this all come down Captain?" Patrick asked.

"Well," the Captain started, "It seems Major Murphy and Sergeant Lyman hatched this plan while they were in Manila to start sending heroin back to a dealer in California. Murphy knew the hospital administrator there and approached him with an offer of a steady monthly supplement to his pay if he helped them. Apparently the money was too good to pass up. After a few months, they decided to cut out their supplier in Manila and deal directly with the source… here in Thailand. Both Murphy and their administrator requested transfers to Korat. The colonel was shipped immediately, but Murphy needed an opening to be vacated before he could join his business partner. When your old boss died in that crash, Murphy was moved in and he brought Lyman and his two goons with him. The colonel told us that they doubled their profit by coming to Thailand… seems he and Murphy were clearing $50,000 per month each after paying all the support players."

"But how did they get it to the States?" Wixon asked.

"Simple," Robbins answered. "They put it in body bags at the morgue. Since some of the casualties from Vietnam were routed through here, they had plenty of cargo to choose from. The ATF and FBI are working on their connection in California. It appears to be a pretty big operation. They had shipments coming in from Cam Rahn until the base was closed down."

Now it all made sense to Patrick. That's why that doctor went after him in Saigon. Probably under orders to retaliate. When Haney relayed his theory to Robbins and Wixon, the lawyer said, "You're probably going to have to watch yourself when you get back to the States. These guys have long memories." The words resonated in Patrick's head. Great, he thought. This will never end.

* * *

Tying up the loose ends was easy. Lyman and the four goons were court martialed in October and after a very short trial, were all sentenced to life in Leavenworth, Kansas. The hospital commander received special treatment… his trial was to take place in the States. Seems the JAG wanted him to cooperate and name his connections. Patrick hadn't heard any more by the time November rolled around, so he decided to concentrate on his upcoming departure. November 22… he'd be home in time for the holidays. He was also excited that the powers that be gave him an extra ten days on top of the usual thirty so he wouldn't have to report to Maxwell AFB, Montgomery, Alabama, until after New Year's Day.

The rest of his time was truly routine. He kept doing his job, but instead of meeting the boys under the tree, he'd have a few beers after chow and retire to an early bedtime. Wixon was assigned to take over Social Actions. It was about time the Air Force got its head out of its ass. They celebrated with a night on the town two days before Patrick was leaving.

On the twenty-second, Haney walked into the departure lounge and was greeted by a host of friends he wasn't expecting. The boys had joined Wixon and Captain Robbins, who both had going-away presents for him. But the biggest surprise was the base commander, who presented him with a distinguished service medal. Patrick was flattered by the commander's words of thanks for risking his life in breaking up the drug cartel... at least on this end.

Chapter 13
"The World"

His homecoming was a carbon copy of his send-off. By the time he got off the plane, his friends had a large head start on the celebration. They were dumbfounded when he knelt down on the floor after exiting the jet way and kissed the ground. None of them knew the extent of his trials in Asia. His mom had let his friends know some of the generalities, but not the details. After saying his hellos he promised to meet up with them at Pete's Bar in the Channel. He rode with his family to his mom's house and settled in for a much needed vacation.

Later that afternoon, he entered Pete's to a full house giving him a standing ovation. Escorting him to a seat at the bar, the two Bobby's unveiled a row of shot glasses filled with Irish whiskey and his first beer to wash it down with. Yep, he thought, some things never change. But you can go home again.

* * *

January, 1973

The forty days seemed to go by like four. It was a relaxing, fun-filled time that he was sad to see come to an end. Well, at least he only had a year and a half to go. At least it was stateside. At least it would be spent in a new job... not in a social actions office. His first mistake was thinking he was finished with the drug/alcohol and race relations duties. As soon as he arrived at Maxwell AFB, Alabama, he'd find out how wrong he was.

Reporting to base administration for processing was his first stop. At first, the master sergeant checking him in said he was to be assigned to the AFJROTC squadron.

"What's that?" he asked.

"Junior ROTC administration," the sergeant answered.

After he got his barracks assignment his last stop was the Base Administration Commander's office for his official welcome... a formality.

General Robert White was one of the original hot shot pilots who joined

Chuck Yeager in the California desert to break the air speed records, making way for the space program. After ending his active flying, he chose Maxwell for his last duty assignment before retiring. The one star general was seated behind a massive oak desk and after returning his salute, offered for Haney to sit down. The master sergeant handed the officer his file and stepped to the side to await the general's orders.

After a few moments of studying the file, the commander said, "Son, you've already been re-assigned before you even start."

Puzzled, Patrick said, "I don't understand, sir."

"You've been re-assigned to the new Social Actions Office," the general answered.

"But sir," Patrick insisted. "I was promised a new assignment…given the… the problems I've had this past year."

"I am well aware of your problems, Sergeant," the general replied abruptly. "This is a new office you'll help open up. The Pentagon thinks your experience is too valuable to let go to waste. Frankly, I agree with them. So, report to Building 212 after you get squared away in your quarters. There will be a Colonel Binder there. He's anxious to get started so don't dilly-dally."

The general wrote something on Patrick's orders and handed it to him. "Dismissed," he told Haney. Patrick snapped to attention and saluted. "Yes, sir," he said.

Man, when is something going to go right, he thought as he drove his new Mercury Capri over to his barracks. The car was a gift to himself a week after he had gotten home. It was a new model that had a six-cylinder with an overhead cam, which his friends told him was too much engine for the car. He didn't care. It had the latest accessory that came in a car… a sun roof. On the way to Montgomery he had gotten the sleek two-door up to 120 miles per hour but had to shut it down when he saw another car coming from the other direction. He promised himself to try and get it up to the 140 that was on the speedometer as soon as he had the opportunity.

With the Air Force going through a downsizing, he found that he had a room all to himself. A real room at that. With four walls and a door that locked. Since there were still two beds in the room, he made a mental note to push them together to form a king-size mattress. He'd just have to figure out a way to cover the separation. Maybe some extra sheets or blankets, he thought as he pulled into the parking lot next to Building 212.

* * *

Colonel Binder was the likeable type. Much like his old boss in 'Nam. But that was the only similarity. Whereas Daly was tall and slender, this officer was short and stocky. Without even being asked, he offered his personal biography on his life up to this point. Haney zoned out as the officer rattled on. The only thing Patrick remembered from his speech was that he was from Virginia Beach where he wanted to go back and retire to. This was his last duty assignment. Great, Patrick thought. Another do-nothing just biding his time.

Although the office was in a good sized building, the social actions space was only given two offices to conduct its business. The first thing Patrick suggested when asked for his opinion of their surroundings was more space.

"Colonel, it will be impossible to run both D&A along with the race relations here," he replied. "We'll need at least two more offices plus a conference room."

The colonel thought for a moment and then said, "Good, I'll work on getting us more space, you make a supply list of things we'll need. That's exactly why I requested you, son."

So I have him to thank for this, Patrick thought to himself as he went to his desk and started writing the list. A list that would be long.

* * *

It didn't take him long to hook up with guys of a like mind at the barracks. They were much like the group back in Thailand who met under the tree. But here it was different. There were no trees in a field on the base. Occasionally they would hide in the bushes next to the barracks and smoke, but most times a couple of carloads would ride out to a vacant farm just outside of the gates. After every field trip, they would stop at a greasy spoon drive-in that they had nicknamed Maggie May's. It had nothing to do with the real name of the place, which they didn't know anyway since the neon sign had been blown down by a storm several years ago. The owner hadn't even bothered putting a new one back up. Its place in the hearts of his base customers needed no advertisement.

Patrick's two closest friends from the group turned out to both be from Hawaii. Mike and Roland hadn't known each other until they both arrived about the same time six months earlier. They naturally hit it off and had been fast friends ever since. Haney found them to be very laid back, even when they weren't high. They obviously took the hang loose motto of their home state very seriously.

A few weeks went by before Patrick felt comfortable sharing his adventures in the Far East with his two new friends. At first, neither believed him. But the more detail he gave them the easier it was for them to believe.

Mike asked, "Did they ever get the importer in California?"

Patrick shrugged, indicating he didn't know. The two Hawaiians looked at each other and Patrick interrupted with, "What... what are you thinking?"

Roland offered, "Man, these guys sound serious. You might want to watch your back."

They continued to smoke but not much else was said. The two dark-skinned friends were truly kicking back, and Patrick was engrossed in his thoughts.

* * *

Sharing the building with Social Actions was the Air War College Administration. Patrick hadn't even heard of it until his boss explained that it was an honor for any officer to be invited to attend. You must be at least the rank of major, hence the reason there were so many high ranking officers on the base.

"Hell," he said. "You can't even get base housing here unless you're a full bird colonel. This base has more officers per capita than any other facility except for the Pentagon."

Coming back from lunch one day, Patrick noticed he was a few minutes early, so he decided to walk through the War College entrance and take the hallway to his side of the building. The building housing the Air War College and Social Actions was a one-story, former school house, square in shape with a courtyard in the middle. Although it had a musty odor, the finely waxed hardwood floors made Patrick think of his grade school, Our Lady of Good Counsel. As soon as he stepped in the door his eyes locked on the receptionist sitting behind the desk to greet all visitors. She was stunning, he thought. She must be fresh out of basic training with only one stripe on her arm. Her hair was a dark auburn that was wrapped behind her ears and held by an elastic band. Dark emerald green eyes and smooth, porcelain doll skin. Even though she was sitting behind the desk, he could tell her body filled out the uniform very nicely. And she was black. Coming from the Deep South, Patrick never had the occasion to be friends with any blacks. The schools were all segregated in New Orleans. Only recently did that trend come to an end. He found himself very attracted to her, a feeling he didn't quite know how to handle.

"May I help you, Sergeant?" the beauty asked. He looked at her like she spoke a foreign language. A little more forceful this time, she repeated, "May I help you?" Her voice was stern, but her smile told him she was friendly.

"Na... no... I mean... I'm just walking through to my office," he stammered, pointing down the hallway.

"Oh, you're with Social Actions?" she asked.

Regaining his composure, he answered by shaking his head up and down.

"Thanks for the visit," she said coyly, "Maybe I'll visit you sometime."

He walked down the hall, glancing back to see her smiling sweetly at him.

The next day he purposely hurried back to Building 212 early and entered through the War College door again. He walked past her but didn't say anything, as she was engaged in a conversation with an officer. He caught her glancing at him and thought he saw a slight smile reach her lips. He waved but knew she couldn't return it.

Less than five minutes later, as he was reading the latest Sports Illustrated, she walked in his office. Quickly with an almost skip step, she entered, looking around with her hand behind her back and said, "So this is how the other half lives." He stood but didn't have a clue as to what to say to her. It didn't matter. She was bold enough for the both of them.

"I'm Carrie," she said sticking a hand out to shake his with. He grabbed hers, noticed the softness and thinking she must take care of herself. When he didn't say anything she asked, "And you are...?"

"Sorry," he answered, "I wasn't expecting anybody. My name is Patrick."

She took the seat just across the desk from him and asked, "Where you from Patrick?"

He told her New Orleans and her eyes lit up. Almost squealing she said, "You're kidding... me too. What part?" After telling her she said, "Ninth ward here. Born and raised. Family's still there." From then on, Patrick was relaxed having a kindred soul to talk to. Someone he could reminisce with.

Their relationship started to blossom. Every day was spent together for a few moments after lunch. Patrick found her to be easy to talk to. He also found her sexually attractive, especially since he hadn't been with a woman since his leave two months earlier. But he found himself reverting back to his upbringing. One of fire bombed churches, civil rights marches and white and black being separated in school as well as socially. He just didn't know how to handle it.

After a week of lunch "dates", she boldly asked if they could go get a bite that evening.

"You mean... like a date?" he asked.

"Well," she answered, "If you want to put it that way. Yeah, a date. You have a car, don't you?"

She knew full well he did, having inquired about him through mutual friends. He didn't hesitate and said, "Sure, why not. Pick you up after work?"

"No," she said. "Meet me at the WAF barracks around 6 p.m.. I've got some things to take care of. It'll give us a chance to see each other in civilian clothes for a change." The rest of the afternoon Patrick waffled between being excited by his first date in a while and doubt because of her race.

* * *

As he pulled up to the front of the barracks, he was slightly relieved to see her coming out on her own without having to go in and have her paged. He felt guilty about his feelings but his mind was quickly taken off the guilt and started to focus on the vision coming toward his car. Dressed in a mini skirt and tight, sleeveless sweater, he easily confirmed his first impression about her body. Hidden behind the uniform during the day, she didn't get a chance to show her pride in her appearance. She walked toward him and her step seemed to take on an air of confidence, relaying her feelings about herself for the world to see.

Dinner was Italian. It wasn't much more than a glorified pizza joint, but on his income it would have to do. Even though the restaurant only had five tables it had enough of a wine list that Patrick could afford one of the less expensive bottles. By the end of the meal, the wine was gone. Feeling better about himself, he ordered one more glass for each of them. With the alcohol taking effect, he felt he had to tell her about his feelings and how embarrassed he was having for them. She listened intently, waiting for him to finish and then lowered her eyes with her head bowed down. You idiot, he thought. Why did you have to tell her?

Only a few seconds went by until she lifted her head, gave him that lovely smile, and said, "I had the same feelings. Why do you think I was waiting for you outside? I had the same upbringing, but from the other side. I was always taught that whites were not to be trusted. If my family knew I was sitting here with you, they'd disown me." He sat back in his chair, took a sip of wine, and then started laughing at the same time she did.

They spent the rest of the evening talking about their childhood and how difficult growing up was in an area ten years behind the rest of the country when it came to civil rights. Driving in the direction of the field where he and his friends sometimes went to smoke, he remembered a small lake that looked like it would be a good place to sit and talk. He was right. Although the lake was small, the full moon shining off the still water made it look like a mirror image of the sky.

They sat under the stars, staring through the sunroof, sharing stories of growing up in their hometown. Looking at her watch, she said he had better bring her back, she had to work tomorrow morning.

"Saturday?" he asked.

"Yeah," Carrie said. "We have a new class starting on Monday and most of them come check in on Saturday. It only happens every eight weeks. My boss gives me off during the week when I do it. It's not too bad."

She could tell he was disappointed, so she leaned over and pressed her lips to his, igniting a reaction from him so that he wouldn't let her go. Her lips were pouty and soft, he thought. The softest he had ever experienced. It wasn't a hard, searching kiss but one more of sweetness and affection, even though it lasted a while. Pulling apart, they looked into each other's eyes and knew that they had a connection that would transcend the race issue. He started the car and pulled away slowly. She leaned over toward him and put her head on his shoulder as he drove. She stayed like that the whole ride back.

* * *

He had walked her to the door of the barracks and they made plans to spend the next evening together. They kissed briefly and she went inside, leaving him to remember her by her smell and the kiss that still lingered on his lips.

The next day he spent looking at the clock on the wall in the dayroom of the barracks. He was watching television but couldn't tell what he was watching because he was just killing time until he picked Carrie up. It was raining all day but was supposed to stop later that afternoon. Thankfully, by the time he pulled up to her building, it had stopped and she bounced into the car smiling and leaned over to kiss him hello.

"So, what's the plan?" she asked.

"Dunno," he answered," what do you feel like?"

"How about picking up something from Maggie May's, grabbing a six-pack and heading out to the lake again," she said matter-of-factly.

"Sounds like you've been thinking about this," he answered. She nodded yes and he said, "Sounds like a plan."

It was a cool night for April. The rain had soaked everything. Driving down the road the car slid from time to time in the mud. But their patience was rewarded when he pulled up to their "spot" and there were no other cars in sight.

They decided to picnic on the hood of the car since the ground was too wet. The warmth from the engine kept them comfortable in the cool night air. After eating, they lay with their backs on the windshield, drinking the beer, and staring at the stars. She asked him about his time in Vietnam and Thailand, curious about the culture there. He shared with her stories of prejudice within the classes in both countries and didn't realize until he said it out loud how much it reminded him of the States in that respect. Carrie kept asking him whether or not he enjoyed his time there. He vacillated about telling her what happened but felt he could trust her and shared his story.

"Aren't you afraid?" she exclaimed.

"What can I do?" he asked. "I can't crawl into a hole and die. Besides, the OSI told me they would probably catch the California connection before I even reached my duty station here."

"Have they contacted you since you've been here?" she asked.

"Nah," he said, "I figure no news is good news." She leaned back down to the glass and shook her head from side to side. He wondered what was going through her mind but didn't have much time to wait as she leaned over and kissed him like she had done the night before. This time was different. It was a much harder, hungrier kiss. One that wasn't going to end. As he wrapped his arms around her he felt the rain starting to fall. Slowly at first, so he thought it might just be a shower. Before either of them could react, the downpour hit like a monsoon. They jumped off the hood and ran into the car, with Patrick closing the sunroof as fast as he could. It only took a few seconds, but it was enough, so he could see the outline of her ample breasts through her blouse. He slowly pulled the car out of the muddy road onto the main highway.

Neither one of them spoke on the way back until just before they approached her barracks.

"Pull around back to that parking lot and wait for me," she said.

As he pulled into a parking space she jumped out the car and ran around to the front of the building. She wasn't gone long. He saw her bouncing down the steps of the fire escape on the back end of the building. Jumping into the car, she tried to shake the excess water from her hair to no avail.

"C'mon in," she said. "I've got the door propped open. My roommate is gone for the weekend. We can watch TV and drink beer."

"What about the other girls on your floor?" he asked.

"Don't worry," she answered, "they do it all the time. Nobody gets turned in."

They climbed out of the car and he thought if she wasn't worried he wasn't either.

Her room was warm and cozy, even for a dormitory-style barracks room. They had decorated it with mementoes from their towns, making Patrick homesick since both of them were from NOLA. She handed him a beer and told him to sit in the only comfortable chair in the room. Going down on her knees she started to take his shoes and socks off and hand him a towel.

"You're gonna have to take those wet clothes off or you'll catch your death," she said as she stood up. He started to unbutton his shirt then stopped to say, "What about you?"

She stepped back and without hesitation pulled her blouse over her head exposing the black, water soaked bra he had already seen earlier. "Your turn," she said.

He wasted no time in getting his shirt off. "Now yours," he countered.

She reached to her side and unzipped her shorts, revealing a matching pair of panties, the kind he had seen in the Frederick's of Hollywood store on Canal Street back home.

"Now you," she continued the game. When he had his pants off she took the towel and started to rub his body to get rid of the water. She snapped the elastic waistband of his underwear and motioned for him to take them off. It wasn't easy since his manhood was already rock hard, but she could already see that.

Sitting naked in the comfortable leather armchair made him feel a little self-conscious, but that disappeared when she leaned over and kissed with the deepest, most soulful kiss he had ever had. Suddenly, she was moving down his chest, walking her kisses towards his vital area, giving him a rush of pleasure he hadn't had in a long time. Not wanting to spoil the moment, she knew just when to pull up as she started to straddle him like a horse.

"Thought black chicks didn't do that," he kidded.

"Just a rumor baby," she answered.

The passion she showed was unmatched by anything else he had experienced. They ended their night of lovemaking in her bed, wrapping legs and arms together in order to fit on the narrow mattress. Sleep came easily. The sun shining through the blinds woke him, and he stole out the back stairs before the possibility of being detected.

* * *

The next few weeks were spent much like that Saturday night. Being bolder about the relationship, they started being together on the base as a couple. Mike and Roland assured him he was the luckiest guy on the base. But Patrick began to feel some resentment from some of the guys in the barracks. One even went so far as to leave a sign on his door saying "nigger lover". Patrick wrote it off as ignorance and decided he would not tell Carrie.

When they went to the chow hall together they could feel the stares as they ate their lunch. Although no one ever said anything, they knew they were being watched. Carrie once told him that she heard the KKK was alive and well in the Montgomery area, but Patrick shrugged it off, not wanting to alarm her any more than she already was.

The first Saturday in May was a special day. It had been raining and cold through most of April, so everyone was eager to get out of the barracks and enjoy the outdoors. The guys from the barracks had decided to have a barbecue out by the lake and invited Patrick and Carrie along. Mike and Roland had a small hibachi and the rest would bring the burgers and beer. It was a beautiful night. There wasn't a cloud in the sky as they drove down the highway with the sunroof open.

Turning off the main road onto the dirt path that acted like a road, Patrick noticed an older Mercedes pulling out of a side road directly behind his Capri. Since it was an older car he figured it to be a local farmer heading to his house somewhere beyond the lake. He hadn't traveled more than a quarter mile before another Mercedes pulled out in front of him. Patrick knew something was wrong. The car in front at first pulled away from him, but then quickly started to slow down. It was at a point in the road that didn't leave any room on either side to go around. Suddenly, the Mercedes slammed his brakes on causing Patrick to do the same, almost losing control. As they both came to a stop, Haney saw in the mirror the car behind had pulled so close there was nowhere to go. With the dust flying up from the road, he never saw the four men jump out of the cars and rush toward him. Before he even realized it there was a gun pressed to the side of his head.

"Don't move a muscle, asshole," the man with the pistol shouted.

Carrie started to scream loudly but was immediately hit on the right side of the head by one of the assailants coming up her side of the car. Her head lunged forward, striking the ridge just above the glove compartment and slumped over against the dashboard. Patrick started to see how she was when the man with the gun said it again and punctuated his intentions with the nozzle of the .38 special, causing Patrick's head to start bleeding.

Afraid to make a move, Patrick felt the blood streaming down his head as the men grabbed him and pulled him out of the car. Standing him up, the two guys on either side of him held him against the car. A tall, deeply-tanned man got out of the rear car and slowly walked up to Haney, sticking his face directly in front of Patrick's, only inches away. The long-haired blond looked like the type to be found on a beach in California.

Patrick's observation was confirmed when the man said, "So you're the bozo who fucked up our supply… not once, but twice. I should've had a professional hit you in Saigon instead of that prick doctor. He begged me to let him have another shot at you. I shouldn't have listened to him."

With that, Patrick felt a blow to the side of his already bleeding head, dropping him like a stone.

He didn't know how long he had been lying there, but he knew he was still alive. Patrick could taste the dirt in his mouth as he realized his captors were still there. The two goons grabbed him by each arm and lifted him up, pinning him on the trunk of the car. His main tormentor then motioned for the other two to get Carrie out and bring her back to him. As they placed her limp body on the trunk, the boss said to Patrick, "You're gonna watch while we take turns on your bitch. Then we're gonna put one in her brain, and then it'll be your turn."

Next thing he knew, there was a gunshot and he figured he had just been hit. All he saw were the thugs diving for cover as more shots rang out, most hitting Patrick's car. It was the last thing he remembered before he completely passed out.

* * *

Waking up in a hospital was getting to be routine for him. This one was different. He remembered being shot at, as he drifted in and out of consciousness, and the last thought Patrick had was a bullet had hit him.

Haney started to feel his body for injuries but found none. As he reached up for his head, a nurse hurriedly ran over to him calling for the doctor. Grabbing his hands as she reached him she said, "No, no, no. Mustn't touch the dressings."

Suddenly afraid of the damage that must have been done he asked what happened.

"You took a serious blow to the head, young man," the doctor said as he started to examine Patrick's bandages. Putting Haney through the usual neurological exam, the seasoned doctor would not answer his questions until he had finished.

"You've had severe trauma to the brain caused by a blow to the side of the head. There is some swelling of the brain with a little fluid buildup which should subside on its own. You'll feel well enough to go home in about a week. Normal activities should resume by the end of the second week," the doctor stated clinically.

"What about Carrie, my friend?" Patrick asked as he tried to sit up but realized his head wouldn't let him. The doctor and nurse parted the way and pointed to a man standing in the doorway to the private room. He was dressed in a black suit, dark tie, white shirt and a black fedora, something Patrick hadn't seen since the early '60s.

The mystery man waited for the medical personnel to leave as he closed the door after them. Pulling a badge and ID out for Patrick to see, he introduced himself as FBI Special Agent Rison, in charge of the Birmingham office and in charge of the case.

"What case?" Patrick asked. "What happened?"

The agent started from the beginning. "We've been aware of the activities surrounding you since you were in Vietnam. After your run-in with the same operation in Korat, we knew they would come after you. This group has a long memory. We've been tailing you since you entered the States."

This information got Patrick's blood boiling and in turn he could feel the pounding in his head. Pausing to calm down, he then asked, "You mean I've been bait for the FBI all this time?"

"I wouldn't put it that way," the agent answered, "but yeah, I guess so."

Seeing the anger on Haney's face, the agent continued, "Look, if we hadn't been following you, you and your friend would probably be dead now."

"Good point," Patrick said, "Speaking of my friend, where is she.... Is she all right?"

"She wasn't as lucky as you," the FBI man said, sighing.

"Is she dead?" Patrick trembled as he asked.

"No, not quite," the agent answered. "The doctors don't know if she'll come out of it or not. She took a .38 shell in the neck and was also hurt by a blow to the head... just like you. But, in her case, the blood supply was cut off for a few minutes."

Patrick knew enough about the human body to understand what he was saying. The guilt settling in was overwhelming.

"Could you excuse me Rison, I'm still a little tired," Patrick requested.

Nodding as he put his hat back on, the agent started to leave when he stopped, saying, "This may end it, but we don't know for sure. The scumbag we got may not have been the number one guy in the cartel. We don't know until we finish interrogations. I'll keep you posted. In the meantime, I've got an agent posted outside your door twenty-four hours a day."

Tipping his hat as he exited the door the agent didn't give a lot of comfort to Patrick. How does this keep happening to me, he thought as he drifted off to sleep.

* * *

The next morning Patrick awoke feeling hungry and much more alert. The doctor paid a visit just after breakfast and told him he had been unconscious for four days, which would explain his famished feeling.

"The JAG office wants to interview you," the doctor said. "Are you up to it?"

Patrick knew he would undergo many interrogations, so he might as well get started. "Sure," he answered.

Less than forty minutes later a colonel and a captain came in accompanied by a WAF sergeant carrying a strange-looking typewriter on a stand.

"Sergeant Haney?" the colonel asked, verifying the right room.

"Yes sir," Patrick answered. The Colonel introduced his staff and said the WAF would be recording the interview for the record.

"We know about everything that happened in Southeast Asia, Sergeant," the colonel began, "So fill us in on your activities since you've been stationed here in Montgomery."

"I don't know what to tell you, Colonel," Patrick started, "I've been working at my job and that's been it."

"Tell me about your friend who was with you," the colonel asked. "Where were you two going?"

Patrick told him about the lakeside spot they had found and their occasional visits there.

"Were you two intimate?" he asked.

Patrick was reluctant to answer the question and hesitated.

"Son, we'll find out one way or another," the colonel said.

"Yes sir," Haney said, "we've been dating for a few weeks."

"Was it serious?" the officer continued.

Patrick could see the disgust on his face. He had seen it before in the eyes of everyone who didn't approve of their relationship.

"I can't answer that, Colonel," he said. "I don't know where things were headed."

"Have you had any contact with these people who attacked you?" the captain interjected.

"I didn't even know they existed until a few days ago," Patrick answered.

"Are you sure, Sergeant?" the young officer continued.

"Yes, sir," Patrick said forcefully, "I'm sure." He waited for the next question but it never came.

"If you think of anything else, Sergeant, contact us at the JAG," the colonel said as the three packed up and walked out.

Patrick wasn't sure what the interview meant. He wasn't sure what they suspected him of being involved in. What he did know was he wanted to see Agent Rison before talking to the JAG again. He didn't have long to wait. Discharged the next day due to a remarkably fast recovery, he hadn't even gotten out of the hospital door before Rison's agents grabbed his arms and escorted him to a waiting car.

* * *

Rison's office in the federal building in downtown Montgomery was much like Rison himself; spartan, Patrick thought. Just like Rison. It didn't take long for the agent to get down to brass tacks.

"Do you know you're going to be arrested when you get back to the barracks, Sergeant?" he said.

Patrick thought for a moment. This didn't make sense. He gets attacked by drug dealers form California, put in the hospital after coming close to being killed, and the Air Force is going to arrest him. Now what?

"What's the charge going to be?" he asked the agent.

"Possession, half an ounce of pot," he said. "They searched your room the night you were attacked and said it was found in the trash can."

Incredulous, Patrick said, "That's bullshit man. I've never even had pot in my room. Somebody is setting me up."

Standing to come around the desk, Rison said, "The thought had occurred to me."

"Well, what are you going to do about it?" Patrick asked.

"We're working on it," the agent countered. "Do you know of anyone who would want to frame you?"

Patrick thought for a moment. Outside of the obvious being the drug dealers, no one else came to mind. "Sorry," Patrick said, "nothing comes up."

"Well, I wanted to warn you before you go home," the agent said. "My men will escort you back. I'll keep in touch."

Standing, Patrick implored the agent, "Isn't there something you can do… vouch for me or something."

Rison stood and looked him straight in the eyes saying, "I don't know you that well. If we find some evidence we'll let you know."

The ride back to the base seemed to speed by. Patrick knew what was waiting for him there… SPs with handcuffs.

Chapter 14
Trying to Get Things Right

May, 1973

As he approached his door, he could see an envelope sticking out of the crack in the side. He grabbed the letter and entered his room. No one waiting for him. At least he had that going for him, he thought. He was expecting the letter to be from the security police. Instead the author truly shocked him. The contents read that because of the president's order to downsize personnel and his harrowing experiences over the last year and a half, Haney was being honorably discharged no later than May 15, 1973. It was signed by Brigadier General Robert White, Commander, Base Administration Services.

He couldn't believe what he had read. He read it again to make sure he hadn't misunderstood. The same result. Going home. Unbelievable! A full nine months early with all VA benefits intact. He could afford to go to school now and not have to have his mother worry about how they would pay for it.

His joy was short-lived as the knock on the door brought him back to the present. Standing outside as he opened the door were two SPs. The master sergeant said, "Sergeant Patrick Haney?"

Patrick nodded in the affirmative and the airman with the cuffs walked in and turned him around, pulling his hands behind his back and placing handcuffs on him.

"Sergeant," the master sergeant said, "you're being arrested for possession of a controlled substance that was found in your garbage last week."

"It isn't mine," Haney insisted.

"I don't give a good crap," the grizzled sergeant said.

* * *

May 14, 1973

For the past week he had been grilled every day by various officers from both the security police and JAG office. Not being able to crack Haney's story that the drugs were not his, the authorities in charge had offered him an Article 15 and discharge. But the discharge would be dishonorable. Something Patrick could not agree to. Losing all VA benefits and the shame his mother would experience eliminated that option. So, it became a waiting game. The lawyer assigned to him was fresh out of law school and had only been in the service for two months. He had advised Patrick to take the deal… at least he would avoid any jail time. The only option he had at this point was to take a court martial and rely on a panel of officers to believe him. It wasn't much, but it was all he had.

Rison had visited him once to give him the news that there was no evidence yet to support him being set up. He was still hopeful that the scumbags in custody would give them something. It couldn't come soon enough for Patrick.

* * *

Colonel Pierce had finally finished reading the list of charges against Patrick. The silence woke Patrick back to the present. It was Patrick's turn to bore the colonel. Recounting the last year and a half wasn't easy. He relived some painful memories and close calls. But he knew if he were to clear his name, he would have to continue telling the story until somebody listened.

When he finished, the little round man from OSI stood up and walked slowly around the desk.

"Young man," he started, "I know you were set up. I just don't know how they did it. We're working on that angle with the FBI, Agent Rison. I believe you've met him."

"Yes, sir," Patrick answered. "So where does that leave us, Colonel?"

"OSI has taken over the case and I've already informed the SP commander to release you, and base administration will process your discharge tomorrow. I told them we knew where to find you if we needed to. Just report to admin by 0800 tomorrow."

Patrick couldn't believe his ears. He had been expecting the worst when the colonel said he was from OSI.

"Apparently Agent Rison's word carries more weight than he thinks," Patrick said.

"It wasn't only that," the colonel answered. "He also raised the question of nothing else being found in your trash can except the pot. Since you had a squadron inspection Friday morning, and hadn't been back there since, two and two says it must have been planted."

Patrick stood and offered his hand to the Colonel. "I don't know how to thank you, sir," he said.

"Don't mention it, Sergeant" the colonel answered.

They shook hands and Patrick started out the door when the Colonel added, "And watch your back."

* * *

Colonel Pierce had been right. Base Administration was waiting for him the next day. It only took one hour to process the paperwork and give him his final paycheck and travel money. Patrick had said goodbye to his barracks mates the night before. He knew he had one more stop to make.

The ICU ward at the hospital was full of elderly patients, mostly retirees who lived in the area. But there was one young patient among the seniors. Carrie's bed was in the back corner and surrounded by machines that had tubes and wires hooked to various places on her body. Her head was completely wrapped and continued on down her neck. She reminded Patrick of the Invisible Man before he took his bandages off. Her head and neck were kept stationary by a brace. Her arms had IV's in each. The nurse told him he could only have three minutes with her. Patrick leaned over to look into her eyes. While open, he could tell she wasn't there. Wasn't cognizant of his presence. He held her hand and squeezed, waiting for a response that never came. The sorrow was too much for him to bear. He leaned down to kiss her on the only spot of skin showing on her cheek and saw tears falling onto her bandages. He hadn't cried since Suzie died in Saigon. The guilt for getting her involved in this was going to haunt him for the rest of his life. Patrick made sure the nurse in charge of ICU would keep him posted on her progress. He promised himself to check on her every few days. The day she woke up, he said, would be the day he came back.

* * *

His first instinct was to gun the Capri up to 100 miles per hour and get home as soon as possible. But Patrick had had enough of law enforcement and decided to do the speed limit and avoid any problems. He was tooling down I-65 about forty miles south of Montgomery when he first noticed the dark blue sedan about one-hundred yards behind. Suddenly, it dawned on him that the same car was behind him leaving the base. Seeing the gas tank was getting low, he decided to pull into the next gas station instead of waiting to gas up when he got hungry.

As the gas jockey pumped fuel into his car, Patrick went to the restroom. On the way back he noticed the same car across the highway at a gas station. Nothing unusual with that, he thought, until he realized the car was not parked near a pump. Instead its two occupants were sitting there with the engine idling. Being a warm day, they had their air conditioning on and it caused the car to vibrate, telling Patrick they were waiting for him to get back on the road.

He wasn't going to waste time with whoever was back there. He gunned it and saw the needle pass 110 mph when he looked back and couldn't see the sedan. Laughing to himself, he slowed it down to the speed limit. Even if they caught up with him they would know he was on to them. He kept glancing back and still could not see his pursuers. It didn't matter. Suddenly he felt another car trying to pass him on the left. In the side view mirror he saw a white Corvette with smoke-tinted windows which prevented anyone from seeing in. As the car pulled even with him, he saw the passenger-side window start to roll down. Halfway down, the blond-haired man in the seat was looking at Patrick with crazed eyes. Before Patrick could say anything the man stuck a .45 out the window and pointed it right at Patrick's head. Survival instincts took over and Patrick slammed the brakes on and steered the car into a sliding stop on the right-hand side of the highway. His momentum carried the car over mile marker 59 and onto the grassy area next to the shoulder of the road. When he finally came to a stop, he looked back and saw the two tire tracks running through the soft dirt for over one hundred feet, bringing him perilously close to the fence keeping people safe from wandering too near the heavily traveled highway.

Haney didn't have time to rejoice from his close call. Coming down the embankment from the highway was the white Corvette. It skidded to a stop thirty feet in front of Patrick. He tried to restart his car but was unable to before the passenger jumped out of the sports car and fired a shot into the radiator of the Capri. Immediately the car started leaking steam, telling Patrick he wasn't going anywhere. Before he could even think of his next move the man with the .45 was within ten feet of Patrick's car and was aiming directly at his head with the pistol. A shot rang out and the thug immediately fell backwards like he had been hit in the chest with a two by four. Patrick wheeled around to see the dark sedan fifty feet behind him with the occupants out and guns drawn. He was thankful to see Agent Rison and his assistant coming to his rescue. Before they got halfway to Patrick's car more shots rang out. This time it was coming from the driver's side of the Corvette.

This time it was a pump action shotgun. The first shot hit the assistant, knocking him to the ground immediately. The second shot was aimed at Rison who had reached the rear of Haney's car, using it as cover. Two more blasts rang out and hit the side of the Capri. With a pause in the shooting, Patrick stuck his head up above the dashboard in order to see the other assailant. He was a large, long-haired blond man with bronzed skin and hippie looking clothes. He was running toward the back of Patrick's car, reloading his shotgun, aiming to finish the job. Patrick, lying across the front seat of his car, thought he had one chance. The thug was concentrating on Rison, so it would give him the element of surprise. He grabbed the door handle and cracked it open, waiting for the right moment. When he saw the top of the man's head appear above the dashboard he used his feet to kick the door open as hard as he could. It struck the tall man directly in the knees and thighs knocking him down on all fours. The shotgun wound up three feet in front of him and he immediately started to reach for it. Patrick knew he could no longer surprise the man and scrambled to get out of the car to reach the gun first. It was too late. The mammoth figure stood up and pointed the double barrel directly at Patrick, causing him to fall backwards into the car. A shot rang out, striking the assailant in the right shoulder. He winched in pain but held on to the gun and continued to aim at his target. Another shot came, striking him just above the right eye, shattering his skull and knocking him backwards. This time, he wouldn't get up.

* * *

With his heart racing and his breath becoming short, Patrick stumbled out of the car and fell on the soft ground. Getting up from his knees from behind the car was Rison, blood coming down his arm from his left shoulder. Patrick looked at him and started to offer help when Rison stopped him and said, "It's just a pellet from the shotgun shell, I'll be fine. The question is: Are you all right?"

"Yeah," Patrick gasped, "I'm fine."

"I thought we lost you back there, Haney," the agent said. "You must have spotted us to take off that fast."

Patrick shook his head and said, "I didn't know who it was, I thought you might be these guys. After all, Colonel Pierce told me to watch my back."

Just then, Patrick heard what was the unmistakable sound of an ambulance and police cars rushing to the scene.

"I can't be sure Patrick," the agent said as he leaned up against the car, "but I think we might have the head honcho here."

Patrick looked over at the first shooter and asked, "How do you know that?"

"Simple, we cracked one of the gang and he ratted out a guy on your dorm floor who was on the payroll. He was easy. Wanted to make a deal before we even sat down. He knew they would be waiting for you after he called in your departure time from the hospital. He'd been following you and was to report the minute you left the gate."

"Who was it... the guy in the dorm?" Patrick asked.

"Roland," the agent answered.

Sonofabitch, Patrick thought to himself. It's gettin' so you can't trust anybody.

* * *

It was the 16th of May. Patrick should have been home by now. The authorities wanted to get a detailed statement from him, so they put him up in a hotel for the night. He learned later that Rison had intervened on his behalf to let him rest for the evening. Rison also convinced his superiors to put Patrick up in the Peabody Hotel instead of the Holiday Inn. Patrick was grateful. His suite had a large hot tub and king-sized bed with 24-hour room service. He'd never lived like that before.

The questioning and statement took all morning. After signing his statement, he asked how the whole drug smuggling system worked. Rison's boss from Washington, Assistant Direct Spears, laid it all out for him.

They were still trying to determine the true identity of the man Rison had killed on the side of the highway, but they knew he went by the name "Juicer". He sent his younger brother into the Air Force to specifically protect his investment in Asia. The middle brother was in charge of the attack on Patrick and Carrie on that dirt road. With the money he had to throw around, it was easy recruiting Major Murphy and Sergeant

Lyman in the Philippines. Murph's axe to grind with the Air Force was not allowing him back to fly, cutting out his flight pay. Lyman was a stone-cold junkie. But he was smarter than most. He got the job done and then would partake in the excess he would skim off the top. The hospital administrator was flat out greedy and wanted more than the service could provide him. All they needed was a connection in KIA retrieval based at Vandenberg AFB, California. This turned out to be the easy piece of the puzzle.

So much so that when a current connection was transferred, he'd just train his replacement before moving on. The FBI estimated Juicer's gross take was in the excess of five million a month. That was if he sold it in bulk here in the States. If he decided to use his own network, the take would exceed ten million. The Thai side would ship no more than twenty pounds at a time so the weight wouldn't raise suspicions. Each body bag was weighed before being placed on the plane. When the non-stop flight would arrive in California it was just a matter of the people Juicer had in place retrieving the package before the bags would be sent to the morgue. Simple, but complicated Patrick thought. With that much money to throw around it was no wonder recruiting was easy.

* * *

Visiting Carrie was awkward at first, given her parents were there. His fears were alleviated quickly by their warmth and compassion. Turned out Carrie had already told her mother of her feelings for him. They said they trusted her judgement completely. Both were unlike Patrick's preconceived notions. Her father was a department head at Xavier University and her mother was a teacher at Nichols High School.

After his visit with her parents, he had one stop to make before leaving Montgomery for good. St. Joseph's Hospital was out of the way, but Patrick felt he had to see Agent Rison. When he approached the room he saw two men, in suits, guarding the doorway. Patrick gave them his name and showed his ID; one of them disappeared into the room, returning a moment later, motioning him to enter.

Rison was in remarkably good shape, having just taken a bullet the day before. With his arm in a sling, the agent was still able to greet Patrick with a handshake.

"I had to come by and thank you, for not only saving my life, but being the only person who believed me. Your boss gave me the whole story about how they had the system set up," Patrick said.

Pausing before he answered Rison said, "Patrick, sometimes in this business you have to go with your gut instinct. I knew from the beginning you were being played for a patsy. I'm just sorry I had to use you as bait."

"Think nothing of it," Patrick said, as they shook hands again. They both laughed knowing that wasn't true.

"Take care of the rest of your life, Patrick."

"Same to you Agent Rison," Patrick said, "same to you."

The ride home was peaceful. The FBI had arranged for a rental car at the government's expense. He would be able to pick up his car at the base garage in a few weeks, again at the government's expense. As he approached New Orleans traveling along Highway 90, he at first cursed the highway people for not having that stretch of the new I-10 completed yet. But, when he saw the sunset reflecting off the calm Gulf of Mexico, he was thankful for the detour.

Epilogue

Patrick's life finally started going the way he had planned it before he joined the Air Force. He was to attend Louisiana State University at New Orleans on the New Orleans lakefront shoreline, majoring in history and creative writing.

His love life took a turn for the better also. Two weeks before his first semester, Carrie woke up. Miraculously, with few lingering effects.

He jumped in the Capri and high-tailed it to Montgomery. The reunion was one they both would remember. Her parents were there and beamed their approval as Patrick embraced Carrie, not wanting to let go.

Her parents had arranged to bring her back to New Orleans after a week. She had a long road of physical therapy, but Patrick pledged to continue to be a part of her life.

Back home, he brought her to doctor and PT visits in between classes. Their relationship progressed to the point that Patrick showed her father the engagement ring he bought her and asked his permission to pop the question. He said yes. So did Carrie. They planned a spring wedding.

Remembering his nurse's offer to contact her husband when he got back, he put in a call to him the day after graduation in 1977. Nurse Baker was excited to hear from him. She had followed what happened to Patrick through the newspaper. Her husband, Terry, was just as excited. When he heard some of the details of what had happened, he offered a plane ticket out to Los Angeles so they could work out the details. Patrick stayed with the Bakers for two months collaborating on a screenplay with Terry. With Terry's track record in Hollywood, it was no problem getting appointments to pitch their story to different studios. It only took them two meetings to secure a deal with Universal Pictures.

Patrick went home with a retainer of $100,000 and a return ticket to come back for the filming. He and Terry would be on set to rewrite as needed. Another $100,000 waited for him upon his return plus a per diem, according to the screenwriter's guild contract that he had become a member of. If the film did well, he and Terry would split two percent of the net profit.

The film was a success, turning a profit and earning an additional

$150,000 for them to split. It wasn't enough for early retirement but enough for Patrick to go back home and do something he'd always dreamt of doing: buying the grocery and bar/restaurant on the corner of the block where he'd grown up. Terry begged him to stay in California and they could work together again. Patrick promised to come back whenever Terry needed him, but this was something he had to do.

Buying the property was easy. For $85,000 Mr. Mura used the money to retire, owning the property since 1938 and having it free and clear for several years. Being over 80, Mr. Mura had let maintenance go and the property proved to be more costly than Patrick had thought. So, $50,000 later he had the best neighborhood spot the Irish Channel had to offer. People would come from across the city to sample its cuisine. He had hired a local chef who had studied at Commander's Palace and gave him free run of the kitchen. Patrick's loyalty was rewarded. The business turned a nice profit from the beginning allowing Patrick to buy a house in the suburbs for his mother. Knowing she would be safe gave him peace of mind. The old neighborhood was changing, and not always for the better.

He would realize the good and bad in the years to come.

TO BE CONTINUED

CPSIA information can be obtained
at www.ICGtesting.com
Printed in the USA
LVHW041222240319
611647LV00016B/743